"I came home because of you, Denny."

"I'm worried about you," J.D. continued. "You think I don't know you're looking for Max's killer? If you'd arrived a little earlier, you might have found him, too. Denny, you could be in a lot of danger!"

Danger? She'd just gone after a prowler with only a phone as a weapon. But her heart pounded harder, her pulse raced faster just being this close to J. D. Garrison again. "I have to go," she said. "I promised Pete—" The lie caught in her throat.

A shadow flickered across J.D.'s eyes. "I guess you and Pete are pretty close?"

"Just like that," she said, crossing her fingers. *Let him draw his own conclusions.*

"Is that right?" J.D. growled, gazing at her from hooded eyes. "Well, you'd better watch out...'cause you're playing with fire!"

W9-DIH-268

Dear Reader,

Be prepared to meet a "Woman of Mystery"!

This month we're proud to bring you another story in our ongoing WOMAN OF MYSTERY program, designed to bring you the debut books of writers new to Harlequin Intrigue.

Meet B. J. Daniels, author of *Odd Man Out:*

B. J. Daniels grew up in Montana listening to scary stories around a campfire. As a newspaper reporter and editor, she has had numerous articles published as well as three dozen short stories, both romances and mysteries. In her first Harlequin Intrigue, she combines mystery and romance in the town where she grew up, West Yellowstone, Montana. B.J. makes her home in the Big Sky state, enjoying skiing, mountain biking and windsurfing when she isn't writing.

We're dedicated to bringing you the best new authors, the freshest new voices. Be on the lookout for more upcoming titles in our WOMAN OF MYSTERY program!

Sincerely,

Debra Matteucci
Senior Editor and Editorial Coodinator
Harlequin Books
300 East 42nd Street, Sixth Floor
New York, NY 10017

Odd Man Out

B. J. Daniels

Harlequin Books

TORONTO • NEW YORK • LONDON
AMSTERDAM • PARIS • SYDNEY • HAMBURG
STOCKHOLM • ATHENS • TOKYO • MILAN
MADRID • WARSAW • BUDAPEST • AUCKLAND

To Kathrina,
who showed me the way,
and Kitty and Judy,
who read every word along the way.
Special thanks to Neil and Dani.

ISBN 0-373-22312-9

ODD MAN OUT

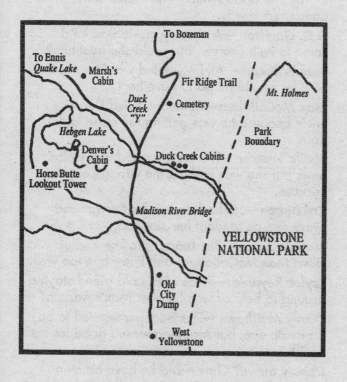

CAST OF CHARACTERS

Denver McCallahan—She was determined to find her uncle's killer—no matter how dangerous it was.

J. D. Garrison—A country music star, he'd come to help Denver, but could she trust him?

Pete Williams—All he wanted was Denver, but how far would he go to have her?

Max McCallahan—Someone killed Denver's uncle because he was getting too close to the truth.

Sheila Walker—The reporter had a nose for news but she was making the wrong people nervous.

Cal Dalton—He had an eye for Denver and every reason to want her stopped.

Maggie Jones—She feared she knew who killed Max McCallahan, and knew him too well.

Taylor Reynolds—Was Max's old friend staying around to help or was he after Max's woman?

Davey Matthews—The teenager wanted to be a private eye, but snooping wasn't good for his health.

Deputy Sheriff Cline—Did he have his own reasons for not wanting Max's killer caught?

Prologue

Rain pelted the tops of the parked cars like rocks hitting tin cans. Rivulets of the icy stuff ran off the brim of J. D. Garrison's gray Stetson as he hung back in a stand of snowy pines on a hillside overlooking the tiny Fir Ridge Cemetery. Hidden from view, he eyed the funeral service taking place beneath the swollen dark clouds covering the valley below. He'd been away far too long. He hunched deeper in his sheepskin coat, his head bent against the cold wetness of the Montana spring day, as he wished it hadn't been death that had brought him home again.

Half the county had turned out for Max McCallahan's burial even in the freezing downpour. Snatches of the service reached J.D. on the hillside. He had to smile at the priest's portrayal of the old Irish private eye. Max must be turning in his grave to hear such malarkey. Too bad the good Father didn't just tell the truth—that Max had been a big, loud, red-faced Irishman and damned proud of it. That he'd loved his ale. And that, if the need arose, he hadn't been one to back down from a good brawl. The truth was, the devil had danced in the old Irishman's eyes most of the time. But there'd also been another side to Max, a gentle, loving side, that a young girl had brought out in him.

As the priest led a prayer, J.D. studied that young girl—Max's niece, Denver McCallahan. She was no longer a girl but she would always have that look because of her slight build. She stood under the dripping canopy at the edge of

the grave, a large black felt hat hiding most of her long auburn hair and part of her face. Her manner appeared almost peaceful.

J.D. wasn't fooled. He knew Denver's composure was an
act. Max had been her only family; she would have killed for
him. J.D.'s jaw tensed under his dark beard as the tall cowboy beside Denver slipped an arm around her shoulders.
He'd have recognized the man anywhere, not only because
of his blond hair and his arrogant stance, but by his trade-
mark—the large, white Western hat now dangling from the
fingers of his right hand. J.D. swore, surprised by his reaction. He didn't like seeing Denver in the arms of his childhood friend, Pete Williams.

J.D. looked up as an older woman joined him in the seclusion of the pines. She wore a worn wool plaid hunting
jacket, Max's, no doubt, jeans, a flannel shirt and boots.

"I've never been so glad to see anyone in my life," Maggie said as she stepped into his arms. He hugged her to him,
feeling her strength. Sturdy. That was what Max had called
her. Sturdy, dependable Maggie. She'd been Max's friend,
his lover, his confidante. Although they'd never married and
had lived in separate houses, Maggie had been the love of
Max's life.

Maggie stepped back, brushing a wisp of graying brown
hair from her face, a face that belied her fifty-five years. She
glanced at the cemetery below them, her expression as grim
as the day. Dark umbrellas huddled around the grave like
ghouls. Denver moved closer to drop a single bloodred rose
on her uncle's casket. Even from the distance, J.D. could see
that she'd grown up since he'd been gone. A lot of things
had changed, he thought, watching her with Pete.

"Shouldn't we be down there at the funeral?" J.D. asked,
still surprised that Maggie had suggested meeting here instead.

"Max knew how I felt about funerals," she said softly.
"And I'd prefer Denver didn't know you're back in town
yet."

His eyebrow shot up. "Why is that?"

"There's something you need to know before you see her." Maggie took a breath and let it out slowly. "Denver's in trouble."

He almost laughed. Ever since they were kids, Denver McCallahan had been in some sort of trouble; blame it on her fiery spirit, but it was one of the things he'd always admired about her. "What kind of trouble?" The moment he said it, he could guess. "She's heard the rumors you told me about Max being involved in something illegal and she's determined to clear his good name, right?"

"You know Denver. And while she's at it, she intends to bring his killer to justice, as well."

That didn't surprise him in the least. "And I suppose you want me to keep her out of trouble while she's doing all that?" He shook his head. "You don't know what you're asking."

Maggie met his gaze and he glimpsed an expression in her eyes that startled him. Anger. Cold as the granite bluffs in the distance. "I'm asking a lot more than that, J.D. I want you to keep her away from Pete Williams."

"You can't be serious." The rain fell harder, dimpling the spring snow's rough surface. He stared at her with a puzzled frown, and realized she *was* serious. "Why would I do that?"

"I know things about Pete—" She looked away. "You just have to keep him away from Denver."

"You're asking the impossible." He'd been gone for nine years and he hadn't left on the best of terms.

Maggie pulled her jacket around her. "Denver knows I've never liked Pete. She won't listen to me."

J.D. watched Denver lean into Pete Williams's embrace as the two stood alone beside the grave. "Denny won't—" he stumbled on the childhood name he'd always called her. "Denver wouldn't appreciate any interference in her life from me."

"Oh, J.D., you know how she's always felt about you."

"She had a crush on me when she was sixteen, Maggie! Believe me, it didn't last." He remembered only too well how angry Denver had been that afternoon at Horse Butte Fire Tower when he'd told her he was leaving town. And how hurt. She'd been like a kid sister to him. He'd never forgiven himself for hurting her.

"If anyone can handle her, it's you," Maggie argued.

"I'm not sure there's a man alive who can handle Denver McCallahan." The umbrellas suddenly dispersed like tiny dark seeds across the snow. The rain turned to snow as the mourners headed for their cars.

"Just promise me you'll do everything you can to keep Pete away from her," Maggie said. "If you don't—" She turned to leave.

"Wait, what are you saying?" J.D. demanded. Surely she didn't believe Denver had anything to fear from Pete. "Give me a reason, Maggie. A damned good reason."

To his surprise, her eyes filled not with their usual resolve but with tears. That anger he'd glimpsed earlier mixed with pain and burned red-hot. "Pete Williams killed Max."

Chapter One

Denver ducked her head to the cold and the pain as she let Pete lead her away from the cemetery. The rain had turned to snow that now fell in huge, wet flakes. She walked feeling nothing, not the ground under her feet nor Pete's steadying hand on her elbow.

"You're Denver McCallahan, right?" A woman in her fifties in a long purple coat and a floppy red wool hat stepped in front of her; the woman didn't wait for an answer. "I'm Sheila Walker with the *Billings Register*." She flipped open her notebook, her pen ready. "I need to ask you some questions."

Pete put his arm around Denver's shoulders. "Ms. McCallahan just buried her uncle. Now is not the time." He tried to pass, but the reporter blocked his way, ignoring him as she turned her full attention on Denver.

"This has to be the second worst day of your life. First your parents, now your uncle." From a web of wrinkles, she searched Denver's face with dark, eager eyes. "You think there's a connection?"

Denver stared at the woman. Her bright red lipstick was smeared and her hat drooped off one side of her head, exposing a head of wiry black-and-gray curls. A scent of perfume Denver couldn't place hung over her like a black cloud. "My parents were killed more than *twenty* years ago." The murders connected? Was the woman crazy? Pain pressed against her chest; she fought for breath. Pete pulled Denver closer and pushed on past the woman.

"Who do you think killed your uncle?" the reporter asked, trotting alongside Denver. "Do you think it was that hitchhiker they're looking for?"

"Please, I can't—" Denver fought the ever-present tears.

"Leave her alone," Pete interrupted in a menacing tone. They'd reached his black Chevy pickup. He opened the door for Denver and spun on the woman. "Back off, lady, or you'll wish you had." Climbing in beside Denver, he slammed the door in the reporter's face.

She tapped on the window. "The rumors about your uncle, is there any truth in them?"

Pete started the pickup and peeled away, leaving Sheila Walker in a cloud of flying ice and snow.

"YOU DON'T BELIEVE IT."

J.D. watched Pete leave with Denver in a fancy black Chevy pickup, then turned his attention back to Maggie. "That Pete murdered Max? No, I don't believe it." He and Pete had been friends and as close to Denver and Max as family. Through the falling snow, he could see workers pushing cold earth over Max's casket with a finality that made his heart ache.

"I don't want to believe it, either," Maggie said. "Max loved Pete. He loved you both like the brother he lost."

"Then how can you suspect Pete of murder?"

She took a long, ragged breath. "The morning after Max's murder, Denver and Pete came over. I'd made coffee and sent them into the kitchen. You remember the photograph Max took of you, Pete and Denver at the lake on her sixteenth birthday?"

J.D. nodded; it had been right before he'd left town. He could still see Denver in the dress Max had bought her. A pale aquamarine. The same color as her eyes. "You gave me a copy of the photo." He still had it. It reminded him of those days at the lake with Denny and Pete. Sunlight and laughter. A long-lost happiness twisted at his insides.

"It was Max's favorite photograph. He always carried it in his wallet," Maggie said. "I saw it the day before he died. It was dog-eared and faded and I wanted to put it away for safekeeping, but Max wouldn't hear of it." She stopped; he watched her fight the painful memories. "When I went to hang up Pete's coat, I saw a piece of the photograph sticking out of his pocket."

"Didn't Pete have a copy, too?"

She nodded. "But I'd written on the back of the one I gave Max. I could still make out the writing. It was the photo from his wallet. Only... it had been torn." She met his gaze. "Someone had ripped you out of the picture."

"That's not enough evidence to convict a man of murder."

"I know, especially since Pete has an alibi for the day of the murder. Supposedly he was in Missoula with his band. But I called to check. The Montana Country Club band was there, but when I described Pete to one of the cocktail waitresses, she didn't remember him. If Pete's good looks didn't make an impression on her, that blue-eyed charm of his would have."

"That's pretty weak, Maggie."

"Pete wasn't in Missoula. I'd stake my life on it."

"I hope you won't have to do that." J.D. tugged at his collar; he wasn't used to this kind of weather anymore.

"I have to go," Maggie said.

J.D. walked with her to her Land Rover parked along the edge of the road in the pines. "It still doesn't make any sense," he said. "Why would Pete want to kill Max?"

"Max wasn't part of anything dishonest if that's what you're thinking." She hugged herself against the cold wetness. "I'll admit something was bothering him."

"What?"

She shrugged and opened her car door. "If Pete finds out that I called you or that I suspect him—"

"Dammit, Maggie, tell me why you're so frightened. It has to be more than a hunch and an old ripped photograph."

She nodded, fighting more than grief. "That last week, Max was . . . afraid."

J.D. had never known the man to be afraid of anything, or anybody—no matter how big or tough they were.

She slid into the front seat and shoved her hands into the pockets of Max's hunting jacket. "He seemed to be looking over his shoulder as if—" She broke off and shivered. "As if something had come back to haunt him. He was obsessed with death and kept talking about his brother's murder."

J.D. fought the chill that stole up his spine. "Denny's father?"

She nodded. "He felt responsible for encouraging Timothy to become a cop. He blamed himself for Timothy's death."

"Maggie, what does that have to do with Pete?" J.D. asked.

She shook her head as if to chase away the memories. "I haven't told anyone this because I was afraid of what Pete would do," she said, her voice barely a whisper. "The last time I saw Max, he was furious at Pete." She bit her lip. "I've never seen Max like that. He said he had to stop Pete . . . before someone got killed."

"I'M SORRY ABOUT that reporter," Pete said as they headed south toward the town of West Yellowstone. "Are you all right?"

Denver nodded, wondering if she'd ever be all right again. Leaning back in the seat, her hat in her lap, she watched the pines and snowfall blur by outside the window. Max dead. Murdered. It wasn't possible. But worse yet were the rumors. She ran a finger through the water droplets beaded up on the brim of her hat, fighting the pain.

"You know, that woman was right . . ." Her voice broke. "People are saying that Max was dirty. That he'd gotten himself involved in something illegal."

"Denver, why do you listen to it?" Pete demanded angrily. "You knew Max better than anyone. If your uncle had a fault, it was being too honest. Naively so."

It wasn't that she believed the rumors. She just couldn't stand seeing Max's named dragged through the dirt. But more than that, she knew the rumors were somehow tied in with the way Max had been acting the past few weeks. Secretive. Something had been bothering him. And Denver felt that if she knew what it was, she'd know who killed him.

"He's gone, Denver," Pete said, taking her hand as if he could read her thoughts. "As much as we both hate it, he's gone. Leave it alone."

Concentrating on the click-clack of the wipers, she closed her eyes. Now wasn't the time to let grief blind her, not when there was something much more important that had to be done—no matter what Pete said.

"I think it would be a good idea if you stayed at my place and didn't go back out to the cabin tonight," he said.

Denver opened her eyes, tempted to take him up on it. Since Max's death, she'd been having the nightmare again. "Thanks, but the cabin's home and I need that right now."

Pete's look reflected a mixture of annoyance and worry. "I don't like the idea of your being out there alone. It's too deserted this time of year."

"You know how I feel about the lake. I love this time of year *because* it's quiet out there." She touched his arm. "I'll be fine."

"I wish you'd change your mind." He sounded angry.

And she wondered if he was talking about her staying at his place or about the argument they'd had earlier.

"I swear, sometimes you're as stubborn as—"

"As Max?" she asked. Max McCallahan had given stubborn a new definition.

Pete's smile faded. "Yeah. Max." She could see him fighting painful emotions as he turned on the radio. Intermittent snow flurries, the newsman said. A slow, sad Western song came on. Pete took her hand. "I just worry about you."

"I know." She smiled, feeling the familiar tenderness she'd felt for him since they were kids. Pete, Denver and J.D. Max had called them the Terrible Trio because of all the trouble they'd gotten into. Pete and J.D. had been the older brothers she'd never had; now Pete was her best friend. She chastised herself for arguing with him earlier; he was just trying to protect her the way he always had.

She studied him, forgetting sometimes how good-looking he was—tall, handsome with his blue eyes and blond hair, and capable of being utterly charming. If only she'd fallen in love with him all those years ago. Instead of J.D.

Another song came on the radio. Denver saw Pete tense and her own heart lurched as it always did when J. D. Garrison's voice filled the airways. "Number ten on the country and western chart and climbing," the radio announcer cut in. "Our own J. D. Garrison with his latest hit, 'Old Friends and Enemies.'"

Pete snapped off the radio. "I can't believe he didn't make the funeral."

Just the thought of J.D. brought back the hurt and disappointment. In her foolish heart, she'd always believed J.D. would come home if she or Max ever needed him. Well, they'd needed him. And he hadn't come.

"I doubt J.D. can just drop everything at a moment's notice," she heard herself say. "Maybe he didn't get the message you left him."

Pete shot her a look. "Still making excuses for him?"

She looked away. Loving J.D. had always been both pleasure and pain. And all one-sided. J.D. had never seen her as anything more than a kid. But sometimes his gaze had met hers and— And then he'd ruffle her hair or throw her into the lake. No, he'd never taken her seriously, even when she'd promised him her heart. Instead, he'd teased her. Just a schoolgirl crush. Puppy love. She'd get over it.

He'd been gone nine years, but she still saw his ghost lounging on the sandy beach beside the lake, heard his laugh on the breeze that swept across the water and felt his touch on a hot summer's night as she stood on the dock, unable to sleep. She'd just never met anyone who made her feel like J.D. had.

But if J. D. Garrison were here right now, she'd wring his neck. For missing Max's funeral. For breaking a young girl's heart. For still haunting her thoughts.

It began to snow harder as they dropped down to the Madison River. A soft mist rose from the water, cloaking the bridge in a veil of white fog and driving snow. A local teenage superstition prophesied that if you didn't honk as you crossed the bridge you'd be in for bad luck. Pete didn't believe in superstitions. "You make your own luck," he'd always said. Denver honked, partly out of superstition, partly out of tradition; J.D. had never crossed the bridge without honking.

As they crossed the bridge, Pete didn't honk. The snow fell in a thick, hypnotizing wall of white in front of the pickup. Denver realized she could barely make out the Madison Arm sign as they passed it. She glanced in the side mirror and was startled to see a huge semitrailer barreling down on them.

"Pete?" Her voice cracked. Her heart caught in her throat. "Pete!" He looked back, his eyes widening as he saw it. At the last moment, the truck swerved into the passing lane. Denver thought it would head on around them, but instead, she realized with growing horror, the truck was edging over into their lane.

"Son of a—" Pete yelled.

Denver could see the huge semitrailer wheels right next to them. A scream lodged in her throat; the truck would either force them off the road or—

Pete hit the brakes. The back of the semi just missed the front of the pickup by inches as it swerved the rest of the way into their lane.

Snow poured over the cab in a blinding rush as the semi roared past. Pete brought the pickup to a skidding stop sideways in the middle of the highway. Denver stared through the falling snow, expecting another vehicle to come along and hit them before Pete got the pickup pulled over to the edge of the road.

He sat there gripping the steering wheel. "Are you all right?" he asked. His voice sounded strained as if the shock of their near mishap was just sinking in.

Denver took a shaky breath. Now that the danger had passed, she was trembling all over. "I think so. What was that guy doing?"

Pete shook his head as he looked at her. "I don't know, but I could kill the bastard."

Denver looked at the highway ahead, half expecting the trucker to come back and finish the job. "I can't believe he didn't even stop to see if we were all right."

Pete swore as he steered the pickup back onto the highway and headed toward West Yellowstone again.

"Did you recognize the truck?" she asked. It had happened so fast she hadn't even thought to look at the license plate.

"I'm sure it was just some out-of-stater who's never been in a snowstorm before." But Pete kept staring at the highway as if he expected to see the truck again, too. And Denver knew she wouldn't feel safe until they reached town. No, she thought, she wouldn't feel safe until Max's killer was caught.

Chapter Two

Pete slowed on the outskirts of town. At first glance, West, as the locals called it, appeared abandoned. They drove down the main drag, past the Dairy Queen, a row of T-shirt and curio shops and Denver's camera shop. All were still boarded up behind huge piles of plowed snow. A melting cornice drooped low over Denver's storefront. Out of a huge drift peeked a partially exposed homemade sign. See You In The Spring!

The only hint of spring was in the rivers of melting snow running along the sides of the empty streets. Dirty snowbanks, plowed up higher than most of the buildings, marked the street corners they drove by. Everywhere, a webbing of snowmobile tracks crisscrossed the rotting snow still lingering in the shadow of the pines. Down a muddy alley sat a deserted snowmobile, its engine cover thrown back, falling snowflakes rapidly covering it.

Only a couple of gas stations had their lights on. Near a mud puddle as large as a lake, two locals sat visiting, with their pickups running.

It was April. Off-season. Snowmobiling was over for another winter and the summer tourist trade wouldn't officially begin until Memorial Day weekend. Denver usually cherished this time of year, a time for the locals to take a breather before the tourists returned. But today, the town seemed to echo her lonely, empty feeling of loss.

"I'm going to get you something hot to drink," Pete said, touching her arm.

Since the near accident with the semi, she hadn't been able to quit shaking. Pete pulled up to a convenience store and came back a few minutes later with two large hot chocolates. "It's beautiful, isn't it?" he said, motioning toward the falling snow. "I love this time of year." His gaze turned from the storm to her. "And I love you."

"Pete, don't—"

"When are you going to stop fighting it, Denver? I love you." He put his finger to her lips when she tried to protest. "I know you don't love me. At least not enough to marry me. Not yet. But you will, very soon."

As she looked at Pete's handsome face, she wished he were right. Marrying Pete was safe, and Max had made no secret of the fact that he had liked Pete for that very reason.

They finished their hot chocolates and drove farther on into town, finally stopping in front of a house on Faithful Street. The place was typical of the older West Yellowstone residences: rustic log with a green metal roof, surrounded by lodgepole pines.

"Let's get this over with," Pete said as he parked in front of Maggie's house.

J.D. STOOD AT THE WINDOW of his room in the Stage Coach Inn, watching snowflakes spin slowly down from the grayness above. He blamed his restlessness on being back in West Yellowstone after all these years, on the weather, on Max's burial service.

Jeez, Garrison, you've been lying to yourself for so long, you've started believing it. He stepped away from the window and went to the makeshift bar he'd set up on the dresser. *It's seeing Denny again that's thrown you.* He frowned, still surprised at his reaction. Denver. He swore under his breath as he ripped the plastic off one of the water glasses and poured a half inch of Crown Royal into it.

All these years he'd remembered Denny as the little freckle-faced girl he'd had water fights with on the beach and beat at Monopoly. Not that there hadn't always been something about her that made her special to him. A fire in her eyes and a spirit and determination that had touched him. But she'd been just a kid. Now he couldn't help wondering about the woman he'd seen at the cemetery—the woman Denver McCallahan had become. How much was left of the girl he'd once shared his dreams with?

The window drew him back again. His dreams. He sipped the whiskey and looked out at his old hometown. It was here he'd picked up his first guitar, a beat-up used one. He'd fumbled through a few chords, a song already forming in his head. It had always been there. The music, the knowledge that he'd make it as a singer—and the ambition eating away inside him.

He stared at the town through the snow. It had been here that he'd performed for the first time, here that he'd dreamed of recording an album of his own music, here that he'd always known he'd end up one day. But not like this.

Nine years. Nine years on a circuit of smoky bars and honky-tonks, long empty highways, flat tires on old clunkers and cheap motel rooms. Somewhere along the way, he'd made it. Even now, he couldn't remember exactly when that happened, when he realized it was no longer just a dream. J. D. Garrison was a genuine country and western star. Grammys and Country Music Association awards, his songs on the top of *Billboard*'s country charts. Since then, there'd been more awards, more songs, more albums, more tours. And better cars, better bars, better motel rooms.

But one thing remained the same. That distant feeling that he was drifting off the face of the earth, that he'd become untethered from life. A few weeks ago, he'd awakened in a strange motel room and forgotten where he was, and when he'd looked at himself in the mirror, he realized he'd forgotten who he was, as well. He was losing the music. The songs weren't there anymore—and neither was the desire to make them.

J.D. spread his fingers across the cold windowpane. The white flakes danced beyond his touch; a tiny drift formed on the sill. "Oh, Denny," he whispered. There was no doubt in his mind that she would try to find Max's murderer. The question was how to keep her safe. And how to keep Pete away from her until he could sort it all out.

But he knew one thing. He'd do whatever he had to do. *Like hell. You're looking forward to coming between the two of them. But is it because you believe Pete might have changed so much in these nine years that he could kill someone? Or is it simply that you don't want Pete to have Denny?*

He frowned as he remembered the woman he'd glimpsed at the cemetery. Denver McCallahan was definitely a woman worth fighting for. And if he were Pete Williams, he'd fight like hell for her.

MAGGIE MET PETE and Denver on the screened-in porch in worn jeans, an old flannel shirt that could have been Max's, and a pair of moccasins. She hadn't attended the burial, saying she preferred to remember Max the way he was. A bag of groceries rested on the step, and from her breathlessness, Denver guessed she'd just come from the store.

The buzz of the going-away party spilled through the door behind her as she hugged Denver. "You okay?"

"I need to talk to you," Denver whispered.

Maggie handed Pete the bag of groceries and asked him to take them inside where friends had already started Max's party—their version of an Irish send-off.

"What's the matter?" Maggie asked after Pete was out of earshot. "Pete isn't pressuring you again, is he?"

Maggie was always quick to blame Pete. She disapproved of him, not because he was a musician with the band he and J.D. had started, the Montana Country Club, but because he'd never gone beyond that. "He's as talented as J.D. but he lacks J.D.'s inner strength," she'd said. "Behind all that charm is a very disappointed, angry young man.'' It was one of the few things Max and Maggie had ever argued about.

Denver wished Pete and Maggie could get along, especially now that Max was gone.

"Pete's fine. It's about Max," Denver said. More guests arrived. She'd known Max made friends easily, but Denver was astounded at the number of people who'd come hundreds of miles to pay their respects to him.

Maggie told Denver to go on through the house to the kitchen, where the noise level was lower and the temperature definitely warmer, and wait for her. "Cal Dalton was here earlier," Maggie said. Since the party was an all-day kind of thing, people kept coming and going. "I just got back so I don't know if he's still here or not."

"Thanks, I need to talk to him."

Denver worked her way through the guests, stopping to accept words of sympathy and visit a moment with friends. She didn't see Cal. In the kitchen, she stood watching the snow fall and thinking of Max. She didn't even hear Maggie come in.

"Has Deputy Cline found some new evidence?" Maggie asked hopefully.

"No." Denver pulled off her hat and coat, and hung them on a hook by the back door. She wandered around the familiar kitchen, too keyed up to sit. "Cline is still convinced Max was killed by a hitchhiker."

Max's body had been found at the old city dump; according to Sheriff's Deputy Bill Cline, he'd been stabbed once in the heart. Cline was looking for a hitchhiker Max had bought lunch for at the Elkhorn Café earlier that day.

Maggie sat down at the kitchen table, her eyes dark with pain. "I can't believe Max was killed by someone he helped."

"I don't think that's what happened." Denver bit her lip, watching for Maggie's reaction. "What if it was connected to one of his cases? Maybe an . . . old case."

"You aren't suggesting it might be—"

"No." Denver fought off a chill. "Even Max had given up on that one." The one old case that had haunted Max for years was the unsolved murders of Denver's parents. Denver stopped beside the table, settling her gaze on Maggie. "I've been having the nightmare again."

"Oh, Denver." Maggie took her hand. "Max's death must have brought it back."

It had been years since she'd had the nightmare, not since Max had brought her to live with him in West Yellowstone. She'd been five at the time and could remember very little of her life before then. Except for images from the nightmare of fear and death from that day at the bank. She'd been with her parents the day the bank robber had killed her father and mother. Her father had just gotten off duty; he was still in his police uniform. Max said that was what had gotten him killed—walking into the middle of a robbery in uniform.

"I thought maybe Max might have mentioned a case," Denver said, changing the subject.

"You know the kind of work he did, small-time stuff, insurance fraud, divorce and child custody, theft—nothing worth getting murdered over."

"What if he'd stumbled across that once-in-a-lifetime case he'd always dreamed of?"

Maggie smiled. "I wish he had, honey. But you know Max. He couldn't have kept that a secret from us."

Denver ran her fingers along the edge of the kitchen counter. "He could if it was too dangerous or confidential or..." The word *illegal* sprang into her mind. Surely Maggie had heard the rumors.

"The last time he mentioned a case, he was tailing a husband whose wife thought he was having an affair," Maggie said. "I remember because Max was keeping odd hours. He wouldn't get in until the wee hours of the morning." She laughed. "I asked him if *he* was having an affair."

"How did the case turn out?" Denver asked.

"He never told me." Maggie looked past Denver, her gaze clouded. "There is one thing, though. A few days before he was . . . before he died, he brought some file folders home from the office. Old ones."

"Where are they now?" Denver asked as she sat down across from Maggie.

"He burned them."

"He what?" Denver couldn't believe her ears.

"That night we were sitting by the fireplace. He was sorting through some things. That's when I saw the folders—right before he tossed them into the fire."

"Did you see what they were?"

Maggie frowned. "I wasn't paying much attention, but a newspaper clipping fell out of one of the files. I don't even remember what it was about, just that it was old. I'm sure that's why Max was throwing the files away."

"Still, that doesn't sound like Max. He never threw anything away."

"I didn't think it was strange at the time. . . ." Maggie's voice trailed off. "You know, he did keep one of those files. I guess he took it back to his office."

"There are too many strange things. Like Max's will. Not even his lawyer's seen it. It seems Max drew it up himself and said he'd put it in a safe place." Denver shook her head. "I wonder what Max would consider a safe place? Probably the middle of his kitchen table."

Maggie laughed softly, her eyes misty with private memories of Max. "The police didn't find it in either Max's apartment or office. Do you think he could have left it at your cabin?"

"I haven't looked yet," Denver said. "And Max's gun is missing, too. Deputy Cline says the killer must have taken it when he took Max's wallet. But you know Max hardly ever carried a gun."

Maggie brushed at her tears. "Max would have given that hitchhiker money before the guy could even ask, and given him his shirt and shoes, as well. Even his car."

"That's just it, Maggie. Why didn't the guy take Max's car? The keys were in it." Denver turned and was startled to find Pete standing just inside the kitchen doorway. She wondered how long he'd been there, listening.

"I thought we'd already settled this." He glared at her, his gaze hard with anger. "You were going to stay out of the murder investigation and let Cline do his job."

Denver drew in a deep breath. Obviously she hadn't made herself clear when they'd argued about this earlier. "I can't stay out of it. How is the killer ever going to be caught when Cline isn't even looking into Max's cases?"

"What cases?" Pete demanded. "Come on, Denver. You're clutching at straws. It was a hitchhiker. You know how bad Max was about picking up strays."

No one knew better than she did just how Max was about helping people in trouble, she thought as she fingered her mother's gold locket at her neck. Fortunately, Max McCallahan had been that kind of man.

"No, it simply doesn't make sense," Denver said, standing her ground. "Maggie said he burned some old files right before he was killed. Doesn't that sound suspicious to you?"

Pete raked his fingers through his hair, not bothering to hide his exasperation. "So what are you going to do? Go after this murderer by yourself?"

"Pete's right," Maggie interrupted, surprising them both, since she seldom agreed with Pete on anything. "Listen, honey, Max wouldn't have wanted you getting involved in this. Obviously it's dangerous. I think you'd better leave it to the deputy sheriff."

Denver stared at her. It wasn't like Maggie to tell her to run from trouble; Maggie had always encouraged her to join Max in the investigation business. It had been Max who wouldn't hear of it, who had insisted she stick to photography, even though she'd helped him by taking photos on some of his cases.

"I'd better get back to my guests," Maggie said, slipping past Pete.

The tension in the kitchen dropped a notch or two in the moments after Maggie left; Denver knew it was because Pete thought he might be able to dissuade her. She looked out the window. The day had slipped away into dusk.

"I'm sorry," Pete said, crossing the kitchen to put his arms around her. "I know you're upset about Max. I just don't want to see you get hurt."

The worry in his eyes startled her. If he believed Max had been killed by some stranger passing through town, why would he be so afraid for her? Clearly he didn't believe it any more than she did.

"Just promise me you'll stay out of this," Pete whispered into her hair. "I want to help you get through it, if you'll let me."

Denver buried her face in his shoulder. She felt protected in his arms. Maybe Pete was right. She was a photographer—not an investigator. But that knowledge did little to cool the fever burning deep within her. She had to see Max's murderer behind bars; she owed Max at least that. And after all those years of hanging around him, she'd picked up a little something about investigative work. She wasn't going after the killer blind; she knew of the danger. But the danger didn't scare her as much as the thought that her uncle's murderer might get away.

"I'm sorry, Pete," she said, lifting her cheek from his shoulder. "I can't make that promise." She felt him tense. He dropped his arms and stepped back, his expression one of disappointment and anger. "I'm going to find Max's killer if it's the last thing I do."

Pete nodded. "It just might be."

J.D. COULDN'T SHAKE the feeling that Denver was already in trouble, more trouble than just being involved with Pete—a possible killer.

He picked up the phone and dialed Maggie's number. Someone pretty well sloshed answered. A moment later, Maggie came on the line. "Is Denny all right?" he asked, feeling foolish.

"She's fine," Maggie said. "She's here and Pete just left." Her voice sounded muffled as if coming from inside a closet. From the party noise in the background, he guessed she probably was.

"Good. I won't worry about her for the moment anyway." He hung up and reached for his coat, trying to shake off the ominous feeling he had.

His options were limited. Confront Pete with what little "evidence" Maggie had against him and have Pete just deny it? Or try to talk to Denver about him. Maggie hadn't taken that route for two good reasons. One was that Denver knew Maggie had never liked Pete, and adding suspicion of murder to that list would only alienate her. The other was that the Denver he remembered would fight to the death to defend a friend, let alone a lover. And it was obvious she and Pete were very close.

J.D. cursed the thought. Nor did he doubt what Denver would do if he told her his suspicions. She'd go straight to Pete. Head-on. That was the way she operated. He assured himself Pete would never hurt her. At least, not the Pete he used to know. He considered Maggie's evidence against Pete flimsy at best. But Maggie's obvious fear for Denver made him think twice about dismissing it. If for some reason Pete *had* killed Max, then what would he do if he thought Denver suspected him? It wasn't a chance J.D. was willing to take with Denver's safety. And sitting around a motel room wasn't going to get him the answers he needed.

AFTER PETE LEFT HER ALONE in the kitchen, Denver stood staring at the snow falling in the darkness outside, thinking of Max. The need to avenge his death tore at her insides, holding her grief at bay most of the time. Except tonight. Tonight she felt alone and frightened.

As a girl, when she'd been afraid, she'd fantasized about J.D. rescuing her. Nothing quite as dramatic as being tied to the railroad tracks with the train coming—but close enough. Always at the last minute, J.D. would appear and save her. But this wasn't a fantasy now. Max was dead. Not even Pete was on her side this time. And J.D. certainly wasn't coming to her rescue.

The noise from the other room had reached a rowdy pitch, music blasting. Denver heard the kitchen door open behind her only because it increased the volume. At first, she thought it might be Pete coming back.

Cal Dalton closed the door behind him and leaned against it. "I hear you've been looking for me."

He reminded her of a coyote, a wild look in his eyes, his body poised for flight. And instantly she wondered what he had to be afraid of; he frightened her much more than she ever could him. Everything about him was cold, from his graying pale blond hair to his icy blue eyes. He had to be hugging fifty but he hung around the bars with men half his age. Cal was known in town as a womanizer and a mean drunk, always getting into fights. One jealous husband had even shot him, and Cal liked to show off the scar, according to local scuttlebutt.

"I'm trying to find out what cases Max was working on," she said. For reasons Denver could not fathom, Max had befriended Cal in the weeks before his death, something she could only assume meant Max was on a case.

"You think I hired your uncle?" Cal scratched his neck. "What would I need with a private eye?" Good question. "Max and I were just drinking buddies."

"He didn't mention a case he might have been working on?" she asked. "Or maybe hire you to do some legwork for him?"

"Legwork?" Cal shook his head. His gaze took her in as if he realized for the first time she was a woman and certainly no threat. "Speaking of legs, yours aren't half-bad," he said, making her feel as if he'd just peeled off her black slacks.

This had been a mistake. "Well, I'm sorry I bothered you."

"Max did talk a lot about you," he said.

She found that more unlikely than their being drinking buddies. "If you'll excuse me, Pete is waiting for me." She tried to get past him, but he blocked her way.

"I don't think so. I saw Pete leave." He was close now. She could feel his breath on her face, smell the reek of beer.

Pete wouldn't leave without telling her, would he?

Cal leaned his hands on either side of her, trapping her. "I'm afraid Pete's thrown you to the wolves, darlin'." His eyes traveled over her with a crudeness that turned her stomach. "How about a little kiss for old Cal?"

"No, and if you touch me—"

He moved closer. "I like feisty girls." He bent to kiss her. Denver dived under his arm, shooting for the space between his body and the counter. He caught her, swung her into him and gave her a smelly, slobbery kiss that made her gag. "How'd you like that?" he asked, leering. "Better than that pansy boyfriend of yours, huh?"

She jerked her arm free and slapped him with a force that drove him back a step.

He rubbed his jaw; a meanness came into his eyes. "You shouldn't have done that. All I wanted was a little kiss."

Denver grabbed the first thing she could find as Cal moved toward her. A pottery pitcher.

"Denver?" Cal turned at the sound of the voice behind him, and Denver looked past him to see Max's old friend, Taylor Reynolds, standing in the doorway. "Is there a problem here?"

Denver set down the pitcher and pushed past Cal to step into the big man's arms.

"It's okay," Taylor said, holding her awkwardly. The old bachelor wasn't a man used to a physical display of sentiment. "Buddy, don't you think you'd better get back to the party?"

Denver heard Cal leave but she didn't look up; she found herself crying, crying for Max, for herself.

"Hey, easy. This is my best suit," Taylor kidded, then pulled back to look at her. "What was going on in here? If he's bothering you—"

She stepped from the shelter of his arms, trying to regain control. "Cal was just being Cal."

Taylor pushed out a chair for her at the table and pulled down some towels from a roll. He handed them to her and joined her at the table.

Denver took a deep breath, wiped her eyes with a towel and looked at the man before her. She remembered Max talking about his buddies from the army, but she'd never met this one before. Taylor Reynolds was a powerful-looking man much like Max had been. Only unlike Max, Taylor was soft-spoken and shy. He'd shown up right after Max's murder.

"Max saved my life in the army—I owe him," Taylor had said, standing with his hat in his hands on Maggie's porch. "I'll be staying at the Three Bears if you need anything."

Denver had taken to him immediately, and so had Maggie. Denver knew it was because he and Max had been so close; in Taylor a small part of Max still lived.

"It's tough, but we're all going to get through this," Taylor said now. He didn't seem to know what to do with his big hands. He took a toothpick and spun it between two fingers.

"Who do you think killed him?"

Taylor's face clouded. "A damned fool."

"Do you think it was the hitchhiker Deputy Cline's looking for?" She had a sudden flash of Max, the flicker of sunlight on the water behind him, the gentle lap of water against the side of the boat, the sound of his laugh floating across the lake. When she looked up, she realized Taylor had been talking to her.

"Denver?" He studied her, his eyes dark with concern. "You're having a rough time with this, aren't you, kid? Be careful. Don't let Max's death become more important than living."

Denver looked away. The noise of the party seemed at odds with the silence of the darkness outside.

Taylor reached across the table and patted her hand, then quickly pulled back, obviously embarrassed by the gesture. He got to his feet. "I think that Cal fellow has had enough to drink. Why don't I see he gets home where he won't be bothering you anymore tonight.''

''Thank you.''

''We're all going to miss Max, kid,'' he said as he left.

For a few moments, Denver stood in the quiet kitchen, thinking about what Taylor had said. She knew he was right; Max would have wanted her to get on with her life. And he would have liked her to marry Pete.

''I want to know there's going to be someone around for you when I'm gone,'' he'd said the last time they'd talked.

Denver closed her eyes. And now Max *was* gone. Had he known there was a chance he might be killed?

The kitchen suddenly felt as if it were closing in on her. Denver took her coat and hat and slipped out through the side door into the night. A chilly wind spun a weathered wind sock on the end of the eaves. She ducked her head against the cold and pulled her coat more tightly around her. The snow had stopped; now it was melting, dripping from warm roofs and dark pine boughs along the street.

Cal had told the truth, she realized with a shock. Pete's pickup was gone. ''Men,'' she groaned as she started the four-block walk to her car.

For days she'd told herself that it was all a mistake, that Max wasn't really dead. Now as she walked the familiar streets, she acknowledged that he was gone. The truth came like a swift kick to the stomach. All the values she'd believed in, Max had taught her. She owed him her very life.

Her Jeep was parked in front of Pete's apartment, where she'd left it earlier before the service. Pete's pickup was nowhere to be seen. As she drove down Firehole Avenue, she realized how tired she was. All she wanted to do was go to the lake cabin and get some sleep. But as she looked down the dark street to Max's office, she wondered again about what cases Max might have been working on, something Cline wouldn't have recognized as a clue since he was so busy looking for a hitchhiker. Finding Max's killer couldn't wait, she realized. And nothing was going to stop her. Nothing. And nobody.

Chapter Three

Pete stood in the snowy shadows of the old log building at the edge of town listening to the night. Normally he loved this hour, when darkness settled in, cloaking secrets and regrets. Tonight, though, he felt vulnerable and afraid. Softly he knocked at the rear door. It opened a crack, then fell open. A hand grabbed his jacket and jerked him inside.

"I've told you not to come here. It's too risky."

Pete stumbled into the dimly lit room; the door slammed behind him. He followed the man to the front of the cabin. "I want to talk to the boss." The man swaggered into the living room. Pete followed, realizing he'd been drinking. "Let me talk to him. Now. Or I'm walking."

The man scowled. "So walk. You're the one who wanted in on this operation."

"If I walk, I walk to the feds," Pete said.

"That would be real smart." The man slumped into a chair before the fire roaring in the small fireplace. He picked up a whiskey bottle from the floor and took a long swig. "But that would be one way to meet the boss. He'd kill you."

Pete looked into the fire. What little he knew about their boss reminded him of hell and the devil himself. "You going to call him?"

"You're signing your death warrant if you mess with him." But he got to his feet and went into the kitchen to the phone. Pete listened to him dial. A long-distance number.

It took a moment and Pete knew the call was being forwarded somewhere else. Then he heard the man in the kitchen talking in a hushed tone, apologizing, explaining. Finally, he called Pete in and handed him the receiver. The look on his face warned Pete he'd stepped over the line.

"You have a problem?" the synthesized voice asked on the other end of the line.

"Look, Midnight, I'm tired of putting up with this bozo," Pete said of the man standing next to him. "I want a number where I can call you. And I want to know why you had someone try to run me off the road this afternoon."

Midnight laughed, the synthesizer turning it into a midway sideshow. "You certainly want a lot, don't you?"

Midnight. How perfectly the code name described a man both dark and dangerous. "I've proven myself in your little organization, haven't I?"

Silence. He could tell Midnight didn't like the "little" part. "So you have."

"I don't like being threatened. You could have killed us both!"

Midnight's voice turned deadly serious. "Yes, I could have. But I didn't. Did it convince you how important it is to keep Denver from looking into Max McCallahan's death?"

"I was always convinced." Pete decided honesty might be the best policy, even with a man like Midnight. "But Denver's determined to find Max's killer."

Midnight let out another carnival laugh. "Well, she doesn't have to look too far, does she?"

Pete glared into the fire. The flames licked at the logs with hot fury.

"You said you could control her," Midnight continued. "I don't like problems."

"I'll take care of Denver. That was the arrangement."

Midnight's voice turned raspy with anger. "Arrangements can be changed."

Pete knew if anyone would renege on a bargain it was this man. Hadn't the truck episode proved that today? Denver had no idea what she was getting herself into if she persisted in searching for Max's murderer.

"You're sure the case file I'm looking for wasn't at Max's office?" Midnight asked.

"Yes."

"Then that leaves the cabin. You haven't said what you found out there. And don't tell me you haven't looked yet."

Pete wanted to tell him to do his own search but knew Midnight hired other men to do his dirty work while he hid on a phone line, behind a synthesizer. Why so much secrecy? All he could figure was that Midnight had to be someone he knew; it made him nervous not knowing with whom he was in business. "I tried to get Denver to stay at my place tonight so I could search the cabin, but she's determined—"

"She's determined?" Midnight let out a string of oaths. "I'm determined. No more excuses. I want that cabin searched *tonight.*"

"And how do you expect me to do that with Denver there?" Pete asked in frustration.

"I've left a prescription in your name at the drugstore."

"Pills?" Pete gasped. "You don't want me to—"

"Kill her?" Midnight groaned. "No. A couple of tablets and she'll sleep like the dead, though. Make sure you don't overdo it or you could kill her." His voice seemed to vibrate with an evil that chilled Pete even in the hot room. "Hit the cabin tonight. And you'd better find that file."

"I told you how Max was. He didn't think like other people. Who knows where he's hidden it, if it even exists?"

"It exists." Midnight sighed. "You realize if Denver finds the file first, we'll have to kill her."

And if anyone could find the file, it would be Denver, Pete thought. She already had her suspicions; it was just a matter of time before she figured it out. "I'll take care of it tonight."

"If you don't—" Midnight paused "—I'll find someone who can."

Pete started to hang up, but Midnight stopped him.

"We have another problem that needs to be taken care of," he said. "It's that kid, Davey Matthews. You know the one who was always hanging around Max's office? I'm afraid he knows too much."

"Just what we need, another murder."

"I'll call you later at the cabin and we can discuss what to do about Davey. He's young and foolish. Young and foolish men have accidents. Put the bozo back on," Midnight said. "Then you'd better get to the drugstore before it closes."

MAX MCCALLAHAN'S detective agency filled the bottom floor of a small two-story log house on Geyser Street; he had lived in a tiny efficiency apartment upstairs. Denver could never understand why he hadn't married Maggie. He'd spent most of his time over at her place, but refused to give up the apartment because he didn't want people to talk. Well, people were talking now, Denver thought bitterly.

A snow-filled silence hung over the street as she walked past Max's old blue-and-white Oldsmobile station wagon parked out front. She'd forgotten the police had left it there. Like everything else, the car reminded her of her loss. She headed up the unshoveled walk, steeling herself for the memories she knew waited inside, but stopped abruptly. Someone else had already climbed these same steps tonight. There were fresh boot prints in the newly fallen snow—coming and going.

Shadows came to life as the large pines flanking the house swayed and creaked in the wind. Water dripped from the eaves and the old house sighed forlornly under the weight of the wet snowfall.

Denver stopped, fighting to shake off the spooked feeling in her stomach. She suddenly thought of a dozen good reasons why she should come back in the morning. She cursed her lack of courage. After her parents died, Max had brought her to West Yellowstone, offering her a safe place to live so she'd never have to be afraid again. For Max—and for herself—she had to find his murderer or she'd never feel that kind of security here again.

With renewed determination, she ascended the steps, her boot heels thudding across the wooden porch. On the window in the old oak front door a sign was painted in gold letters: McCallahan Investigations. Behind the letters, the drapes were drawn. Nothing moved. She dug for her key, then reached to unlock the door.

But it was already open. The hinges gave a sigh as the door swung into the dark room. With fingers cold and shaking, Denver flipped on the light. She feared what she'd find, but nothing prepared her for this.

File cabinets lay over on their sides, folders sprawled everywhere, their contents crumpled and strewn across the floor. All the drawers on Max's big oak desk were upside down. Even the photographs she'd given him had been pulled from the walls and thrown into the pile of debris.

Denver clung to the doorjamb fighting for breath. Why would anyone do this? For several moments, she just stared. What had the burglar been looking for? No doubt the same thing she was. That was some consolation. Maybe there *was* something to find. Or had been, anyway.

She glanced around the office, wondering if it could still be here. If Max was on a hot case, something explosive, what would he have done with the evidence he'd collected? Good question.

Max had no concept of organization. His files were always a disaster with some filed by first names, others by nicknames, even a few by last names. He had once hired a part-time secretary to straighten them, but when she had gone to lunch, he couldn't find a thing and made such a mess of the file cabinet that she finally gave up and quit.

Denver bent to retrieve a handful of folders from the floor. It would take hours to make any sense out of this mess. And she had to face the probability that any clues Max might have left had already been stolen. Not only that, she might be destroying evidence that could lead Deputy

Cline to the culprit who did this, she realized, dropping the files on the edge of Max's desk.

She righted the huge oak office chair and sat down, more certain than ever that Max had left something behind to help her solve his murder. *Think like Max,* she told herself. She put her feet up on the desk and leaned back with her hands behind her head, imitating Max's favorite pose when he was pondering a case.

Where, Max? Where would you put something that would incriminate the person you were after? She surveyed the ceiling lights. Max jotted down everything; that was how he worked through his cases. Usually it was just a lot of scribbles. Sometimes it might be only a few words. Then he filed the notes until he solved the case. If Max was working on a job, there'd be scribbles and there'd be a case file.

And that was what the burglar had been looking for. That had to be it. And the same person was probably spreading those rumors about Max. Muddying the waters. But why bother, with Cline convinced that Max was killed by a hitchhiker for no other reason than robbery?

Denver was so preoccupied that at first she thought she'd imagined the sound. Then it happened again—a floorboard creaked overhead, followed by the scraping sound of wood. It was coming from upstairs in Max's apartment. She froze. Why hadn't it crossed her mind that the burglar could still be in the house?

Carefully she slid her feet off Max's desk and, slipping off her boots, tiptoed to the bottom of the stairs. No sounds, except the thunder of her pulse in her ears. She picked up the nearest object from the floor—the telephone—and unhooked the cord, then, carrying it as a weapon, started up the stairs.

Halfway up, one of the steps creaked under her weight and she stopped, afraid to move. Reason invaded her brain. What was she doing?

Why didn't you think to call Deputy Cline *before* you unplugged the phone, the rational little voice in her head asked.

Nice that you should suggest that *now,* Denver retorted silently as she looked from the disconnected phone in her hand to the creaky steps behind her. And Max used to think she was a little too impetuous. If he could see her now.

She stood on the step, listening. Silence so strong it seemed alive answered her back. She shifted the phone to her right hand and continued up the stairs, willing herself to remain calm, knowing she wouldn't.

At the top of the steps, she cautiously pushed open the door to the apartment, phone ready. When nothing jumped out, she reached in hesitantly and switched on the lights. She expected the apartment to resemble Max's office; she hadn't expected it to be destroyed. An overstuffed chair was up-ended, the mattress hung off the side of the bed, its guts spilling out on the floor. The contents of all the dresser drawers had been thrown around the room. She hoped the destruction meant that the burglar hadn't found what he was looking for.

She exchanged the phone for a brass lamp base, checked the closet and started to breathe a little more easily. Across the room, a shutter banged softly against the side of the house. That explained the noise she'd heard. No ghosts. No burglars. Just the breeze.

The state of the apartment and Max's office reinforced her theory that Max had left something that would incriminate his killer. All she had to do was figure out what it was and find it before the killer did. If he hadn't already found it.

That was when she noticed the partially closed bathroom door. She headed for it, thinking about what she'd tell Deputy Cline. Surely when he saw this place, he'd have to give up his hitchhiker theory. Reaching into the bathroom, she fumbled for the light switch with her free hand.

Cold fingers clamped over her wrist in a deathlike grip. Denver let out a cry of total terror as she was jerked into the darkened bathroom. She swung the lamp. It connected with something solid and veered off. She heard a male voice swear as the fingers on her wrist let go, and a loud thud followed. Denver retreated, fumbling for the bathroom light switch on her way out, this time with the lamp in her hand ready to swing again.

She found the switch. The bathroom light flashed on. Denver blinked. At first because of the sudden brightness, then out of disbelief. Sitting crosswise in the bathtub swearing and holding his head was none other than J. D. Garrison.

Denver stumbled backward and fell over, tripping on the overturned chair. She landed on her bottom in a pile of mattress stuffing. J. D. Garrison leaned over her.

"Hello, Denny," he said, offering her a hand. "It's been a long time."

Chapter Four

Denver lay staring up at the man standing over her, unable to move. J.D. J. D. Garrison. After all these years.

She'd envisioned the day he returned thousands of times, always in Technicolor, always with the same basic plot. He'd come riding in like John Wayne, all handsome and charming. He'd beg her to forgive him for not taking her with him, sweep her off her feet, promise his undying love, maybe play a few songs on his guitar. And then she'd tell him to drop dead.

Never would she have imagined it quite like this.

She ignored his offer of help and got to her feet on her own power, dusting herself off. The gesture gave her a few moments to compose herself; J.D. was the last person she'd expected to see in that bathtub.

"What are *you* doing here?" she demanded, her pride as well as her bottom still smarting. Damn. The effect he had on her! Her heart was pounding and not from fear anymore; she felt sixteen again. The feeling made her all the more angry with him.

"It's nice to see you again, too," he said, his smile widening.

She'd practiced at least ten thousand times what she'd say to him if she ever *did* see him again. But nothing came to her lips. He'd changed; he wasn't that lanky young man she remembered. A dark mustache and neatly trimmed beard nearly hid his deep dimples. His eyes, always a blend of moonlight silvers and midnight grays, seemed darker, but there was an older look about them, almost a sadness....

She realized he was holding his head where she'd hit him with the lamp. His gray Stetson dangled from his other hand. "Are you all right?" she asked guiltily.

He nodded and tried to get the hat back on his head over the lump she'd given him. "My head's too hard for most lamps. But the fall into the bathtub I could have done without." As he rubbed his backside, she noticed the flashlight stuck in his belt. "I'm sorry I scared you. I heard a noise and thought the prowler had returned." He grinned.

Prowler indeed. His grin sent her heart racing around in circles. Just what she needed. "So you're back in town," she said, before adding, "you missed Max's funeral and you better have a damned good reason."

He leaned back and laughed. "You had me worried for a moment there. I thought you'd lost that charming way you've always had with words." Those wonderfully deep dimples were now just a hint under the beard, and little wrinkles had been added around his eyes. It didn't matter. He still had that same heart-thumping effect he always had on her.

She frowned and turned away from the look in his eyes. What was it? Affection on his part? Or imagination on hers? Without another word, she hurried down the stairs; she could hear J.D. right behind her.

"Don't you want to hear my damned good reason?" he asked.

"I didn't really expect you'd make it anyway," she said, pulling on her boots. "I figured you were probably busy making a new album or performing for all those fans of yours." Bitterness and hurt crackled from her words and she wished she could bite her tongue. She bent down to pick up files and loose papers from the floor, forgetting all about saving evidence for Cline. "I told Pete not to bother calling you."

"Pete called?" J.D. sounded surprised.

"Don't pretend you didn't get the message." She heard the soft tread of his boots on the floor as he came up behind her.

"Denny, I was so sorry to hear about Max." His voice was soft. So was the touch of his fingers on her shoulders. "I wanted to be at the funeral for you."

She shrugged his hands away and spun on him. "I thought you cared about Max. I thought you cared about—" Tears brimmed in her eyes. She fought the culprits, determined not to cry. She'd shed enough tears for J. D. Garrison. Damned if she'd cry in front of him.

"I do care," he said, lifting her chin to meet her gaze. "I caught the first plane out. But getting to West Yellowstone this time of year is kind of tricky. You might remember the airport's closed until Memorial Day weekend." He flashed her a sheepish grin that beseeched her to give him a break. "I'm here now, though."

She wished he'd just take her in his arms and hold her, but he didn't, and she stepped back, all the hurt flowing out of her in place of tears. "I'm sure we'll probably read in the tabloids next week just how hard it was for you to get back for the funeral." The tabloids had followed his exploits with one woman after another for years now. "I suppose there'll be flight attendants involved this time."

J.D.'s jaw tensed as he shook his head at her. "I'm surprised you read the tabloids, let alone believe them." He met her gaze and held it as gently as a caress. "Come on, you know me better than that."

Know him? She thought she knew him. She'd shared his dreams. And a lot more. She'd given him her heart. No, she'd given her heart to J. D. Garrison, the boy she had grown up with, not this stranger in designer Western wear.

"Did you find what you were looking for?" he asked, motioning to the mess in the room, probably thinking a little humor would soften her up.

Fat chance. "Don't you remember? This is the way Max liked his office. Everything out where he could find it."

J.D. nodded, his eyes darkening. "Yeah, I remember that about Max." He stood, just staring at her. "You've changed."

Her chin went up instinctively. "I've grown up, if that's what you mean. I'm not a kid anymore."

"I can see that." The look in his eyes blew the devil out of her theory. Those weren't the eyes of a stranger. She looked away. "I assume you won't be staying long?" she asked, bracing herself for his answer.

He tipped up one of the drawers with his boot toe, and then let it back down gently. "I've taken a room at the Stage Coach Inn for a few days."

She nodded. In a few days he'd be gone again. That old pain gripped her heart. What had she expected? "A few days? And Max's funeral is what brought you home?" She wanted to clarify it for her heart, just in case the silly thing wasn't getting it straight.

"I came home because of you, Denny."

Her head snapped up.

He grinned at her surprise. "I know you, Denver McCallahan. And I know what you're thinking."

"You do?" She let her eyes travel the length of him. If he knew what she was thinking, he'd be blushing.

But when her gaze returned to his silver-eyed one, she realized with a shock that he *did* know what she was thinking. She felt her face flush red-hot and looked away first.

"I'm worried about you," he continued, his voice gentle. "You think I don't know what you're doing here tonight?" She watched him step over a pile of papers on the floor. "You're looking for Max's killer, and if you'd arrived a little earlier, you might have found him."

"I can take care of myself," she said, her chin coming up again.

He smiled. "I don't doubt that for a moment—under normal circumstances." The smile faded. "But Max is dead and someone tore this place apart with a desperation that scares me even if it doesn't you. You could be in a lot of danger."

Danger? She'd just gone up the stairs after a burglar with only a phone. Her heart pounded harder, her pulse raced faster just being this close to J. D. Garrison. "I have to go." She glanced at her watch, seeing nothing. She had to get away. She couldn't bear spending another minute in the same room with him, wanting to touch him, to feel his arms around her, to kiss those lips. "I promised Pete—" The lie caught in her throat. Who was she kidding? She didn't even know where Pete was.

A shadow flickered across J.D.'s eyes as he turned to look at her. "I guess you and Pete are pretty close?"

She crossed her fingers. "Just like that." It didn't bother her at all to let him think they were more than friends. He frowned. "You've made a lot of . . . friends yourself," she said, unable to stop herself. "Weren't you engaged to a Hollywood starlet, if I remember right?" Which she did. "And not six months after you left Montana." She glared at him. "Didn't take you long, did it, Garrison?"

His grin was the old J.D.'s. "You haven't called me Garrison since the last time you were mad at me. I've kinda missed it."

"I'll just bet." She edged her way toward the door, trying to put space between them; she felt like an out-of-balance washing machine.

As she passed J.D., he reached out and grabbed her arm. His gaze settled on her, solid as a rock. "Where do you think you're going?"

"I beg your pardon?" She shook off his hold.

"Look at this place, Denny," he said, sweeping an arm out. "What do you think the burglar was looking for?"

"How should I know?" If she knew that, she wouldn't be standing here talking to *him*.

"Then let me ask you this. Do you think he found what he was looking for?"

"No," she said, not sure why she felt so confident that the burglar hadn't.

"So, Denny, where do you think he'll look next?"

She stared at him, all cocky and sure of himself, standing in the middle of the mess in Max's office. But he was right. Why hadn't she thought of it? Because seeing J.D. again had put her mind on a permanent spin cycle.

"You bet," J.D. said. "Your burglar will more than likely head straight for the lake cabin because that's the next logical place to search. He'll probably be waiting for you when you get there." He raised an eyebrow at her. "Unless you aren't going home tonight?"

"I *was* planning to go to the cabin." His gaze narrowed. "Alone."

A grin played at his lips. "I thought you promised Pete—"

Oh, what a tangled web we weave... "I promised ... I'd call him when I got home."

He looked pleased to hear that was all there was to it. "Then change your plans and stay in town at the hotel. I'll get you a room and you can call him from there."

She glared at him. "And just let the burglar have the cabin for the night?" No burglar or even a murderer was going to force her out of her home. And no man was going to start running her life—especially when that man was J. D. Garrison. "Guess again."

J.D. let out a long sigh. "Then I'm coming out to the lake with you." She started to argue but he stopped her. "If there's no sign of trouble, I'll just stay for a while."

She relented, seeing how hard that concession was for him to make. Unfortunately he was right; it made sense that the cabin would be the next place the burglar would hit. "All right."

J.D. held the door open for her. "I'm glad to see you're not as impossibly stubborn as you used to be."

She made a face at him as she swept past. "Don't push your luck, Garrison." She could hear his laugh as he walked to a pale green Ford pickup parked down the street.

Denver climbed into her Jeep and started the engine, thinking how funny life could be. Well, maybe not funny. No, not funny at all.

She made a U-turn and headed toward the lake. A few miles out of town, she glanced in the rearview mirror to see the lights of the pickup right behind her. J.D. was home. Just like in her dreams. Almost. It made her want to laugh. And cry.

"DAMMIT." J.D. FOLLOWED Denny out of town, telling himself that it wasn't seeing her again that had him in a tailspin. But he couldn't get over his reaction to her. Or hers to him, he thought with a grimace. The woman he'd seen in Max's office certainly wasn't the girl who'd had a crush on him at sixteen. No, she'd definitely gotten over her infatuation with him.

He tried to concentrate on the problem at hand. The destruction to Max's office and apartment had convinced him of just how much danger Denny was in. But not from Pete. J.D. just didn't believe Pete capable of tearing apart a place like that—let alone murder.

And keeping Denny away from Pete was even more impossible than he'd first thought, now that he knew how Denny felt. About Pete. And about J. D. Garrison.

He smiled ruefully to himself. He'd hoped to charm her as a last resort. Ha. That would be like trying to charm a hungry grizzly bear away from a Big Mac.

As they neared the lake cabin, J.D. realized his only hope would be for Max's killer to be found. And fast.

The lights from Denny's cabin spilled from the windows and shot like laser beams through the pines. "Damn." The burglar had already been there, he thought as he followed Denny up the narrow, snowy driveway.

What if the burglar was still in the cabin ransacking it? Denver slowed, and he knew she must be thinking the same thing. Her headlights lit up a vehicle parked at the edge of the driveway. J.D. stared at Pete's black Chevy pickup. "Double damn." He pulled in behind Denny.

Before he had a chance to get out, Denny walked back to talk to him. He rolled down his window.

"Pete's here," she said, resting her hands on the window frame. "There's no reason for you to stay now. I'll be perfectly safe."

Right. "Then you won't mind if I make sure." He opened the pickup door, and with obvious reluctance, she stepped back.

"You should talk about stubborn," she mumbled as they walked up to the cabin.

A slice of moon peeked through a break in the clouds and splashed the partially thawed lake with thin metallic light. In the crisp night air, he smelled pine and lake water and... smoke. He looked up to see smoke curling up from the chimney. "Looks like Pete built you a fire."

She scowled. Clearly she hadn't expected Pete to be here nor did she seem that happy about it.

"Looks like he made himself at home," J.D. added, fighting a grin. He heard Denny mumbling under her breath.

The moment they entered the cabin, J.D. smelled peppermint. Denny looked puzzled by the scent, too, as she closed the door behind them. The cabin was as J.D. remembered it. The living room had a fireplace at the entrance and huge glass windows at the other end, looking out on Hebgen Lake. To the left was an adjoining kitchen and down the hall was a bath, small office and laundry room. Max had converted the laundry room into a darkroom before he gave the cabin to Denny, Maggie had told him. Upstairs were two bedrooms along with another bath.

J.D. was glad to see that the place hadn't changed. He was even more delighted to see that it hadn't been ransacked. In fact, everything appeared perfectly normal. Except maybe for the man-size pair of cowboy boots by the front door.

Denver called out a tentative hello. J.D. wasn't sure what he expected. But it wasn't Pete coming out of the kitchen in his stocking feet and carrying a teapot.

"Surprise!" Pete said, then stopped in his tracks as he spotted J.D.

"Surprise," J.D. said. Pete hadn't changed at all; he still had those boyish looks J.D. had always envied. Nor did he look like a murderer, standing there in one of Denny's aprons holding that teapot. Feeling foolish for suspecting Pete, J.D. extended his hand to his former best friend. "How have you been?"

Pete didn't move. Something J.D. couldn't quite read flickered across his face. He quickly covered it with a smile and reached to take J.D.'s hand. "J. D. Garrison. Boy, has it been a long time."

Out of the corner of his eye, J.D. saw Denny frown.

"I guess I should have made more tea?" Pete directed the question to Denny. There were already two cups and saucers on the coffee table in front of the fire. And a single red rose.

How touching, J.D. thought and growled softly to himself. "Yeah, let's have some tea and catch up on old times."

Pete didn't look thrilled by the idea, to put it mildly.

"Not tonight," Denver said. She motioned to the orderly state of the cabin and lowered her voice. "As you can see, I'm in good hands."

"Yeah," J.D. said, unable to come up with a reason not to go. Blurting out that Maggie thought Pete was a murderer didn't seem like a great idea at the moment. And even if Pete were Jack the Ripper, it was doubtful he'd do anything to Denver with J.D. knowing he was there. "If you need me—"

"I have more than enough baby-sitters for one night, thank you." She opened the door for him.

But he still didn't want to leave her there alone with Pete. And not because of Maggie's suspicions. He tried not to think of Pete and Denny in front of the fire, or the single red rose on the coffee table, as Denny closed the door in his face.

He stood for a moment in the dark, lost. The idea of sitting outside the cabin posting guard seemed ridiculous as well as emotionally painful. Denny was right; she didn't need him. He stalked to his pickup, trying to remember something important he'd meant to do at Max's office earlier. All he could see in his mind was that cozy little scene back at the cabin. *What's wrong with you, Garrison? You're acting jealous as hell.* He jerked open his pickup door. *Jealous? What a laugh.* But as he climbed into the cab, he couldn't get Denny out of his mind. Or Pete's damned little tea party for two.

That was when he recalled what had been so important. He'd spotted what looked like a wallet wedged behind the old radiator in Max's apartment. He had started to work it out of the hole when he'd heard what he thought was the burglar returning. Later, when he'd looked up from the bathtub to find Denny standing there . . . well, he was just lucky he remembered his name.

He turned the pickup toward West Yellowstone and Max's office, promising himself he'd be back within the hour to check on Denver. As he raced toward town, he realized he was humming the same tune over and over again as he drove. With a curse, he recognized the song—"Tea for Two."

DENVER TURNED TO FIND Pete looking a little guilty as he set the pot on the coffee table by the two cups and saucers and the sugar bowl.

"So J.D.'s back, huh?" he asked. "Did he say how long he's staying?"

Exhaustion pulled at her. All she really wanted was to go to bed and sleep.

"I know you said you wanted to be alone and I promise I won't stay long." He brightened. "I made tea."

"Tea?" Max used to make her tea when she couldn't sleep.

Pete sat down and proceeded to pour the tea. Denver had to stifle a smile as she took off her coat and hung it in the closet. The teapot appeared so small and fragile in his hands. She'd bet money this was the first tea he'd ever made.

"I mixed the spiced kind with some other one that sounded good," Pete said, confirming her suspicions. It also explained the peppermint scent. He bent over, the spoon clicking against the china cup as he stirred.

"No sugar for me, please," Denver said, feeling like the visitor. J.D. was right; Pete had certainly made himself at home. She could see that the laundry room door was ajar. She'd closed it before she left for the service, having souped some photos that morning to keep her mind off Max. What had Pete done? Searched every room to make sure Max's killer wasn't here waiting for her? It would have been funny, if he wasn't so determined for her to stay out of Max's murder investigation.

"Oh, a little sugar never hurt anyone," he said, handing her the china cup and saucer, her treasured rose-patterned dishes Max had brought her back from Canada. "Anyway, I'm afraid I put sugar in them both. I hope you don't mind."

She didn't have the heart not to drink the tea after he'd gone to so much trouble—sugar and all. Sitting down across from him, she said, "I looked for you at the party but you'd left."

He grinned sheepishly. "I thought I'd come on out and surprise you. I remembered where Max hid his spare key so... here I am."

Yes, here he was, even though she'd told him she wanted to be alone, she thought resentfully as she got a whiff of the strange brew. The last thing she wanted to do was drink it.

"Do you like it?" Pete asked, sounding hopeful.

The truth was she hadn't even tried it. "It's good." She took a sip; it was too hot to taste, fortunately. The warmth seemed to take away some of the day's pain. Max was gone. She'd have to learn to accept that. If only she could throw off the memory of J.D. in Max's office. Max's ransacked office. And J.D. grinning at her.

Realizing Pete was waiting for her to drink her tea before he left, she took another sip and burned her tongue. Exhaustion had numbed her muscles and made her feel as if she were sinking into the chair. All she really wanted to do was put this day behind her.

"So J.D. followed you home?" Pete asked.

She saw his jaw tense and remembered the animosity she'd felt between the two of them earlier. "He's like you, worried I might be in some sort of danger."

"Oh, really?"

The phone rang. Pete offered to get it, but Denver was only too anxious to have an excuse not to finish her tea. She put her cup down and went to answer it.

It was Taylor. "Denver?"

She smiled. He always sounded a little embarrassed.

"I was thinking about that trouble you had earlier with Cal. You're all right out there, aren't you?"

Another man worried about her. If only they'd just let her get some rest. "I'm fine," she said, thinking how much Taylor reminded her of Max.

"I gave Cal a ride home but I was afraid he might decide to show up at your cabin. No trouble?"

Denver thought about Max's ransacked office. And J.D. "What kind of trouble could I get in?" She laughed guiltily but didn't want to mention either problem in front of Pete. "No trouble. Pete's here with me."

"Good." He seemed to hesitate. "You know, if you need anything..."

"I know. I appreciate it." She hung up the phone and returned to the coffee table but didn't sit. Pete was in the kitchen washing the teapot. Denver thought of excusing herself, but decided it would be rude not to at least drink some of her tea.

Hurriedly she picked up the cup from the table and drank it down, trying not to gag. When she went to replace the cup in the saucer, though, she realized she'd finished Pete's instead of her own. She was switching the cups when Pete came back into the room. Quickly she handed him the full cup.

"Who was that?" he asked.

"Taylor."

He seemed annoyed that Max's friend had interrupted their little tea party. "What did *he* want?"

"He was just checking on me."

Pete frowned. "It seems I'm only one of a long line of men concerned about your welfare."

She let that pass. "I think I'm going to call it a night," she said with a wide yawn and a stretch.

Pete glanced at Denver's empty cup on the coffee table and smiled. "I can take a hint." He drank his; from the face he made, he didn't like it any better than she had. "I'll just throw a few more logs on the fire and make sure both doors are locked before I leave."

Denver started up the spiral log stairs to her bedroom. "Good night, Mother Hen."

Pete looked sad to see her go. "Good night, Denver. Sleep well."

J.D. PARKED IN THE darkness of a lodgepole pine outside Max's office. Denny had locked the front door, but thanks to the burglar, all he had to do was put his shoulder against the old door and it fell open. He took the stairs two at a time to Max's apartment. Images of Denny in the middle of the mess made him smile. He rubbed the lump on his head in memory. Hadn't he always known she'd grow into a beautiful, strong, determined woman with a helluva right-handed swing?

He went to the old radiator. Sure enough, there was something down there. He picked up a thin bent curtain rod and worked to pry what looked like a wallet from the radiator's steel jaws.

The wallet tumbled out onto the floor. He picked it up and opened the worn leather. Max's face looked up at him from a Montana driver's license. J.D. thumbed through the rest of the contents. There was no doubt it was Max's wallet. The question was: how did it get behind the radiator?

J.D. shook his head, remembering what Max had been like. Absentminded about day-to-day things.

He took the wallet downstairs and dumped out the contents on Max's desk. There wasn't much—a few receipts, some business cards he'd picked up, Denny's graduation photo, a yellowed, dog-eared photo of Denny and her parents, forty dollars in cash and a MasterCard.

J.D. stared at Denny's photo for a moment, realizing how many years he'd missed by leaving. Then he looked at the picture of Denny and her parents. She couldn't have been more than two at the time. Denny's father, Timothy McCallahan wore his police uniform, and the threesome stood on the steps of the Billings Police Department. Timothy looked like Max, only younger. Denny had his grin. Her mother was the spitting image of Denny, the same auburn hair, same smattering of freckles and identical intense pale blue-green eyes.

J.D. stared at the happy family, unable to accept the fact that someone had killed Denver's parents. Somehow Denny had escaped being hit in the gunfire. He hoped that same luck held for her now.

It took him a moment to realize what finding the wallet meant. Maggie's strongest evidence against Pete was the photograph from Max's wallet because she assumed Max had the wallet *and* the photo on him the day he was killed.

If the wallet was behind the radiator the day of the murder, then Pete didn't get the photograph at the murder scene. But the fact that Pete even had the photo made him look suspicious. How had he gotten the photo and why had he taken it?

J.D. just hoped there might be a clue to Max's murder among the receipts, scraps of paper and business cards as he stuck the wallet inside his jacket pocket. Maybe Denny could make some sense of it.

On the way out, he turned off the lights and closed the door. As he stepped into the darkness of the porch, he felt a chill on the back of his neck.

Denver.

A premonition swept over him. He had to get to her; she needed him. As he hurried across the porch, he caught the slight movement of something in the night. He turned, but too late. An object glistened in the streetlight for an instant, and then there was only pain and darkness.

Chapter Five

Chapter Five

J.D. woke, cold and confused. He glanced around, surprised to find himself on Max's office porch. He was even more surprised to find he was alive. His head ached and he couldn't remember a thing. Except Denny. He could see the light in her auburn hair, hear the sweet sound of her voice. And ... feel the lamp as she knocked him into the bathtub. He groaned. It was all starting to come back.

Rubbing the bump on the side of his head, he tried to get up. A wave of nausea hit him and forced him back down. Where was Denny now?

As he stumbled to his feet, bits and pieces of the night began to return, ending with him leaving Denver at the cabin with Pete. He swore—and reached into his coat. Max's wallet was gone.

Except for his pickup parked at the curb, the street was empty. His watch read 3:52 a.m. Damn. One thing was for sure. Investigating Max's murder was turning out to be more dangerous than he'd realized—than he was sure Denny realized. He had to protect her. He smiled at the humor in that; he wasn't even doing a very good job of taking care of himself. But now more than ever, he feared for Denny's safety.

As he headed for the lake cabin, he wished he could come up with a logical explanation for waking Denny and Pete at this time of the night. Instead he knew he was about to make a first-class fool of himself. At least it was something he was good at. But he had to make sure Denny was safe. A vague uneasiness in the pit of his stomach warned him she wasn't.

IN THE DREAM, DENVER skipped through the bank door ahead of her parents, singing the song her mother had taught her. The words died on her lips; her feet faltered and stopped. Everyone inside the bank lay on the floor on their stomachs. A silence hung in the air that she only recognized as something wrong. As she turned and ran back to her parents, she saw the other uniformed policeman on the floor. Her father's hand came down on her shoulder hard. He shoved her. She fell, sliding into the leg of an office desk. She heard her mother scream. Then the room exploded.

The phone rang.

Don't answer it, her father said in the dream. He wore his police uniform and he was smiling at her. The phone rang again. Don't answer it unless you want to know the truth. But as she looked at him she already knew—

Denver sat up, drenched with sweat. The phone rang again. For a moment, she couldn't remember where she was. Then familiar objects took shape as her eyes adjusted to the dark. The phone rang again. She fumbled for it. "Hello?"

Silence. Heavy and dark as the night. The dream clung to her. Alive. Real.

"Hello?" Denver shivered. Just nerves. And that damned dream. "Is anyone there?"

"Denver McCallahan?" a voice whispered.

The dream had left her with an ominous feeling. She tried to shake it off. "Yes?"

"I have information about your uncle."

"Who is this?" The voice sounded familiar. She sat up straighter and rubbed her hand over her face. The dream and the last remnants of sleep still hovered around her like a musical note suspended in the air. "You know something about Max's murder?" Her head started to clear a little. It was just a crank call. "If you know anything, why haven't you gone to Deputy Cline?"

The caller coughed. "You'll know when you meet me at Horse Butte Lookout under the fire tower. But hurry."

Now fully awake, Denver clutched the phone. "You can't expect me to come to an abandoned fire tower *now*." The voice sounded even more familiar; if only she could keep the person talking.

"Look, if he finds out I called you, I'm dead meat." The caller sounded genuinely frightened. "The fire tower. Hurry. I won't wait."

"Please just tell me—"

But he'd already hung up.

"Damn."

Denver stared at the receiver in her hand. Then at the clock beside her bed. It read 4:05 a.m. She hung up the phone and hurriedly pulled on warm clothes. The fear in the caller's voice made her think he really might know who murdered Max. That hope ricocheted around in her head, forcing out everything else. If he really knew . . .

Denver opened her bedroom door and started down the stairs. Her heart thudded. Someone was downstairs. She listened, trying to recognize the noise floating up from the living room. It sounded like— Cautiously she crept down the stairs and stopped, staring in surprise.

The fire had burned down to smoldering embers. The warm sheen from the firebox radiated over the living room, bathing the sleeping Pete Williams in a reddish wash. Sprawled across the couch, Pete snored loudly.

Denver shook him gently; he didn't stir. She tried again, a little more forcefully. He groaned and started snoring again. Well, she'd tried, she told herself as she covered him with the quilt from the back of the couch. She knew he would have tried to stop her from going, anyway.

Hastily she wrote him a note—"Gone to Horse Butte Fire Tower"—and propped it against his teacup. Trying to protect her must have worn him out, she thought with a laugh as she closed the front door behind her. Just as she reached her Jeep, an arm grabbed her from the darkness. Only someone's hurried words stopped the scream on her lips.

"Take it easy, slugger," J.D. said. "It's only me. You don't have a lamp with you, do you?"

"What are you doing?" Denver demanded in a hushed tone as he released her. "Trying to scare me to death a second time?" As her eyes adjusted to the darkness, she could see his pickup parked in the trees.

"I think the question is where are we going at this hour of the night? And why are we whispering?"

Denver planted her hands on her hips. "I thought you left."

"I did." He gave her an embarrassed shrug. "I came back. I had a feeling you might need me."

She liked the sound of that. And, although she'd never admit it to him, she was glad he was there.

"Maybe I'm psychic when it comes to you." He grinned. "Or maybe I just know you."

She mugged a face at him. "Well, as you can see, I'm fine." She reached for the Jeep's door handle. J.D.'s gloved hand covered hers.

" 'Fine' isn't going for a drive at four in the morning, Denny. What's going on?" He glanced at Pete's pickup. "Where's Pete?"

Out like a bad light bulb, she thought. "I don't have time to argue—"

From inside the cabin, the phone rang. Denver started to run back to answer it in case it was her mysterious caller changing his mind. But it stopped on the third ring. Maybe it had been the caller, checking to see if she'd left yet.

She turned to find J.D. already in the Jeep. He grinned at her. Maybe it was the grin. Or the late hour. Or just plain common sense. She might need him when she got to the fire tower. But at that moment, she didn't mind the idea of the two of them in the close confines of the Jeep together.

As Denver backed down the driveway and started up the narrow road through the pines, she realized she hadn't thought about where her caller had phoned from. There was no telephone near the fire tower. She'd just assumed he was calling from West Yellowstone, but he wouldn't be able to reach the tower quickly if he'd phoned from town. No, he either had to call from a private residence near the lake, or—

As she tore up the road, she remembered the phone booth at Rainbow Point Campground.

"Where exactly are we going in such a hurry?" J.D. asked. Denver smiled as she took a corner in a spray of snow, ice and gravel, and he fumbled to buckle up his seat belt.

"Horse Butte Fire Tower."

His gaze warmed the side of her face. "Really?"

She'd made the mistake of kissing him at the tower the day he said he was leaving. She'd foolishly thought one kiss would change his mind. She shot him a look. "I can promise you you're not going to get as lucky as you did the last time." She couldn't believe she'd said that.

To her surprise, he laughed. "That's too bad."

But she could feel him studying her, and when she glanced over at him, she saw what could have been regret in his gray eyes. Probably just lack of sleep, she assured herself as she concentrated on the next curve, waiting for the campground phone booth to come into view. As she came around the corner, her foot pulled off the gas pedal unconsciously.

The phone booth stood in the darkened pines, door closed. The overhead light glowed inside. She stared at it half expecting someone to materialize inside it. The pines swayed in the wind. The booth stood empty. Had that been where he called from?

"I think you'd better tell me what's going on," J.D. said, frowning at her as she hit the gas again and barreled past the campground. Denver glanced back into the darkness, then took a sharp curve on the snowy, narrow road with the familiarity of someone who'd driven it for years. J.D. hung on. "Come on, Denny, I'm sure you have a good reason for trying to kill us. I'd feel better, though, if I knew it *before* the wreck."

She smiled. "You were the one who insisted on coming along."

"So true."

Freewheeling around the next curve, Denver shot down a straightaway and looked back. No headlights. "I got a call tonight from what sounded like a man. He claimed he knows something about Max's murder. He told me to meet him at the fire tower."

"I'm sorry I asked." J.D. let out a breath after Denver successfully maneuvered the Jeep around another sharp curve in the road. "Let me ask you this—are you completely crazy?"

Denver looked over at him for just a second, then back at the road. Yes, she'd been crazy once. Crazy in love. Then just plain crazy when she realized J.D. had walked out of her life and not even looked back. Meeting a possible murderer in the middle of the night was nothing compared to that.

"I know it probably sounds foolhardy to you," she said.

J.D. let out a laugh. "No, it sounds suicidal to me. Have you considered you might be driving right into a trap?"

Why had this made a lot more sense back at the cabin when she was half-asleep? A sudden chill raced up her spine and the first stirrings of real fear made the Jeep seem even colder inside.

The dark pines that lined both sides of the road blurred by blacker than the night. Occasionally the moon broke free of the clouds to lighten the slit of sky where the road made a path through the trees. Her headlights flickered down the long, narrow tunnel of a road. Behind her, darkness fought the silver-slick reflection of the snow hunkered among the pines.

"If you wanted to kill someone, can you think of a better place than an abandoned fire tower?" J.D. asked.

"No." She reached over to bang on the heater lever; the darned thing wasn't even putting out *cold* air. When she looked up, she saw the reflection of a large mud puddle dead ahead. She tried to avoid it and plowed through a pile of deep slush instead. The windshield fogged over. Hurriedly she rolled down her window. As she wiped a spot clear on the glass with her mitten, she heard what sounded like an-

other vehicle close behind her. Her caller? Or just a rever-
beration in the trees?

"What's wrong?" J.D. asked, glancing over his shoulder.

"I think we're being followed."

"Great."

Not slowing down, Denver leaned down to rummage under her seat.

"What now?" J.D. asked.

"You don't happen to have a weapon on you, do you?"

"I'm a guitar player, Denny, not a gunslinger."

She dug blindly until she felt the screwdriver, then pulled
it out and held it up to the lights from the dash.

"Get serious," J.D. said.

One thought of Max stabbed to death and she tossed the
screwdriver back under the seat. She reached under again,
the Jeep sliding dangerously around a curve, and pulled out
a wrench. It was just a small crescent but it was better than
nothing. She handed it to J.D. He groaned.

"Is there any way I can talk you out of this?" he asked as
they neared the fire-tower turnoff.

She leveled a look at him.

"I didn't think so."

At the bottom of Horse Butte, Denver took one look at
the snowy road zigzagging up into the darkness and shifted
into four-wheel drive for the climb. Half a dozen tracks
etched the mud and melting snowdrifts, giving little indi-
cation as to the last vehicle to climb the single-lane switchbacks up the mountain, or when. Her caller couldn't have
picked a more remote spot. Denver glanced down at her
wrist. Her watch read 4:19. She hoped she wasn't too late.

A shiver of dread ran through her, followed quickly by
growing fear as she began the climb up the mountain. J.D.
was right; this was crazy. She rolled down her window to
listen. Nothing. If someone had been following them, they
weren't anymore.

J.D. glanced back at the darkness. "Only a lunatic would
have tried to keep up with you on that road without lights."

"Or someone who knows the road as well as I do."

A gust of wind slammed against the side of the car, rocking the Jeep. In the distance, the wind whirled snow across the frozen surface of Hebgen Lake in the faint moonlight. At the thawed edge of the ice, waves slapped the deserted shore. Air crept in through the cracks around the car door. Denver shivered.

"You suspect you know the caller?" J.D. asked.

Denver nodded as she maneuvered the car up the first of the switchbacks, mud and snow flying. "I think Max's *killer* is someone I know."

J.D. stared at her in shocked surprise.

"Max was stabbed. Cline thinks he got too relaxed around the hitchhiker."

"But you don't."

"Max was too smart for that. I think he knew and trusted the person who killed him." She met J.D.'s gaze for an instant. In the cloudy darkness, his eyes were silver, his beard black as the night. He was more handsome than she remembered.

"And you're afraid you know, and trust, this person, as well?"

Denver nodded and slowed a little as a cloud covered the moon and darkness dropped over the mountaintop. "I'm not sure this is such a good idea."

J.D. laughed, throwing his head back. "I can't believe it. You're actually admitting that we'd be damned fools to come up here in the middle of the night to meet someone who just might be a murderer?"

She frowned at him.

"Well, it's too late to call Cline," J.D. said softly. "And too late to turn around." He motioned to the single-lane road. They wouldn't be able to turn around now until they reached the shortcut fork almost at the top of the mountain. "But once we get up there, I doubt I can get you to leave if you really believe this caller knows something, right?"

She glanced over at him. "You know me better than I thought you did."

"Yeah. And this won't be the first time you and I were ~~fools at~~ this particular fire tower."

She smiled at him. "And we always have our wrench if there's trouble, right?"

J.D. HELD HIS BREATH. He'd done some crazy things in his life; they were nothing compared to this. His heart contracted with each switchback as Denny maneuvered the Jeep up the mountainside. He recognized her apparent calm for what it really was: bravado. She had to be as scared as he was. He couldn't shake the feeling that they were driving into a trap.

And how did Pete fit into this? "Where did you say Pete was?"

"Asleep on my couch," she said matter-of-factly.

"Oh." J.D. touched the lumps on his head tenderly. It had been a long day. While he was glad to hear that Pete was on the couch, he wondered why she hadn't awakened him. Maybe Pete and Denny weren't as close as she was letting on, he thought with a grin. That was the only explanation he could come up with. And it was one he rather liked.

He stared up at Horse Butte. What if someone really knew who had killed Max and would be waiting for them? He let his gaze return to Denny. Then he'd have no reason to stay in West, no reason to hang around this woman. Her hair, dark waves of polished copper, hung free around her shoulders. He imagined the feel of his fingers buried in it.

The image came so sharply and painfully he closed his eyes against it. But it wouldn't go away. Instead, he could see her beside the lake in summer, the sun dying behind Lionshead Mountain, its golden rays spilling over Denny's skin like warm water...his fingers following the path of the sun. He moaned softly and opened his eyes to find Denny staring at him.

"My driving isn't *that* bad," Denver said as she swerved to miss a rock in the middle of the road. The Jeep started to slide in the mud toward the drop-off and the gaping darkness below. The car slipped toward the abyss. She could sense the chasm coming up at her side.

"Denny," she heard J.D. whisper. His hand touched her thigh. And just when she thought they were going over the side, the car stopped.

"Wanna drive?" she asked, a little breathless.

"I thought you'd never ask."

By the time they reached the fork in the road, Denver had stopped trembling a little. And J.D. wasn't holding on to the steering wheel with white knuckles anymore. The right fork of the road went on up to the fire tower; the left dropped down the far side of the mountain, a shortcut back to the lake cabins. J.D. turned the Jeep up the fire-tower road.

"Wanna change your mind?" he asked.

She shook her head.

"Just checking."

Denver looked at her watch. Four thirty-three. "I hope we're not too late." J.D. didn't answer, and when she looked over at him, he was staring at the fire tower silhouetted in black against the night.

The Jeep's headlights shone on the wooden legs of the tower as he made a sweep of the mountaintop. Only a few wind-warped trees, an old outhouse and the fire tower itself shared the mountain with them. The parking lot was empty with only a few snowdrifts melting at the edge of the road.

J.D. turned the Jeep around and parked facing back down the mountain so they'd be able to see approaching headlights. Only a hint of the lake lay in the blackness beyond. The wind howled across the top of the mountain. An awkward silence grew between them.

"I'm sorry about the last time we were here," J.D. finally said, sounding as young and unsure of himself as he had nine years ago.

"It was just a silly girl thing." Right. She could still remember every moment, including J.D. telling her he was leaving. The words didn't even register because he'd touched her cheek with his fingers. Her heart had pounded so loudly she didn't hear half of what he'd said. Instead she'd blurted out how she loved him, would always love him. And, impulsively, she'd stood on tiptoes and kissed him. "I got over it."

"Yeah, I noticed."

She took a breath and let it out slowly. "I always knew you'd have to leave one day because of your career. I just had this crazy idea that you'd take me with you."

"You know I couldn't have done that. You were only sixteen. Max would have had my head." His tone softened. "Anyway, all I could think about back then was my music. And you were just a kid who couldn't possibly know what she was saying. I mean offering me your heart—"

"Let's not talk about it," she interrupted. It had been bad enough nine years ago; she didn't need him reminding her how she'd thrown herself at him. "What are you *really* doing here?" she asked.

"Here?" He looked up at the fire tower. "I wish I knew."

"Not here. *Here* in West Yellowstone." She turned on the bench seat to face him. She'd thought it would be different, the two of them on this mountaintop again. It wasn't. She wasn't a kid anymore, but she still wanted this man. Damn him. "What are you doing here with me right now? And don't give me that line about your being worried about me."

J.D. smiled. "I wish you'd just say what you think for once, Denny." His eyes darkened. "I'm here because I can't let you go after Max's murderer alone."

She stared at him. "Does that mean you're going to help me—or try to stop me?"

"I'd rather talk you out of it—" he held up his hand before she could protest "—but since I know that would be impossible, I guess I'm going to... help you."

She hated herself for being suspicious. "Why do you want to help me after all these years?"

"Let's just say I owe it to Max."

"Oh." Her heart whispered, I told you so. And the wall she'd built around it called for reinforcements. "What makes you think I want your help?"

He laughed. It was a wonderful sound that made her smile. "You're something else, Denver McCallahan. Most women would be anxious for any assistance. Even mine."

"I guess I'm not most women."

His gaze met hers and held it. "No, Denny, I'm beginning to realize that."

He said her name with an intimacy that rattled her. But he seemed serious and it wasn't like anyone else was offering. "If you mean it, then here's the deal," she said, still studying him intently. "No logical arguments. And no trying to protect me from myself."

He grinned and pulled off his glove. "You drive a hard bargain, but you've got yourself a deal," he said, extending his hand.

Reluctantly, Denver pulled off her glove and took his hand. It was warm and soft, but strong. She suspected it would be the same feeling in his arms.

"With a little luck, maybe it will all be over tonight," she said quietly, the memory of his touch still making her hand tingle. If she cared anything about her heart, she had better hope this was over soon. Spending time with J. D. Garrison could definitely be harmful to her health.

J.D. followed her gaze down the mountain. He couldn't believe he'd agreed to help her find Max's murderer. He blamed the late night, his growing exhaustion, the nearness of Denny. But what choice did he have? It was the only way he could stay close to her, the only way he had any chance of protecting her.

Stop deluding yourself, Garrison. You're looking forward to spending time with her. He smiled to himself. While he wanted Max's killer caught soon for Denny's sake, he didn't mind staying around for a while, staying around her. She intrigued him in a way no other woman ever had.

Overhead, the tower swayed in the wind; the clouds ate up the starlight as quickly as it appeared. A light flashed in the distance. J.D. sat up, staring down the mountain. It took him a moment to realize the lights he'd seen were headlights and they were coming up the mountain road. He watched the vehicle inch up the mountainside, then looked over at Denny. He wanted to take her in his arms and hold her, but the look in her eyes warned him that would be a mistake. She didn't trust him anymore.

"Even if this turns out to be nothing, we're going to find Max's killer," he whispered. "Together."

She didn't look convinced. And he wondered what it would take to make her believe in him again. For some reason he couldn't understand, he wanted that more than he'd wanted anything in his life—even his music.

The headlights neared the top of the mountain. J.D. looked at the lights without seeing them, as he realized it could be Pete Williams coming up that road. As the car came around the second-to-last switchback, he knew he'd do whatever had to be done to protect Denny. No matter who the killer turned out to be.

Then his heart stopped in midbeat as a second set of lights flashed on from the shortcut road. And in the time it took him to take a breath, the second vehicle leaped directly into the path of the oncoming car. The car veered to the left, away from the sudden bright lights, and dropped over the abrupt edge of the road.

"Oh, my God," J.D. breathed. He heard Denver cry out beside him as the car cartwheeled like a toy down the mountainside, its headlights rotating in the darkness.

J.D. jumped from the Jeep and ran to the edge of the road. The second vehicle sped back up the cutoff road, into the twisted pines and disappeared from view. J.D. stared after it for a moment, then looked down to where the car lay at the bottom of the mountainside, its headlights slicing up through the darkness at a frightening angle.

Beside him, Denver began to cry.

Chapter Six

Dawn came with a bloodred sun over Horse Butte Fire
Tower. Denver stood huddled in the scratchy wool blanket
J.D. had found in the back of the Jeep, his arm around her,
warm and reassuring. She couldn't remember J.D. leaving
to go to the pay phone at Rainbow Point to call Sheriff's
Deputy Cline or him returning to Horse Butte to wait with
her for Cline to arrive with the ambulance and wrecker. But
the memory of the car being forced off the road kept coming back, a slow-motion nightmare, and the sound of the
ambulance wailing into the last of night still clung in the air.

"It's hard to believe," Cline said as he looked back up at
the mountain. "You'd think a fall like that would have
killed him. Damned lucky kid. Course if he comes to, he's
in a pile of trouble."

"What do you mean?" Denver asked.

"Car theft. Not to mention no driver's license."

"He stole the car?" she asked in surprise.

Cline grinned. "Stole it from behind the Elkhorn Café.
Probably just forgot to mention to the cook who owns it
that he was taking it." The deputy flipped through his
notebook. "Okay, let me get this straight. You don't find it
strange that a fifteen-year-old kid calls you in the middle of
the night and tells you to meet him out here?"

"We've already been over this," J.D. interjected.

Cline ignored him. "And you say you didn't know who
it was until you saw him."

"The voice sounded familiar. Then when I saw Davey—" Denver stopped, remembering the horror of finding the boy in the crumpled car. "When I saw him, I realized it was his voice I'd heard on the phone."

Cline smirked at her. "And rather than call me, you decided to meet the kid yourself?"

"The voice on the phone said he wouldn't wait long. All I was thinking about was getting here as quickly as possible. You probably couldn't have gotten here in time anyway."

Cline smiled coldly. "But wouldn't it have been nice if you'd have let me try?"

Denver stomped her feet, trying to warm them, and glanced over at J.D. He looked sick, as if what he'd witnessed last night had hurt something critical inside him. "All I can tell you is that someone tried to murder Davey Matthews. They came out of the shortcut road and forced him off the mountain."

"Now why would anyone want to hurt a high school dropout working as a dishwasher at the Elkhorn Café? Except maybe the cook whose car he stole," Cline added.

Denver took a calming breath. "Davey told me on the phone that if someone found out he'd called me, that person would try to kill him."

"Someone?" the deputy asked.

She pulled the blanket more closely around her. She was cold and tired, and she didn't want to deal with Cline. Whoever that someone was, he'd stopped Davey from talking to her. Now Davey was unconscious and Denver knew no more than she had yesterday at Max's funeral. "Davey called him a 'he.' Isn't it obvious to you that Davey knew something and that someone tried to keep him from telling me what it was?"

Cline frowned. "How long have you known Davey Matthews?"

She sighed. "I don't really *know* him. He did odd jobs for my uncle. Davey wanted to be a private investigator. Max was trying to get him to go back to high school and graduate. He also used to hang around the band some."

She called up a blurry picture of Davey in her memory: a boy in his teens with large brown eyes and stringy, long brown hair. She immediately felt guilty because she'd never paid much attention to him. Then she remembered him the way he looked when she and J.D. had found him at the bottom of the mountain. At first, she'd thought he was dead. She shivered despite the wool blanket she clutched around her. "I haven't seen him in months."

"What band? The Montana Country Club band?" Cline asked.

Denver nodded. A chill ran through her as she watched the wrecker operator hook onto the demolished car. "Davey would hang around asking questions about drums, guitars, sound systems." She glanced up to find J.D. studying her. He seemed surprised by something she'd said.

The deputy stopped scribbling in his notebook to give each of them a searching glance. "Isn't that the band you started, Garrison?"

"Pete and J.D. started the band," Denver said quickly. "About ten years ago. Pete kept it going when J.D. left."

Cline rubbed his chin. "What happened? You two have a falling out over something?" He shifted his gaze from J.D. to Denver; a smile played at his lips. "Or over someone?"

"Could we get this over with? It's cold out here," J.D. said.

Cline grinned at Denver but directed his question to J.D. "Your timing's interesting, Garrison. What was it you said brought you *back* to West?"

"Business." J.D.'s gaze narrowed. Denver could feel the heat of anger coming from him. "*Personal* business."

Cline cocked an eyebrow at him. "I'll bet. And how was it you just happened along tonight when you did?"

"I had stopped by Denver's—"

"At four in the morning?" Cline interrupted.

"I was worried about her," J.D. said, his voice deadly soft.

"Worried?"

J.D. nodded.

"And with good reason, it appears," Cline said, slamming his notebook shut.

"When will I be able to see Davey?" Denver asked.

Cline scowled at her. "This is sheriff's department business now. But I wouldn't put much hope in Davey knowing anything about your uncle's death."

"I guess we won't know until Davey comes to," J.D. said tightly.

"If he does." Cline shoved the notebook into his pocket. "I've got some forms for the two of you to fill out."

"We'll meet you at the office," J.D. said.

Cline seemed about to say something, but apparently stopped himself. He frowned at J.D. "Make sure you do that."

PETE WOKE TO THE SOUND of the phone ringing. He sat up on the couch and immediately grabbed his head. "Damn." He looked around, surprised to find himself not in his apartment but in Denver's cabin. The phone rang again. He stumbled after the sound, confused, head aching. It felt like he had a ferocious hangover, but the last thing he could remember drinking was that awful tea.... "Hello?"

"You blew it." The words were little more than a harsh breath but Pete recognized the synthesized voice right away. Midnight. "Your precious Denver could be dead right now."

Panic cramped his stomach. "Denver? What's happened to her?" He glanced up the stairs, realizing that if she were here, she'd have answered the phone. "Where's Denver? Is she all right?"

"*She's* fine. But what the hell happened to you last night?" Midnight demanded.

Pete rubbed his hand over his face, trying to recall. The pills. And the tea. Something clanged, and Pete realized that Midnight was calling from a phone booth. "I . . . guess the teacups got . . . switched."

Midnight let out an oath. "And just how did that happen?"

Pete didn't have a clue. He'd been so sure Denver wasn't on to him. "I don't know. But I won't mess up again. You have my word on that."

"Your word?" Midnight laughed. "I have your *life* on that."

So true. "What did you mean, Denver could be dead?"

"Take a look at your pickup."

Pete stepped to the door. He swallowed hard. "It's covered with mud." Mud? The West Yellowstone basin was miles of coarse obsidian sand. Where could he have gotten mud on his truck?

Midnight chuckled. "Don't remember going to Horse Butte last night?"

"Horse Butte?" He rubbed his temples. How many pills had he put in that damned tea anyway? "I couldn't have driven up to Horse Butte last night." But obviously his pickup had.

"I would suggest you wash it before anyone sees it," Midnight said.

"Wash it?" Pete tried to shake off the effect of the pills. His life depended on it, and even drugged, he was smart enough to know that. "Don't tell me you woke me up at this time of the morning to tell me to wash my truck?"

"The question you should be asking is how it got muddy."

Pete stared at his pickup as the puzzling question wove its way into his hurting head. "How *did* it get muddy?"

Midnight laughed. "You'll find out soon enough." He hung up.

Pete stared at the phone for a moment, then stumbled to the door and pulled on his boots, feeling sick. What the hell *had* happened last night? He had a feeling he didn't want to know.

The phone rang as he was shrugging on his coat. Pete hurried to it, thinking it might be Denver.

"Pete Williams?" a female voice asked.

"Yes." He held his breath.

"This is Helen, the dispatcher at the sheriff's office. Deputy Cline asked me to call you. He said to tell you, and I quote, 'Your girlfriend is on her way to the sheriff's office with J. D. Garrison and maybe you'd better get your butt down there.'"

"What's this all about?" Pete asked, his heart lodged in his throat. Why would Denver and J.D. be on their way to the sheriff's office this time of the morning, together, when the last time he saw her she was headed up to bed alone?

"There was an accident on Horse Butte last night."

Pete darted a look at his pickup. "Horse Butte?" His heart pounded. "Was anyone hurt?"

"I really can't tell you, but I'm sure Deputy Cline will fill you in when you get here."

"I'm sure," Pete said and hung up, his gaze never leaving the muddy pickup. Horse Butte. Looking outside, he could see that Denver's Jeep was gone, but J.D.'s pickup stood back in the pines, mud free.

"What the hell's going on?" he said to the empty cabin. All he knew for sure was that he had to wash his truck before he went to the sheriff's office.

J.D. SEEMED LOST in thought all the way into town. Denver didn't mind. She didn't want to talk anyway; she kept turning over Cline's questions in her mind. By the time they'd reached the sheriff's office, some of the shock had worn off, making things seem a little clearer to her.

The dispatcher sent them into Cline's office to wait for him. After a good while, the deputy sheriff came in, eating a big gooey doughnut and slurping a giant-size cup of coffee.

"Why don't you believe someone tried to keep Davey from talking to me?" Denver asked him before he could sit down.

He shoved the last of the doughnut into his mouth and made a place on his desk for the coffee. "Not a very sure-fire way to shut somebody up permanently, wouldn't you say?" He sat down; the office cháir groaned under his weight.

"I told you, the vehicle came off the shortcut road from the far side of Horse Butte. From the angle it came at Davey, his immediate reaction would have been to go to the edge," Denver said.

"She's right," J.D. cut in. "Even an experienced driver might have done the same thing at that spot on the road."

Cline shrugged as he began riffling through a stack of papers on his desk. "Maybe. But let's look at this reasonably. Davey Matthews was driving up the mountain probably to extort money from Miss McCallahan. He'd just stolen a car. And it was pretty dark and spooky out. Then all of a sudden another car appears on the road in front of him. It's no wonder he overreacted."

"We don't know for a fact that Davey planned to extort money from Denver," J.D. reminded him.

"Nor do we know for a fact that the other vehicle purposely tried to run Davey off the road," Cline said, slamming his hand down on his desk. "What we do know is that Davey Matthews is a dropout, a small-time car thief and—"

"I know what I saw," Denver interrupted. And what she knew in her heart. Davey had come up the mountain to tell her who'd killed her uncle. And if Max had trusted Davey to run errands for him, the kid was all right. "I witnessed an attempted murder."

Cline met her gaze. "You witnessed an unfortunate accident." His tone softened. "Look, it's probably only natural that you'd start seeing attempted murders at every turn after what happened to your uncle."

"I am not a hysterical woman," she said, trying to control her anger. "It was four in the morning. Don't you think it odd that another vehicle was even up there, let alone that it used the shortcut road and took off again the same way?"

Cline shook his head. "You both grew up here. I don't have to tell you about the keggers at the old fire tower."

"A kegger this time of year?" J.D. demanded. "And if it was an accident, why didn't the other car stop?"

Cline made a face. "Probably another kid like Davey who wasn't supposed to be up there at that hour and got scared."

Denver stared at him. "Maybe we should contact the sheriff in Bozeman and see what he thinks."

Cline leaned back, folded his hands over his stomach and let out a long sigh. Then his face tightened with anger. "Let's not blow this out of proportion. You were sitting in the dark on top of a mountain with your...friend here." His eyes narrowed. "Maybe you weren't paying a lot of attention at the time, you know what I mean, missy?"

She felt heat radiating from her anger. "It's Denver. Or Ms. McCallahan. Not missy. And I'm sick of your chauvinistic, simpleminded—" She felt J.D.'s hand on her arm.

"Cline, I'd like to talk to you in private," J.D. said.

Cline had his mouth open about to say something to Denver. He looked from Denver to J.D. and back again. "I'd watch my step, *Ms*. McCallahan." He turned to J.D. "And it's *Deputy* Cline to you, Mr. Garrison."

J.D. tipped his hat and followed the deputy into a small room at the back of the sheriff's office.

"You got a problem?" he asked.

J.D. closed the door. "Several. But the only one that concerns you is what I saw at the fire tower last night."

Cline rubbed his jaw. "I already heard this story."

"No, you haven't." J.D. hesitated, wondering if Cline was just a fool or if he could be trusted. "When I saw the lights coming out of the cutoff road, I ran to the edge of the mountainside. I recognized the rig."

Cline chewed at his cheek, his eyes bright with interest. "Why didn't you mention this before?"

"It was Pete Williams's black Chevy pickup. The same one I saw him drive away in from Max's burial service yesterday."

Cline's mouth sagged and he swore loudly. "You don't expect me to believe that?" The deputy pushed past him, started to open the door, then stopped. "I know there's bad blood between the two of you and I know why.'' He shot a look into the outer office at Denver. "But you aren't going to use me to settle any old scores, Garrison. There are a lot of black Chevy pickups around."

J.D. shook his head. "This one had the fancy running lights Pete had put on. And the matching camper shell."

Cline swore again. "There are probably other trucks like that around. I know Pete Williams. And his family."

"You knew my family," J.D. said, anger building in him like one of the geysers in the park. "Aren't you going to look into what I've told you?"

"I don't have to," Cline said, reaching for the doorknob again. "I know for a fact where Pete Williams was last night. Miss McCallahan is his alibi." Cline grinned. "She said she left him sleeping at her cabin."

"For how long? You'd defend him no matter what. You're his second cousin by marriage and everyone knows that blood always runs thicker than the truth."

Cline turned, eyes blazing. "Watch yourself, Garrison. You're no famous country and western star here. You're just some punk who happened to grow up here." The deputy stormed out, heading straight for Denny. He handed her a stack of forms, tossed another pile on the opposite desk and looked back at J.D. "Be sure you just put down the facts."

J.D. met Denny's gaze as he took a seat.

"What's going on?" she whispered.

"We have to talk, but not here," he said to her. When he thought about the pickup he'd seen at Horse Butte, he realized he should have warned her about Pete last night. Pete Williams was a dangerous man.

DENVER HAD ALMOST finished her paperwork when Pete rushed into the sheriff's office. He came straight to her and pulled her into his arms. "You scared the hell out of me," he declared. "When I heard what happened ... What were you doing on Horse Butte?"

She tensed in his arms at the clear reprimand. "Trying to find Max's murderer."

"Smart move." Pete pulled back slowly, anger making his movements tense. "Are you all right?"

"How did you hear about it?" she asked.

"I had my dispatcher call him," Cline said from behind her.

"Hello, Pete," J.D. said. Denver saw something pass between the two of them; she didn't like the look on J.D.'s face.

"Can I speak to you for a moment, Pete?" Cline said. They went into the small room where Cline had taken J.D., and the deputy closed the door. It looked like Cline was doing most of the talking, and not in his usual loud voice, either.

"Remember that phone call you got as you were leaving last night?" J.D. asked. Denver looked up from the form she had just completed. "Could that have awakened Pete?"

"I suppose so," she said cautiously.

"Is there any chance he would have known where you went?"

"I left him a note. Why?"

J.D. ran his fingers through his beard. "Denny, I think I know who may have been driving the vehicle that ran Davey off the road last night."

His words didn't have time to sink in before Cline and Pete came out of the office. Pete closed the door a little harder than necessary, Denver noticed.

"Don't say anything right now," J.D. added in a whisper as Cline and Pete started toward them.

Denver wondered why he wouldn't want Cline to know, but kept silent. Maybe he didn't trust Cline any more than she did. Cline took the forms from her and reached for J.D.'s, not looking all that pleased about doing it.

"If I have any more questions, I'll call you," the deputy said, steering the three of them toward the door. "In the meantime, I'll be keeping my eye on you, Ms. McCallahan, and on your friend."

As Denver walked by the dispatcher, she asked, "Have you heard any word on Davey Matthews's condition?"

Before the woman could answer, Cline came up behind her. "I hope you don't plan to interfere in police business the way your uncle did."

"All I want to know is if Davey's all right," she said evenly.

"You and your friend—" Cline threw a dark look at J.D. "—are treading on thin ice, young lady. Don't get involved. I'm warning you."

"It sounds more like you're threatening her," J.D. said.

Denver could feel tears at the back of her eyes. She was too tired and too emotionally drained to take Cline on, but she was also fed up with his attitude. "The next thing you're going to tell me is that Max wasn't murdered. Maybe he stabbed himself. Suicide." She took a breath, fighting tears. "I would think you'd want to solve this murder as fast as possible. That is unless there's some reason you can't—or don't want to."

"Hold it right there!" Cline took her arm and steered her toward the door, away from the attentive ears of the dispatcher. "I'm warning you about making any wild accusations," he muttered through gritted teeth. "You stay out of my damned investigation or I'll put your little butt behind bars. Is that understood?"

"Let her go," J.D. said, his voice hard and cold as he laid a hand on Cline's arm.

Cline looked down at J.D.'s hand, then carefully removed it. He smiled. "Did your old friend here tell you what he thinks he saw up at Horse Butte?"

A muscle twitched along J.D.'s jawline. "Cline—"

"He says he recognized that vehicle you say purposely ran Davey Matthews off the road," Cline continued, a wide grin stretching his lined face. "He says it was Pete Williams's."

Denver shot a surprised look at J.D. Then at Pete. Pete looked shocked. "How can you be sure?" she pleaded with J.D. "It was so dark and it happened so fast."

"I'm sure," J.D. said softly.

"You're wrong," Pete cried. "I wasn't near Horse Butte last night and Denver knows it. I was asleep at her place."

Denver looked from J.D. to Pete and back again. "There must be another explanation."

"This isn't the time or place to get into this," J.D. said, lowering his voice.

"You're right," Pete agreed. "Denver needs rest."

Denver looked into J.D.'s gray eyes. "Why didn't you mention this last night?"

His gaze caressed her face. "You were already so upset...." He grazed her hand with his fingers. "Denny, there are some things I need to tell you."

"Can't you see how exhausted she is?" Pete demanded. "She needs food and sleep. We can talk about your crazy allegations later." He opened the door and started to usher Denver out into the spring morning.

"I'll be all right," Denver said, surprised by the fear she saw in J.D.'s eyes. Surely he didn't believe it had been Pete on that mountain last night.

J.D. reached for her. "Denny, I can't let you—"

"It's all right," she repeated as Pete led her toward his pickup. "I need to talk to Pete. Alone."

"No, Denny." J.D. tried to get past Cline.

"Not so fast, Garrison," Cline said, blocking his way. "You're not going anywhere. I just thought of some more questions I need to ask you."

J.D. pushed past him and started after Denny.

Cline's hand closed over his arm. "Either we talk now, Garrison, or I can have you held over in jail for the next twenty-four hours for questioning. Which is it going to be?"

J.D. looked down at the hand on his arm, then up at Denny. She'd walked out with Pete to his pickup. The two stood next to it talking but neither looked very happy. Twenty-four hours. J.D. glanced up into Cline's grinning face. The deputy would have liked nothing better than to put him behind bars. "I think we'd better talk now, don't you?" J.D. said.

"GARRISON, I SUSPECT you planned to come in here like Rambo and save the damsel in distress," Cline said, rocking back and forth in his large, worn office chair. "Tell me I'm wrong."

"If you're asking if I plan to protect Denver in any way I can, the answer is damned right. And I know what you're up to, Cline. You just detained me to keep me from leaving with Denver."

Cline studied him for a moment. "Let me set you straight on a couple of things. I can do whatever I want in this town. And I'm not going to have any trouble when it comes to you or this case. None. As soon as I find that hitchhiker, this case is going to be closed."

"Wanna bet?" J.D. said.

Cline stopped rocking abruptly and leaned forward. "What did you say?"

"Your killer isn't making tracks down some highway with his thumb out." J.D. got to his feet. "He hasn't even left town. And if you don't believe it, you'd better have a look at Max's office. Someone tore it apart."

"How do you know that?"

J.D. put his palms on Cline's desk and leaned toward him. "You got a murderer loose in your town, Deputy. And you'd better find him soon before someone else gets killed."

"Stick to your guitar playing, son. I know what I'm doing, and if you get in my way—"

J.D. turned and walked out, slamming the door behind him.

PETE'S APARTMENT WAS on the top floor of a two-story log structure in the heart of the town. After he'd put some toast and a glass of cold milk Denver didn't want in front of her, he sat down at the kitchen table. "You realize you could have gotten yourself killed last night. Dammit, Denver, you've got to quit playing Nancy Drew."

Denver broke off a piece of toast, crumbled it and dropped it back on the plate. "I don't want to argue about this. I need to ask you about something else."

"What, that ridiculous claim of J.D.'s?" Pete got up angrily and poured himself a glass of water. His reaction made it even harder for her to ask him what she had to. But she couldn't forget the worry in J.D.'s eyes.

"Why would J.D. say you were at Horse Butte last night if you weren't?" she asked carefully.

"I don't know." Pete sounded hurt and confused. "I guess there's just bad feelings between us I didn't realize."

"But why?"

Pete frowned as he sat back down. "That's the part I can't understand. Why would he purposely try to hurt me? He has everything he ever wanted."

Denver couldn't argue that; she knew firsthand how much J.D.'s career meant to him. Nothing and no one could ever come before it. He'd made that clear years ago.

"You must have really been tired last night," she said.

She could feel his gaze on her. "Dead to the world," he said. "Why didn't you wake me? Going to Horse Butte alone..." He paused and turned the water glass in his fingers. "But then, you weren't alone, were you?"

"I tried to wake you, but I couldn't," Denver said. "I left you a note. You probably saw it this morning when Cline called. That is where Cline reached you, wasn't it?"

Pete rubbed his temples as if he had a headache. Suddenly he grabbed her shoulders, knocking over his water as he turned her to face him. "Remember me, Denver?" His gaze searched her face, his eyes bright. "I'm your best friend, the guy you grew up with, the one who helped you with algebra, who taught you how to play a guitar, who took care of you when you got your heart broken by J. D. Garrison."

Denver felt tears burn her eyes. "Pete, I—"

He got up and returned with a towel to clean up the water he'd spilled. "Yes, Denver, that's where Cline reached me this morning. He had his dispatcher call. And, no, I wasn't on Horse Butte last night. You know where I was—asleep on your couch." He turned to face her. "The question you should be asking yourself is what the hell J.D.'s doing back here after all these years? It can't be because of Max. He didn't even make the funeral."

"That's something else," she said, voicing her doubts. "J.D. seemed surprised you'd left a message for him about the funeral."

"Where are all these doubts about me coming from?" She watched him wipe up the water and toss the towel onto the kitchen counter. "From you? Or J.D.?"

She stared into Pete's handsome face, the ache in her chest growing. "Why would J.D. lie?"

"Why would *I* lie?" Pete demanded. "Look, Denver, maybe J.D. just didn't see what he thought he did. There's probably a reasonable explanation for all of this." Pete glanced at his watch and groaned. "I was supposed to meet the band to practice an hour ago. I have to go. Stay here, get some rest." On his way to the door, he lifted his white Stetson from the hook on the wall and turned to look back at her.

She brushed distractedly at a dirty spot on her jeans, avoiding his gaze.

"If you care anything about me, Denver, you'll stay away from J. D. Garrison." He turned the hat brim in his fingers. "And if you don't care, then do it for your own good. He hurt you once. He'll do it again. And about Max's murder..." She looked up at him; their gazes met and held. "Keep digging around in it and you'll get yourself killed."

She stared at him, shocked by the threat she heard in his voice, saw in the cool blue of his eyes.

"Get some sleep," he said gruffly. "I'll be back later to make you lunch." He slammed the door on his way out.

Denver pushed back the plate of toast and hurried to the window. As she watched Pete pull away, her stomach did a slow, sick spin. When had he washed his pickup? She remembered it parked in front of the cabin last night; it had been dirty, but not *that* dirty. Pete had to have washed it early this morning *before* he came to Cline's office. Why would he do that? She glanced down at her jeans and the spot she'd been brushing at. Mud. She gripped the windowsill as she remembered brushing against Pete's pickup when she stood outside the sheriff's office with him. Where would Pete get so much mud on his pickup this time of year? Enough to feel the need to get it washed. Denver felt herself turn to ice as she looked at her mud-covered Jeep. Horse Butte.

"I DON'T LIKE any of this," Maggie said when Denver called her from Pete's. She could hear Maggie relating the story of Max's ransacked office and the incident at Horse Butte to someone in the background, and stopped short of telling Maggie of J.D.'s accusations against Pete. Or her own doubts about his story since seeing the mud on her jeans and Pete's washed pickup.

"Tell me that's not Cline you're talking to," Denver whispered.

Maggie laughed. "No, Taylor's here. He's as worried about you and this mess as I am."

Taylor. Denver was surprised how much he'd been hanging around Maggie since Max's death. She felt jealous for Max's sake, then uncharitable for such thoughts. Of course Taylor was just there because he was Max's friend and was trying to help Maggie get through this. But Maggie was also a nice-looking woman; Taylor would have to be blind not to notice. He'd even mentioned that he might hang around longer than he'd planned.

"I hate to keep repeating myself," Maggie was saying, "but maybe you should stay out of this. Taylor agrees."

"Don't worry. I'm going to Bozeman this afternoon. With a little luck, Davey will be conscious. By this time tomorrow, the murderer could be behind bars."

"I hope so," Maggie said thoughtfully. "In the meantime, please be careful. Max would have a fit if he knew what you were up to. And worse yet, that I'd let you." Maggie seemed to hesitate. "Can you hold on just a second?" Denver could hear her telling Taylor goodbye. "I just wanted to let you know I'm going to Missoula sometime soon," Maggie said. "I have a friend up there whose mother died and she could use some help getting the house ready to sell. Why don't you take down the number where I'll be staying in case you need to reach me.''

"Just a minute." Denver looked around for something to write on. Digging in the wastebasket, she found a piece of paper and wrote the number on the back of it.

After she hung up, she glanced at her watch, the watch Pete had given her. It had been such a thoughtful gift. "I just wanted you to know that I was thinking of you," he'd said the morning he'd returned from his gig in Missoula, the morning after Max was found murdered.

She stared at the watch, remembering all the things Pete had done for her over the years. She thought of the tea he'd made her last night, of him passed out on her couch, of the mud that remained on his pickup. There had to be an explanation. Because if she couldn't trust Pete, then whom could she trust?

Chapter Seven

Denver knew she couldn't sleep until she talked to Davey Matthews, no matter what Pete said. She took a quick shower and left his apartment.

Once outside in the bright spring sun, she felt a little better. The strong scent of pine and the sun filtering down through the snowy branches promised a new warmer season. She stuffed Maggie's number into her jeans pocket, breathed in the sweet familiarity of the small town and headed for her Jeep. Her steps faltered when she spied the figure leaning against her car. Desire took a trip through her bloodstream at the speed of light.

"Hi," J.D. said, straightening. The sun caught in his eyes, moonlight on water. She fought the urge to wade in, to take even a little dip, no matter how warm and inviting they appeared.

"I'm on my way to the hospital in Bozeman to see Davey Matthews." She dared him to argue with her.

"I'll drive," J.D. offered.

She did a double take. "What, no argument?"

He smiled. It had its usual heart-thudding effect on her. "I believe the deal was no logical arguments. No trying to protect you from yourself. Right?"

"Right. So why did I think you'd change your mind?"

He frowned. "Probably because you don't trust me."

She nodded.

"Give me a chance?" he asked.

His smile warmed something deep inside, thawing the wall of ice around her heart. She looked into his eyes and wanted nothing more than to curl up in his arms.

"Have you heard anything more on Davey's condition?" he asked as he walked her toward his pickup.

"No. I couldn't get any information on Davey from the hospital. At least there, he should be safe."

J.D. opened the door for her. Just as she started to get in, she turned to look behind her, feeling that they were being watched.

PETE LEANED AGAINST the wall of the building across the street, fighting the sick feeling in the pit of his stomach at seeing Denver and J.D. together. He swore under his breath, his love for Denver almost overwhelming him. He gritted his teeth, wanting desperately to be the one she turned to, the one who would take her in his arms and make love to her. Instead it looked like it would be J. D. Garrison.

That realization squeezed the blood from his heart. For years he'd lived in J. D. Garrison's shadow. Denver had never seen him as anything but a friend. Just recently, he had felt as if he were winning her over.

Now J.D. was back in town.

And as long as J.D. was in the picture, Pete knew he didn't stand a chance. He watched them get into the pale green Ford pickup. If J.D. was gone, Denver would turn to him just as she had years ago. Only this time, he wasn't going to chance J.D. ever coming back again. He'd stop J.D. from ruining everything. And at the same time, get him out of their lives forever.

DENNY TURNED ON THE RADIO as J.D. started up the engine. "What's this?" she asked, sounding surprised. "Rock and roll?" She thumbed over to the country and western station. He could feel her studying him out of the corner of her eye.

One of his latest songs, "Heart Full of Misery," came on the radio. He reached over and turned it off. "Denny, we have to talk."

"So what's it really like being a star?" she asked, turning in the bench seat to face him.

J.D. looked over at her, knowing she wanted to talk about anything but Pete—the one thing they really needed to discuss. The sun spilling through the window caught in her still-damp hair, firing it to burnished copper. She smelled of spring, her skin pink from her shower. Just the sight of her made him ache with a need for her like none he'd ever known.

"A star?" he asked, trying to concentrate on the question. He'd never thought of himself as anything but a guitar picker. Certainly not a star. Stars had a tendency to fall. "What's it like? Months on the road playing concerts, months of trying to write new songs, months in a recording studio." He looked into her eyes, the color of a tropic sea, and felt a pull stronger than the tides. "It's not all it's cracked up to be."

"But it's what you always wanted."

He pulled up to a stop sign and looked over at her again, letting his gaze caress her face the way his fingers wanted to do. "Is it?"

"Everything comes at a price," she said.

Didn't he know it. He stared into those aquamarine eyes of hers for a long moment and forced himself to pull away. *You just want to protect her, just like when you were kids.* He laughed softly to himself as he turned onto the highway. *I think it's a little more than that.* Because right now the last thing he was thinking about was protecting Denny. And, boy, did she *need* protecting. But not just from Pete.

"Denny." He took her hand in his. Just the feel of it made him want to stop the car and take her in his arms, to hold her, to feel her body against his. When this was over— "We have to talk about Pete."

She pulled her hand free, closed her eyes and leaned back against the seat.

"I was at Max's burial service yesterday," he said. Her eyes flew open and she turned to look at him. "I met Maggie in that stand of pines overlooking the cemetery."

She narrowed her gaze at him, the old fight coming back into her. "You and Maggie? I don't understand."

He saw her marshal forces against what he was about to say, knowing she understood only too well. "Maggie thinks Pete is somehow involved in Max's death."

Her next words came out controlled, careful, but her gaze crackled like Saint Elmo's fire. "Why would Maggie think that?"

"Max seemed worried in the few weeks before his death, Maggie said." He saw reluctant agreement in Denny's expression. "The day he died, he told Maggie he was going to see Pete. He was very upset, and told her he had to stop Pete before someone got killed."

"That doesn't mean—"

J.D. told her about the photograph Maggie had found in Pete's coat pocket. Denny started to argue but he stopped her and explained, "When she found it, the photo had been torn. Someone had ripped me out of the picture.

"Hang on, it gets crazier," he continued before she could argue further. "Last night after I left you and Pete at the cabin, I went back to Max's place. I'd seen what looked like a wallet caught between the radiator and the wall in his apartment."

"A wallet?" Denny asked, sitting up a little straighter.

"It was Max's."

She frowned.

"It looks like Max didn't have it with him the day he was killed."

"Then that means Pete could have gotten the photo at any time. Max could have even given it to him."

J.D. nodded.

"Where is the wallet now?" she asked.

"As I was leaving last night, someone relieved me of it." He motioned to the latest lump on his head.

"Are you all right?" she cried.

He smiled, touched by her concern. "I'll live, but this whole thing is getting more dangerous all the time."

She turned to look out the window. A wall of pines, dark green against snow white, blurred past the pickup, throwing her face in shadow. "Pete couldn't kill anyone, especially Max."

They topped Grayling Pass, went by Fir Ridge Cemetery and dropped into Gallatin Canyon, the road twisting through snowcapped pines and granite cliffs, skirting the Gallatin River. The once-frozen river now flowed around huge slabs of aquamarine ice—another sign that spring was coming.

He could tell that her mind was elsewhere by the way she worried her lower lip with her teeth. "You were right, though," she said softly. "Pete's pickup *was* at Horse Butte last night." She turned a little in the seat to show her backside to him. "Do you see that?"

He slowed down as he stared at her posterior. Oh, yes, he saw that. He'd admired it numerous times lately.

"See it?" she asked, pointing to a spot on the thigh part of her jeans.

He glanced at the highway, then back at the spot on her thigh. "I see some dirt."

"It's mud. I brushed against Pete's pickup this morning and got it on my jeans."

It was the same as the stuff all over Denny's Jeep.

"And that's not all. Pete washed his pickup early this morning." She straightened in her seat. "In his haste, he missed a few spots. He's hiding something, but it's not because he's involved in Max's murder."

"How do you know that?" J.D. demanded. How could she keep defending Pete in light of everything they'd learned?

"I know Pete." Her eyes clouded as she leaned back against the seat, her hair tumbling around her shoulders in a fiery waterfall.

She's in love with him. The thought struck him like a fist. He felt sick. Then shocked that he could feel such pain. *My*

God, you're falling for her. He drove on, trying to sort out his feelings. He'd always cared for Denny but not like this. *You just need sleep. And getting hit in the head can't be helping, either.* He laughed to himself, no longer able to blame the way he felt on anything but the truth. He was falling for her like a boulder off a high cliff. All he could think about was taking her in his arms. He'd never wanted to kiss anyone so much in his life.

He realized she was staring at him again. "What about Pete's alibi?" she asked.

Reluctantly he recounted Maggie's story about the barmaid in Missoula.

"So Pete wasn't his usual charming self that night and the barmaid just didn't remember him," she said. "Why wouldn't Pete be there if his band was there?"

She turned those wonderful green eyes on him. He wondered what they would be like fired with desire. And he wondered if he'd ever get the chance to see anything but anger in them.

"And what possible reason could Pete have to kill Max?" she demanded.

"I'm not saying it makes any sense," he said, dragging himself away from her gaze.

Suddenly Denver bolted upright. "Oh, no. Maggie's going to Missoula. She said to help a friend but I'll bet she's going up there to check out Pete's story."

J.D. sighed, wishing Maggie wouldn't do that. "She could be in real danger. Do you know where she's staying?"

Denver dug out a piece of paper from her pocket. "She gave me a number." He watched her turn it in her fingers for a moment as if trying to read something written on it. "No." He watched her bite her lower lip, tears shimmering in her eyes as she fought the tears, and knew whatever was on the paper had upset her deeply.

"What is it?" he asked.

She closed her fingers into a fist, crumpling the paper, and for a moment he thought she wasn't going to tell him. "When I was on the phone with Maggie, I couldn't find

anything to write on. I found this in Pete's wastebasket."
She held it out to him with shaking fingers. "It's a receipt
for the rental of a semitrailer." She closed her fingers around
it again.

"Pete rented a semi?" J.D. asked.

Her voice came out a whisper. "A semi almost ran Pete
and me off the road on the way back from the funeral yesterday."

"You think Pete rented a truck and hired someone to
drive it just to scare you?" he asked, astounded to hear
himself defending Pete. "Do you have any idea what it costs
to rent a semi?"

"Sounds pretty ridiculous, doesn't it?" She smiled a little. "Also, he was in the pickup with me and could have
been killed, too."

J.D. nodded. "Didn't you tell me Pete sometimes does
odd jobs around town? He could have rented it for one of
his employers."

"That must be what it is," she said, looking relieved as
she stuffed the receipt back into her pocket. "And I'm sure
there's an explanation for his pickup being on Horse Butte."

"And why he washed it in such a big hurry this morning?" J.D. pressed as they neared the outskirts of Bozeman. The snow-covered Bridger Mountains glowed white
gold in the sunlight, a backdrop for the bustling western
college town.

"Yes," she said, giving him a hard look. "When did you
lose your faith in people?"

He glanced over at her, taken aback by the question. He
had lost faith in people. And he knew exactly when it had
happened. "I'm sure you read in the tabloids about my ex-
business manager. I trusted him, Denny. He robbed me
blind."

He recognized the determined set of her jaw. She said, "I
know Pete."

He nodded, afraid just how well she knew him. "I
thought I knew my business manager. Sometimes people
disappoint you. Even people you care about." And J.D. was

afraid Pete Williams was going to disappoint them both. Either way, he intended to keep Pete as far away as possible from Denny.

DAVEY HAD REGAINED consciousness. As J.D. pushed open the door, he spotted Deputy Cline beside Davey's bed.

"I figured you two would show up," Cline said, not looking at all pleased. "Don't you ever stay home and clean house or bake cookies or sew or something, Ms. McCallahan?"

"How are you doing?" Denver asked Davey.

"Okay, I guess," he mumbled.

"Don't you have some records to make or something, Garrison?" Cline asked.

Denver flashed J.D. a warning not to take the bait. He just smiled at her. "You don't mind if we visit with Davey for a few moments in private, do you?" she asked Cline.

"This is the sheriff's department's business, Ms. McCallahan," he said, crossing his arms over his belly. "And I'm the deputy sheriff for West Yellowstone, you might recall. I'm not leaving this room."

J.D. gritted his teeth, but kept his mouth shut, just as he'd assured Denny he would. But it wasn't easy.

"Do you feel up to talking?" she asked Davey as she took the chair beside his bed. He turned his face to the window and chewed at his cheek. "Last night you called me and asked me to meet you at Horse Butte—" she began.

Davey shot a look at Cline. "I don't know what you're talking about."

"What?" Denver exclaimed. J.D. saw the shock on her face. "Are you telling me you didn't call and tell me to meet you at Horse Butte Fire Tower?"

"I'm telling you I don't remember anything. All right?"

Denver stared at the boy. "I don't understand."

"The doc says it's common with concussions," Cline interrupted, sounding almost pleased by the turn of events. "He may never remember what happened."

"Oh, I'm sorry, Davey, I didn't realize . . ." She touched his hand. He turned it only a fraction, just enough so that J.D. could have sworn it held a small scrap of paper.

"Look, I don't know anything, okay?" Davey insisted.

J.D. watched the boy stealthily slip the scrap into Denver's palm before he turned to the wall. "I just want to be left alone."

"Satisfied?" Cline asked Denver. "Why don't we step out into the hall?"

"I hope you're feeling better soon," she said to Davey, pocketing something as she followed Cline from the room. J.D. took one last look at the boy, then trailed after her.

"Too bad about the kid," Cline said once Davey's door closed behind them. "But I do have a lead on your uncle's murder. You know that hitchhiker Max picked up at the Elkhorn Café just before he was killed?"

Denver made a face. "What about him?"

"Did you know Max gave him a ride out of town?" Cline asked. "Davey saw it. He just told me."

"I thought he couldn't remember anything," J.D. objected.

"Selective memory," Cline said. "I imagine he won't remember stealing that car, either, or trying what I suspect was extortion. I figure he planned to give you the information about the hitchhiker for a price. Of course."

"You think that's all he intended to tell me?" Denny asked.

Cline nodded. "The hitchhiker did it."

"And how do you explain Max's ransacked office?" J.D. asked. Denver shot him an "I-told-you-reporting-it-to-Cline-wouldn't-do-any-good" look.

"This kind of thing happens all the time," Cline said. "Someone gets himself killed, it hits the papers and kids sneak into the dead guy's house and fool around."

"If you thought it was just kids, why did you dust the place for fingerprints?" Denver asked.

"Police procedure."

She glanced back at the boy's room. "I suppose you can also explain why Davey seems ... scared—as if he's being threatened not to remember."

Cline's eyes narrowed. "You aren't suggesting—"

"I didn't say *you* were threatening him," Denver quickly amended.

Cline took off his hat and turned the brim in his thick fingers. He glanced over at J.D. "You're being awful quiet." J.D. shrugged and looked away. "It's obvious why the boy's acting the way he is," the deputy said, turning his attention back to Denver. "He's looking at a minimum of a year in Miles City."

Reform school? J.D. glanced back at Davey's room. It all seemed too convenient. When the boy was well, he'd be shipped off. Denny seemed to be thinking the same thing.

"You'll let me know when you pick up this hitchhiker?" she asked.

Cline grinned. "Trust me. You'll be the first to know." He walked them to J.D.'s pickup and waited until they'd driven away. J.D. watched in the rearview mirror as Cline went back into the hospital.

He looked over at Denny. She sat with one hand in her pocket, the same pocket he'd seen her stick the note from Davey in.

He waited for her to tell him about the note as they started back up the canyon. But when he looked over, she'd fallen into an exhausted sleep. He gently pulled her toward him so that her head rested in his lap. As he studied her angelic face, the first lines of a song came to him, clear and strong, just like they used to. He hummed softly, writing the song in his head as he drove, and Denny slept.

IT WAS THE SAME DREAM. Denver skipping and singing into the bank. Her parents behind her. The words dying on her lips. Her feet stopping as she saw the people lying facedown on the floor. The silence. Her father calling her name. As she ran back to him, she saw the other policeman on the floor. Her father grabbed her and shoved her down as he reached for his own gun. She hit the floor and slid into the desk leg. The pain made her cry out. Only this time, Denver saw herself crawl under the office desk, felt the cold floor beneath her cheek as she looked out to see the masked man turn, shotgun in his hands. She saw the silver flash, and something flickered in the light as it spun. Her mother screamed. And the room exploded.

Denver sat up with a scream in her throat, her fingers clenched into fists.

"It's all right," J.D. murmured as he drew her to him. He pulled off the road and held her, rubbing her back, soothing her with whispered words. She nestled against him, fighting off the nightmare, feeling safe in his embrace. "Bad dream?" His voice was soft and gentle, like his touch. She nodded. "About Max?"

"No. My parents and the day they were killed." She shuddered and he held her tighter. "I remembered more of it. I saw the bank robber."

"The man who killed your parents?" he asked, sounding not altogether convinced.

"I know it sounds crazy, but ever since Max's death, I've been having the dream again. Each time, I remember a little more. Or maybe I just think I remember. Maybe it's just my imagination. But this time, the robber turned and I saw him. He wore a ski mask but there was something about him...."

J.D. frowned. "I suppose it could be a memory. I can remember things when I was very young." He seemed to hesitate. "Denny, have you ever thought of *trying* to remember? I know Max encouraged you to forget, but what if you got someone to help you bring it all back?"

Her heart pounded; just the idea of reliving it paralyzed her. "Someone?"

"Maybe a psychologist who uses hypnotism."

She stared at the highway ahead, suddenly more afraid than she had ever been. "I'm not sure I could go back to that day, J.D."

"I just thought it might make the nightmare end," he reassured her softly.

"The nightmare will end when we find Max's killer," she said, telling herself she believed it as she snuggled against him. His shirt against her cheek was soft and warm and smelled of J.D., a scent she'd never been able to forget.

"I've always wondered about your parents," he said, sounding cautious.

"I can't remember very much. Max always wanted me to put that part of my life behind me because their deaths had been so violent, and I have so few memories before that. Maybe he was right."

He released her just enough to get the pickup going again. Denver found herself studying J.D. out of the corner of her eye. In broad daylight, he looked even more handsome, strong and muscular from his broad shoulders to his thighs. She mentally shook herself. Being attracted to him was one thing; falling for him was another.

"How are you going to handle our suspicions about Pete?" he asked, back on the road.

Pete. "The more I've thought about it, the more I'm convinced of Pete's innocence," she said, anticipating J.D.'s reaction.

He tensed, and she heard him mutter an oath under his breath. With regret, she moved out of the shelter of his arm and slid across the seat to her side of the pickup. She could see West Yellowstone in the distance.

"You're going to have to be careful with Pete," J.D. said. "If you're wrong and he turns out to be—"

"I know." She stuffed her hands deep into her jeans, not wanting to think about Pete. Her fingers hit the note Davey had slipped her. "Could you drop me by Max's office?" she asked as they entered town.

He shot her a look as he pulled up in front of Max's and started to cut the engine.

"I really need to be alone for a while," she said, opening the door.

"Denny—"

"I'll talk to you later," she said, jumping out and not looking back.

J.D. swore, slamming his fist on the steering wheel. He'd done it again, pushing her away when that was the last thing he wanted to do. He thought about the note he'd seen Davey pass her at the hospital. Damn. Denny hadn't trusted him enough to even tell him about it.

"What do you expect?" he demanded out loud. "The woman has no reason to trust you." *No,* he thought, *instead she trusts Pete. No matter how much evidence piles up against him.*

J.D. headed for Maggie's, thinking of the Denny who'd slept on his lap on the way home and the music that had come back into his head. The music and the words were gone again; just like Denny, they'd slipped away from him.

As he climbed Maggie's steps, he wished he was a detective instead of a musician. A damned good detective could solve this and save Denny from any more sorrow. He knocked, then remembered that Maggie was probably on her way to Missoula. She surprised him by opening the door.

"I was afraid you'd already left."

"Something's come up," she said quietly. She motioned him inside. "Oh, J.D., maybe Max *was* involved in something illegal. A hundred and fifty thousand dollars' worth of illegal."

THE WORDS WERE WRITTEN in a childlike scrawl. "Gralin Pas. Sunriz. Tommarro. Brng yur karma. And yur skiis."

Denver stared at Davey's note. At first she thought it was in some form of code but soon realized it was just horrendous spelling. "Grayling Pass. Sunrise. Tomorrow. Bring your 'karma'?" Denver moaned. "Bring your camera. And your skis."

Not another one of Davey's secret meeting places! Maybe Cline was right. Davey was just trying to extort money from her. Well, if he thought she was going to meet him at another isolated place, he was wrong. She wadded up the note and threw it into the trash. Davey was in for a surprise. No more games. This time he was going to talk to her.

"Davey Matthews?" the head nurse repeated over the phone.

Denver held her breath. Had Davey gotten worse? Surely he hadn't—

"Are you a relative?" the nurse asked.

"No. I'm a friend. His relatives all live out of state. He's not worse, is he?"

The nurse seemed to hesitate. "Mr. Matthews has left."

"Left? He was released this quickly?"

Silence. "Not exactly. It appears he's run away."

Denver hung up, her hands shaking. Davey had run away, all right, but not to avoid the law, she thought as she looked around Max's ransacked office. Davey was running for his life.

"Oh, Max, what were you working on?" she whispered. The killer was looking for something. But what? Max's office was in a worse mess after Deputy Cline and his fingerprinting team had come through; everything was covered with gray powder.

She began picking up the mountain of papers and putting them into stacks. It was probably fruitless, but right now she needed something to occupy her mind—something besides images of J.D. She thought about the man she'd spent the last twenty-four hours with. Something was desperately wrong. The music industry had acknowledged his talent; his fans had made him rich. He had women falling at his feet. What else would it take to make him happy? she wondered.

Forcing aside the image of J.D. in his snug-fitting jeans, she sat down at the desk and assumed Max's thinking pose. Max had picked up a hitchhiker. They'd gone to the old dump. Not logical, but possible, she supposed. Max liked the place. It was all tall pines and grassy slope now, but years ago it had been the city dump. Many nights she and Max had driven to the edge of the embankment and parked in his Olds wagon above the dump, waiting and listening.

About midnight, Max would snap on the headlights. The beams would shine down the slope, where a handful of black bears scrounged in the day's pickings of people's leftovers. But Max's favorite part was what happened at about two in the morning. The black bears would suddenly get nervous and run off. Then the grizzlies would come out.

Max never tired of watching the grizzlies at the dump. It was a ritual for him. And Denver guessed it was his fascination with the huge, powerful animals and his concern that ordinary people would never get the chance to see a grizzly out of captivity.

Max had taken it personally when the city closed the dump. It wasn't that he wanted the bears munching on tin cans and plastic sandwich bags; he was just sorry to see the grizzlies go when the dump closed. And he missed those late nights, talking, waiting for the grizzlies. So did Denver.

No, it didn't seem strange that Max might go out to the old city dump. Maybe even to meet someone he couldn't meet any other place. That seemed to leave Pete out. Max had no reason to meet Pete secretly as far as she knew. She thought about the hitchhiker. Max would have given him a ride as far as the dump. That was Max. A lover of old city dumps, grizzlies and people in trouble. Maybe when Cline did find the hitchhiker—if he ever did—the man would know something about Max's death. Maybe that was why he was so hard for Cline to find.

She stared at the room and all the work that lay ahead of her. Too many questions still plagued her. And thoughts of J.D. kept pushing in. The way his face softened when he smiled, the way his eyes shone silver— She shook herself, bumping her knee against the desk. It gave out a hollow thud. She stared at the desk, suddenly remembering the secret compartment.

Denver reached under and pushed the worn panel. It swung inward, and there in the hollow space was the last thing she'd expected to find. Max's gun.

MAGGIE HANDED J.D. the bank receipt. "Max deposited $150,000 in his account the day before he died," she said, her voice wavering.

J.D. looked down at it. "Could he have saved that kind of money?"

She shook her head. "Every penny he saved, he put in a special account for Denver. Her account hasn't been touched." Maggie punched the couch as she plopped down onto it. "Dammit, J.D., you have to find out what's going on. Max couldn't have been dirty. Not Max, please."

He took a chair across from her. "I'm trying, Maggie, but none of it makes any sense and Denny—"

Maggie wiped at the tears. "She's going to have to be told."

"It would be better coming from you considering the way she feels about me right now." His suspicion of Pete had driven a wedge between them. He told Maggie about finding Max's wallet.

"It's strange that the attacker took his wallet and not yours," Maggie said after a moment. "Obviously there was something in there the attacker didn't want anyone to find."

"Like what?" J.D. tried to remember the contents. "I wanted Denny to take a look. She might have recognized something significant that I wouldn't." He rubbed his temples. "I feel like I'm making a mess of this."

Maggie smiled at him kindly. "Just think what might have happened if you hadn't been with Denny last night at Horse Butte."

He grimaced. "But she still thinks Pete's a prince and I'm a first-class jerk." J.D. picked up the bank-deposit receipt from the table. "When she hears about this, she isn't going to be happy, Maggie."

"That's why he couldn't be involved in anything illegal," she said. "Max would never hurt Denny."

J.D. hoped Maggie was right about that.

SLOWLY, DENVER PULLED the revolver and the box of shells from their hiding place. Then she reached back into the compartment and felt around again. Nothing but dust.

She stared at the gun, angry with Max. Why had he hidden it? If he'd had it, he might still be alive. She rubbed her hand over her tired eyes. Had he left the gun behind because he'd known the person he was meeting at the city dump and felt safe? He would feel safe meeting Pete. Or

Deputy Cline, for that matter. Or just about anyone she could think of.

Denver continued to put Max's office back into some kind of order, knowing it was the only way she'd ever be able to make sense of his case files. The files Max had burned nagged at the back of her mind. Had he been trying to protect someone? The same person who'd killed him? She thought about the "Case of the Wandering Husband" Maggie had mentioned and promised herself she'd search for it as soon as she had everything picked up.

Tired and dirty, she lifted the last batch of papers from the floor and made room for them on a corner of the desk. One sheet floated to the floor and she bent under the desk to retrieve it. A noise made her come up too fast and bang her head on the underside of the desk.

"Ouch!" She rubbed her head, staring at the open front door. Sheila Walker stood framed in the doorway, that same goofy hat hanging off the side of her head, that same hungry look in her eyes.

"You and I have to talk, honey," Sheila said. "It's a matter of life and death."

Chapter Eight

The reporter strode into the room, shoved papers aside and plopped down on a corner of Max's desk. "I've been doing some digging. Sometimes I get this feeling in my gut. I got that feeling now, honey."

Denver didn't have the foggiest idea what the woman was talking about.

"I heard you were on Horse Butte last night," she said. "Deputy Cline says it was an accident. You buying that?" Denver didn't get a chance to answer. "Me neither."

The woman slipped her large handbag off her shoulder and onto the desk. She got up and stalked around the office.

"What do you think your uncle was hiding?" she asked, poking a finger into one of the holes the burglar had made. When Denver didn't answer, the reporter turned toward her. "You know, they never caught the bank robber who killed your folks. He got away with over a million bucks—and murder. Did you know that?"

Denver felt her head swim. The woman jumped around so fast, it was impossible to follow her line of thinking. "No."

Sheila cocked her head. "Off the record, did your uncle ever talk about the money?"

"What money?"

"I'm on a money trail, honey. And I'm afraid I'm thinking it leads right to your uncle." She came over to the desk to pick up her purse. "Max's murder and that boy being run off the road are just the beginning. A caper this size... Who knows where it will end. Or how many more people are going to die."

Denver stared at her, dumbstruck. What money trail? Surely she didn't think Max—

"Just answer me one question. Did Max leave you a bundle of money?"

"Max never had a bundle of money."

Sheila nodded. "So you're saying you don't know where he stashed the money."

"There is no money."

Sheila Walker smiled. "Take some good advice, honey. Watch your backside. As naive as you are, you're bound to be next."

FOR A LONG TIME AFTER the reporter had left, Denver found herself staring after her. The woman had to be nuts. Did she think Max had something to do with the bank robbery? Max hadn't even been in Billings. She remembered the wait at the police station and a woman police officer finally taking her home to wait until Max arrived. Sheila Walker had to be looking for a connection between the two cases, but if she thought Max was it, she was dead wrong.

Max's pistol lay on the desk beside the box of shells. Sheila's warning that she'd be next ricocheted around in her head. She picked up the pistol and, trying not to speculate on whom she had to fear, loaded it.

Then on impulse she called the Stage Coach Inn and asked for J. D. Garrison. When no one answered in his room, she left a message, then headed home, anxious for the peace of the lake cabin—the healing place Max had given her as a child.

As she left Max's office, she noticed another storm had turned the sky to slate gray. Wasn't spring going to ever come?

THE MOMENT DENVER OPENED the front door of the cabin, she knew something was terribly wrong. A cold breeze hit her in the face along with the knowledge that someone had been there. She flicked on the overhead light to find the cabin ransacked, but not as badly as Max's office. She fought between anger and tears; the tears finally won.

Damn the person who had done this. She stepped farther into the cabin, pushing open the laundry room door. Her photography supplies, detergent powder and dirty clothes were scattered everywhere.

What in the world was the person looking for? Did he really think Max would hide a case file in the laundry-detergent box? The thought gave her a sudden chill. A hitchhiker would look in obvious places, but someone who knew Max would look in the detergent.

She strode down the hall to Max's old office and closed the side door to the cabin, cutting off the cold air. His big old rolltop gaped open, everything pulled out onto the floor.

The phone rang. "Hello?" Silence. "Hello?" It hit her that it might be Davey again, but then she heard Taylor's deep voice. Outside, the storm clouds had dropped over the cabin, a dense, dark cover, as dark as her mood.

"Denver?" He sounded almost surprised and she thought for a moment he might have dialed the wrong number. "I'm trying to find Maggie. You don't happen to know where she is, do you?"

"She said she was going to Missoula to help a friend whose mother died, but I'm not sure when she planned to leave."

"Oh, right, Maggie did mention she might go," he said, sounding a little dejected. "I didn't think she'd already left. I didn't even get to tell her goodbye."

"I'm sure she'll be back soon." They talked a little longer, with Taylor asking about her health, if Max's will had turned up, if Cline had found any new evidence. He sounded lonely.

She snapped on a light and began sorting through the mess from Max's desk.

"Are you sure you're all right?" he asked, obviously feeling he had to fill in as her protector now that Max was gone. Did he also feel protective toward Maggie or did he have something more romantic in mind? The thought didn't bother her as much as it had at first.

"Oh, I'm as well as can be expected," Denver said, looking around the ransacked room. She knew if she mentioned what had happened, he'd come out. And as much as she liked him, she didn't know what to say to him. He was so quiet, so different from Max, who would have entertained her while the two of them cleaned up this mess.

She hung up, anxious to get busy. She felt a sudden chill as the side door flew open behind her. An arm locked around her neck and pulled her backward. She fought for breath as the pressure against her throat increased, cutting off her air. A hint of a man's cologne drifted across her senses; the familiarity of it stunned her. Her head pounded as she ripped at the arm around her throat with her fingers. Panic seized her as black spots danced before her eyes. She felt the darkness coming up for her and realized he planned to kill her. She kicked frantically behind her, connecting with a shin, and got a loud curse.

Then the lights went out. Literally.

"Get out!" She heard a man yell from down the hallway, the voice muffled as if behind a mask. "Now."

Her attacker let go, shoving her forward. She stumbled into Max's desk and hurriedly groped for the pistol in her purse. She could hear her attacker stumbling down the dark hall. She pulled out the gun, planning to go after him, when a wave of cold air hit her, then a body. The body hurled her to the floor. The pistol went flying.

"Stay down. And keep quiet," the man on top of her commanded.

Denver moaned as she recognized the voice. "Great timing, Garrison." The cologne scent was gone, along with the man who wore it.

"I knew you couldn't keep quiet," J.D. growled, rolling off her. In the other room, the front door slammed. "Stay here!"

She heard J.D. run down the hall toward the living room. He knocked over something large, swore loudly as it rumbled to the floor, then a door opened again, followed by silence.

Denver felt around for the pistol and, not finding it, got to her feet and made her way to the dark living room. The front door stood open, cold air rushing in; snow had begun to fall, making the day even darker. She tried the light switch, then when it didn't come on, felt around on top of the fireplace mantel for a flashlight.

"J.D.?" Denver called as she stepped outside into the storm. "J.D.?"

A car engine cranked over, its headlights cutting a swath of light through the snowflakes. Denver could make out two shadowy figures wrestling in the snow near the edge of the road. J.D. and...another man. Denver ran back to the cabin, grabbed the poker from the fireplace and ran toward the two, screaming at the top of her lungs.

The sight of her, or maybe it was just the sound of her, made them both look up. One man stumbled to his feet and ran toward the waiting car. The other kneeled in the road, an arm over his face as the car turned around, roaring away in a tidal wave of ice shards and chunks of frozen obsidian sand. As the car's taillights died away in the pine trees, J.D. slowly got to his feet.

"Are you all right?" Denver called out.

"I thought I told you to stay where you were," he snarled as he started back toward the house.

"And miss seeing you get killed?"

J.D. pushed Denver through the open doorway and slammed the door behind them. Denver flicked the beam of her flashlight over him. He took it from her hand, along with the poker she still carried, and laid both on the hearth.

"Did you get a look at him?" she asked.

"No." She heard him snap the light switch. "How about you? Did you recognize him or the car?"

"Just his cologne." She could hear J.D. stumbling over things in the living room. She told herself that anyone could buy the same designer cologne Pete wore, anyone with money, but it didn't help ease the sick feeling in her stomach.

"Where's the breaker box?" J.D. asked as if he hadn't heard her. He seemed to be running on straight anger and she wasn't sure how much of it was aimed at her.

She took the flashlight from the hearth. "In the laundry room. I'll get it."

J.D. followed her into the multipurpose room. Denver held the flashlight on the electrical box behind the wall calendar near the door, while J.D. flipped the breakers. The lights came on.

She caught sight of J.D.'s face. "My God." She stared at him, the ransacked room and the assailant quickly forgotten. "J.D., you're hurt."

Gingerly he touched his left eye with his fingers. "Just a lucky punch, that's all. I'm fine." But Denver was already running warm water in the laundry tub. She reached into the overhead cabinet and took out a washcloth.

"Come here," she said, motioning for him to sit down on a footstool. She touched the washcloth gently to his face. "What about these cuts?"

"It was just a little gravel," he mumbled. "Ouch."

"Hold still." Her fingers found a bump on the side of his head, probably where she'd hit him with the lamp. The tears came without warning. Denver bit her lip and tried to step away from him. "I'll get some antiseptic for those cuts."

He caught her hand and pulled her into his arms. She clung to him, feeling his strength, his warmth, the steady beat of his heart against her breast. He hugged her tightly against him as if he needed her in his arms as much as she needed to be there.

"You could have been killed," she whispered.

"I'm all right, Denny." He cradled her head with one hand, her back with the other. "I'm fine."

She brushed at her tears, pulling back a little to look at him, but didn't move from his arms. "What do you think they wanted?"

"I wish I knew because you won't be safe until we do," he said, pushing back a strand of her long hair from her face. His gaze shifted to her neck. "Oh, Denny, your throat."

She touched it gingerly with trembling fingers. "I don't know what would have happened if you hadn't come along when you did."

He pulled her against him, cradling her in his arms, rocking her. "It's all right, baby. It's all right now."

The room seemed to shrink, pressing them even closer. Denver fought for breath as J.D. held her. She could feel his heart pick up a beat next to hers, feel his breath against her cheek become ragged. Warning signals began to go off in her head. *Dangerous territory! Red alert!* Except she couldn't move.

He pulled back a little; his look flamed her cheeks and sent her temperature skyrocketing. She watched his gaze touch her lips as tenderly as a kiss. And as he stole up to her eyes again, she felt her heartbeat go from a two-step to a cowboy jitterbug.

"I should get the antiseptic," she whispered, but didn't move.

The phone rang. She stared at it, not wanting to leave his arms but knowing if she didn't—

"You get the phone. I'll get the antiseptic," J.D. said, his voice thick with emotion.

Reluctantly she stepped from his arms; he didn't seem any more anxious to let her go than she was to leave. As she answered the phone, she put the washcloth to her face and fought to quiet her thundering pulse. She heard J.D. draw in a ragged breath. "Hello?" she said. Silence. Then a click.

"Who was it?" J.D. asked behind her.

She shook her head as she ran more cold water over the cloth and put it to her still burning cheeks. "They hung up."

"Probably just a wrong number."

Under normal circumstances, Denver would have agreed. But before her caller had hung up, she'd heard the distinct opening of a phone-booth door. She couldn't shake off the feeling that whoever it was had been calling from just up the road—and that that person had just tried to kill her.

She flung the washcloth over the tub and took the antiseptic from J.D.'s hand. He didn't even flinch as she touched it to his scrapes and scratches. Instead, he kept his gaze on her face.

"Thanks," he said softly. He was so near her she could feel the heat of his body.

"I guess I'd better start putting this place back together." She put the antiseptic away, then knelt to pick up the pistol. After stuffing it back into her purse, she stepped past J.D. He threw her completely off guard.

"What were these, Denny?" he asked. He was holding several long strips of exposed film. A couple of the cassettes still hung from the ends of the film.

"Just some promo shots I was doing for a free-lance project."

"Doesn't it seem odd that the burglar destroyed them?"

All she could think about was that she'd have to reshoot them.

"What else have you been working on that someone might find interesting?" J.D. prodded.

Denver shrugged. "I've got some shots of celebs for the free-lance writers I work with. Montana's hot right now, you know. Lots of movie stars and TV moguls moving here."

"I heard."

"And there's some film I was getting ready to soup for a travel brochure I've contracted to do." She grumbled under her breath as she picked up more strips of exposed film dangling out of film cassettes. "I guess I'll have to shoot these again, too."

"Nothing more?" J.D. asked.

"Just Max's birthday party. That's it."

"Max's birthday?" he asked, taking the film from her. "Do you think any shots can be saved?"

"Not of the film that's out of the cassettes. If there's any shots still inside . . . maybe."

"Let's take a look," J.D. said, hitting the light.

"Sorry there isn't more," she said later as she hung up the processed film to dry. Only a few photos in three of the rolls had survived.

"That's all right. It was a long shot anyway, but it just seems strange that they'd destroy your film." There were several pictures of the buffalo jump near Three Forks and a nice scenic landscape of Big Sky with Lone Mountain Peak. On the other roll, three shots of Max's birthday party had turned out.

"Damn," Denver said, holding the frames up to the light. "These are the last photos of Max and most of them are ruined."

"Can we put these on your light table?" J.D. asked.

"What are we looking for?" Denver asked as she spread out the negatives.

J.D. picked up the loupe and bent over to study them.

"See anything?" she asked.

He handed her the loupe. "Here, take a look. At the back of the room by the fireplace."

Denver bent over the negatives. "I think we'd better blow this up."

A few minutes later, she held up the photograph from Max's birthday for J.D. to see. It was a wide-angle shot of the entire party; the photo as well as the cabin overflowed with people. But now she could see the two people at the rear clearly. Pete Williams was having a very serious conversation with Cal Dalton.

"It almost looks like Pete and Cal are arguing," J.D. said.

"I wonder what they have to argue about? I didn't even know they knew each other." Her gaze skimmed the rest of the photo. "Oh, my God, look," she said, pointing to the right-hand side of the picture.

"Max is just washing up some dishes," J.D. said, sounding confused.

Denver shook her head. "See how he's carefully wrapping up that glass in a towel?" Her gaze met J.D.'s. "I've helped him collect evidence before to send to the crime lab in Missoula. He's getting someone's fingerprints from the party."

J.D. stared at her. "Why would Max run a fingerprint check on anyone at the party?"

"I know it doesn't make any sense. We knew everyone who attended the party." She shivered. "But it would mean that even two weeks ago he suspected someone close to him."

"Come on," J.D. said, taking her hand, "I'm going to build a fire so you can warm up." He pulled a chair up to the fire for her and began pulling kindling and old newspapers out of the wood box. "Why would Max take one of the guest's fingerprints? It's not like most people's fingerprints are on file somewhere, right?"

"Unless the person had been arrested before or worked in a high-security job that required them," Denver agreed, sitting forward. "Or Max might have needed the prints to compare to some he'd picked up at a crime scene."

While J.D. got the fire going, Denver went to the phone. He listened while she called the crime lab in Missoula.

"They received a fingerprint request from Max," she said after she hung up. "But they can't give me any other information. They did say that their findings have been mailed." She picked up one of her framed photographs from the floor. "Another dead end unless we can dig them up at Max's office."

"You were very lucky this time, Denny," J.D. said as he joined her and hung the photo back on the wall. "Whoever tried to strangle you obviously meant business."

"Speaking of luck, you must have gotten my message right after I called."

"You called me?" He sounded pleased to hear that.

She had stooped down to pick up a stack of spilled magazines; now she looked over at him. "If you didn't get my message, how did you—"

"Just luck." He smiled that all-too-familiar sexy smile of his. She wished he wouldn't do that when she was feeling vulnerable, then realized that around him she was *always* vulnerable.

"There seems to be a lot of luck going around," she said quietly.

"I followed you out of town," he confessed with a shrug and a sheepish grin. "I just thought—"

"That I might need help again." She laughed and shook her head at him in amazement. "You *do* know me, don't you." He knew her in a way no other man ever had; he'd seen into her heart and she'd invited him in. She quickly looked away from those knowing gray eyes of his.

"You said you recognized the guy's cologne?"

Denver picked up a couch cushion and put it back in place. So he *had* heard her. She hugged herself but couldn't shake off the cold chill as she looked over at him. His gaze was so filled with compassion she thought she would cry if she kept looking at him.

"It was the kind Pete wears," she said, realizing J.D. had probably recognized it, too.

"That's what I thought."

She waited for him to say, I told you so. He didn't. "Thanks for coming to my rescue."

His laugh was low, directly behind her. "A knight in armor I'm not, Denny. In fact..." His fingers touched her shoulder and his voice dropped.

"You were doing fine without me," she said, realizing she could mean both the fight in the driveway or his life in California.

"Don't kid yourself. I needed you."

Her body stirred beneath the warm touch of his fingers. His voice found its way to her heart and chipped away at the wall of ice she kept trying to build against him. Slowly she turned and looked up into his eyes. His gaze softened. How had she ever forgotten the depth of emotion in those eyes?

"You're scared to death it's Pete, aren't you?" He caressed her face, tracing his fingers along her cheek.

"Pete's been my best friend for years."

His fingers stopped short of her lips. "He's asked you to marry him?"

She nodded reluctantly.

He pulled his hand away. "Have you given him an answer yet?"

How could she tell J.D. that he'd been the only man who'd ever interested her let alone had a chance with her heart? "Yes. I can't marry Pete when I gave my heart to another man years ago—" The words caught in her throat.

"Denny," he said, his voice low and soft.

How many times had she wondered if J.D. ever regretted leaving West Yellowstone—and her? He looked as if all he wanted to do was kiss her, as if his lips wanted nothing more than to touch hers. But then he stepped back over to the fire.

"I'm never going to hurt you again," he said, making her wonder if he was telling her—or reminding himself. He tossed another log onto the fire. "We'd probably better have a look upstairs to see how much damage was done."

She stood, staring at his strong, muscular back, his slim hips, wanting him in ways she'd never even imagined at sixteen. Then she followed him upstairs.

Her intruder had obviously started his search upstairs. Clothing hung out of dresser drawers; closet doors stood open, their insides tumbled about. With J.D.'s help, she quickly put things away. Then she saw her old cloth doll on the floor. Denver picked it up; she held it against her chest fighting tears of joy to see that it hadn't been damaged.

"At least they didn't destroy the house as badly as they did Max's office," she said, unable to let go of Hominy. She touched the doll's worn face, thinking of Max. And her parents. She couldn't remember if it had been Max or her parents who'd given her Hominy. She thought she remembered her mother giving her the doll on her birthday but she couldn't be sure. Maybe she just wished her mother had given it to her. She had so little left of that life.

"You think this all ties in with Max's death?" she asked.

"It seems likely, don't you think?" J.D. replied, watching her. "Come on, let's clean up the other bedroom."

When they finished the bedroom, J.D. led the way back downstairs. Denver picked up a throw pillow and replaced it. When she turned, she caught the expression on J.D.'s face.

"What is it?" she asked. Her legs turned wobbly under her and she gripped the back of a chair J.D. had righted. "You're scaring me."

"I'm sorry, I didn't mean to," he said, going to her. He led her over to the hearth and sat down beside her.

"Tell me what's wrong," she pleaded. "You didn't just come out here tonight because you were worried about me, did you?"

He shook his head. "Look around this room, Denny. Look at the bruises on your neck. You have to be straight with me if you want me to help you find Max's killer." Firelight caught in his eyes, making them bright as winter moonlight on new snow.

Automatically Denver reached for her mother's locket at her throat as she got up and walked to the window facing the lake. The glow of the fire flickered behind her, searing her silhouette to the glass.

"You're right not to trust me with your heart," he said. "But you have to trust that I'm here to help you."

She was right not to trust him with her heart? The words made her ache inside. Didn't he realize that trusting him meant surrendering not only her heart to him? There was no half way, no possibility of compromise, not between them. They could never just be friends. At least she couldn't.

"I saw Davey slip you a note, Denny." The hurt in his voice tugged at her heart.

She turned slowly, searching for the words. "I needed to open that note alone." Her desperation to find the name of Max's killer printed on that scrap of paper in that boy's young hand had pushed her away from J.D., the one man she longed to be close to. The fire danced wildly behind him, throwing his face in shadow. "It wasn't you. It was me." She began picking books up off the floor without even realizing she was doing it.

"Denny..." She continued gathering up things from the floor. Pictures from the walls, pillows, an overturned chair. Suddenly she felt J.D.'s hand on her arm. "Talk to me, Denny." She looked up and saw some of her own fears mirrored in his eyes. J.D. pulled her to him and held her with a force that comforted her as nothing else had since Max's death. She pressed her cheek against his shirt, listened to his heart thunder next to her ear. "Talk to me, please."

She breathed in the scent of him. "I feel like my world is falling apart, like nothing is real—or ever was."

He stroked her hair, his hand sure and strong. "I'm going to help you put it back together. I'm not going to let anyone hurt you, Denny. I promise you that. But you have to trust me. No more secrets."

She struggled to find solid ground beneath his silver gaze. Instead, what she saw deep in his eyes made her heart dance to a beat she'd never known before. Overwhelming desire. It raced through her blood, melting the wall of ice around her heart. "Did I destroy any chance of you ever trusting me?" he asked, his eyes darkening like the storm outside.

She shook her head and looked away. "I'm just afraid your music will call you back before we can find Max's murderer."

He took her face in his hands; his eyes met hers. "I won't leave, Denny, until you no longer need me."

Then you will never leave, she thought.

Chapter Nine

"Here," Denver said, handing him the note. "And don't bother to say it."

J.D. read the words, then looked up at her. "Say what? That you'd be a fool to meet him in an even more isolated place than the fire tower—that is, if he bothers to show up, if he has any information for you, if it's not a trap, if he could even spell?"

"That about covers it." She dropped into a chair by the fire. He could see the day's events had taken their toll on her, but a steely determination still burned in those incredible eyes.

"But you're going to do it anyway, aren't you?"

As she curled her feet up under her, she met his gaze. "You saw him at the hospital. He's obviously scared. Why would he have run if he didn't know something?"

J.D. hadn't the heart to tell her that the kid might have taken off just to avoid reform school. "I'm going with you."

She smiled. "I had a feeling you'd say that."

God, she was beautiful. The firelight played in her hair, igniting it. And her eyes. Light, mysterious eyes. He wanted nothing more than to drown himself in them.

"As long as I'm being truthful, I guess there's something else you ought to know. I found Max's pistol and a box of shells he'd hidden in a compartment in his desk. If it's some kind of message to me, I don't know what it could be."

He felt his heart expand, his desire for her growing with the trust she was putting in him. She was still as defiant, stubborn and fiery spirited as anyone he'd ever known, only now there was an elegance to it that made her all the more fascinating. The last thing he wanted to do was hurt this woman. He promised himself he'd protect her—not only her life—but her heart.

He thought about his music. He'd come home, running scared. Nothing had mattered. Or hadn't until he'd seen her standing over him holding a lamp base.

Denver brushed a strand of hair back from her face. "The only lead I have to go on is a case Maggie said he was working on before his death. He'd been trailing a possible cheating husband and spending late long hours following the man."

"Any chance Max would have cross-referenced his files?" She laughed. "You knew Max."

"It was just a thought." J.D. wondered if either of them really knew Max. "Denny..." Her gaze held a warning, almost convincing him it would be better if she found out from Deputy Cline. Almost. "Max made a rather large deposit in his account the day before he was murdered."

"How large?" she whispered.

"One hundred and fifty thousand dollars."

"Where would he get that kind of money?"

"I was hoping you might know."

She shook her head, her eyes filled with dread. "There's this reporter in town from the *Billings Register.* She stopped by Max's office earlier. She asked me where Max got his money and insinuated he'd been in on the bank robbery."

J.D. swore. "That's ridiculous. Your parents were killed during that robbery."

Denver shook her head. "The woman didn't know Max." She took a breath and let it out slowly. "But it doesn't look very good for him, does it?"

"No, it doesn't."

Denver buried her face in her hands for a moment. "He's innocent, J.D.," she murmured sadly, lifting her gaze. "But then, I want to believe Pete is innocent, don't I?"

WITH VERY LITTLE prompting, Denver agreed to spend the night in town at Maggie's. J.D. knew she was running from all the evidence building against Max, from her dreams about her parents, her worries about Davey, her fears about Pete. Max looked like a crook, and that, J.D. knew, was much more frightening to her than anything else that was happening.

As Denver gathered her ski gear for their meeting with Davey and her overnight bag to go to Maggie's, the phone rang.

It was obvious from the frown on her face that she wasn't delighted about what was being said on the other end of the line. Nor was that person letting her say much.

J.D. watched, suddenly frightened, knowing Pete was on the other end of that line. And that Pete wasn't happy about something. It scared him.

What bothered him most was the $150,000. Did the reporter really suspect something, or was she just following up on the rumors?

"I don't want to talk about this right now," Denny was saying, irritation in her tone. She twisted the phone cord around her fingers. "Fine, I'll see you then."

He didn't like to hear that last part. "Everything all right?"

"Pete just wants me to stop by the Stage Coach. The band's playing there tonight."

J.D. nodded. "Denny, you wouldn't—"

"Don't worry, I haven't forgotten," she said, touching the bruises on her neck.

He wanted to say something to take the hurt from her eyes. "Until we find out who killed Max, we're going to suspect everyone."

She nodded and glanced toward the window. It had stopped snowing and the first stars had popped out over the mountains.

"You still want to go dig through Max's files? I'll help you."

THEY SPLIT A PILE OF Max's papers in the middle of the floor. And began sorting through them looking for the "Case of the Wayward Husband," as J.D. called it, as well as the fingerprint results from the crime lab. She was glad for the company and even happier that he'd suggested it.

"I love Max's system," J.D. said, holding up a file marked RoadKill. "What do you think goes in here?"

Denver shook her head. "Knowing Max, it could be anything." She read a file name. "How about this one—Rock 'n' Roll." They laughed together, their gazes locking. "I guess we'll have to rename the files."

J.D. nodded. "We could even use last names. What do you think?"

His hand brushed hers as he reached for more papers. Her pulse took off running. Her heart yearned to go chasing after it. His touch earlier seemed like an appetizer and she was one starved woman.

"Hungry?" J.D. asked.

She blinked at him. "What?"

"You just said you were starved."

"I did?" She ducked her head to hide her embarrassment.

J.D. got to his feet. "Why don't I get us something? I'll be right back. Want me to surprise you?"

"Great." Not that anything could surprise her after that. She sat in the middle of the floor trying to still her panic as she listened to his pickup leave. When was she going to learn not to say what she was thinking? She could just imagine what she'd say one of these days if she continued to hang around J. D. Garrison, feeling the way she did about him.

J.D. returned with two chili dogs loaded, fries and large Coke floats.

"You remembered," Denver said when she saw the food.

"Who could forget what you like?" he joked. "Not that many women like jalapeños and tortilla chips on their chili dogs."

"I have an odd appetite," she admitted, studying him through her lashes. As much as she loved chili dogs, right now all she really wanted was J.D.

He groaned softly, a smile playing at his lips, as he sat down beside her. "You know, I've always admired your appetite. Among other things." When he looked at her, she could have sworn he was reading her mind.

They wolfed down the food, then leaned against the wall to finish their Coke floats. Denver idly thumbed through a stack of Max's papers, thinking more about J.D.'s long legs than the words on the pages. One word jumped out at her. *Affair.* She plucked the sheet from the pile and checked the date. The last entry was less than a week ago.

"This is it!" she cried, sitting up straighter.

J.D. moved closer to read it with her. "Lester Wade? Is that the one I know?"

Denver nodded, momentarily mute from the scent of him. "Lester still plays in the band." She read down the page through a series of surveillance times and dates, all late at night even after the bars had closed. "That's strange. He had to be cheating on his wife, Lila. What else would he be doing out this hour every night?"

"Not so." J.D. pointed to the last notation on the page. It read simply: "No other woman."

They looked at each other. "You don't think—"

Denver flipped the page. Written in Max's scrawl was the comment:

Informed wife Lila, Lester not having an affair. Paid in full.

"Well, I guess that takes care of that," Denver said, then squinted at the notation Max had made at the bottom of the page:

Bil 69614. Pearl file.

"Pearl file?" J.D. asked. His leg touched hers; the jolt rivaled any faulty toaster she'd ever known. "Do you know anyone named Pearl?"

Denver shook her head.

"How about the numbers?" J.D. asked.

She shook her head again. He was so close she thought for sure he'd kiss her. He must have thought the same thing because he moved over and got to his feet.

"Maybe it's some kind of billing code," J.D. suggested.

She groaned at the loss she felt when he moved away from her. "With Max, they could be just about anything." But she wrote them down, noticing it was late. "I didn't see a Pearl file, did you?"

"No. I didn't see anything with Bil on it, either," J.D. assured her. "Our burglar could have taken it, too, I suppose."

"That and the fingerprint results," Denver reminded him. She glanced at her watch. "I told Pete I'd stop by the Stage Coach."

The closeness she'd felt with J.D. all evening disappeared in one blink of his gray eyes. "I don't think that's a good idea, Denny. If you say anything to him—"

"I know," she interrupted. "I'll be careful."

As they were leaving, Denver reached into the mailbox, amazed she hadn't thought to check it before. She thumbed through the stack of bills and junk mail, then thumbed through again, this time paying closer attention. The return address of the crime lab in Missoula caught her eye. She plucked it from the pile and handed it to J.D. with trembling fingers. He took one look at it and tore it open.

"Who?" she asked, her voice no more than a whisper.

"I don't know. The prints belong to a man named William Collins. Do you have any idea who that is?"

"J.D., I knew everyone at Max's party. Whoever this William Collins is, I know him. I just don't know him by that name."

WHEN THEY WALKED INTO the Stage Coach Inn's bar, Pete spotted them right away. The band was just finishing a number and Pete looked up. Just the sight of J.D. seemed to make him angry.

"Why don't you wait for me at the bar," Denver said.

"You're calling the shots." His gaze warned her to be careful. "But if you need me, I won't be far away." He strode off into the bar, where a group of fans was already on their feet with pens and paper in hand.

Denver felt as if someone had dumped a bucket of ice water on her as she watched the women huddle around J.D. for autographs. Sometimes she forgot about his fame.

Pete said nothing as he came toward her but grabbed her arm and propelled her out of the bar to the lobby.

"Where have you been?" he demanded as he pulled her over to the side of the wide, sweeping staircase. "I asked you to wait at the apartment for me."

Denver jerked free of his hold and glared at him. "I had to talk to Davey Matthews."

"Davey Matthews? When is this going to end?"

"When Max's killer is caught," she said.

"I'm trying to protect you. Can't you see that? And what is J.D. trying to do?" He pulled off his hat and raked his fingers through his blond hair. "You still believe that I hurt that kid up at Horse Butte?" Pete looked toward the lounge, anger in his eyes.

"I don't know what to believe." The sweet scent of his cologne was the same as the man's who'd attacked her at the lake cabin, but in her wildest imagination, she couldn't conceive of Pete trying to kill her. She could hear J.D.'s warnings but she couldn't stop herself. She'd worn a turtle-necked sweater to hide the bruises on her neck. Now she pulled the collar down so Pete could see her neck.

He let out an oath; his eyes filled with shocked horror. "Who did this to you?" he demanded.

She shook her head. "There were two men. They ransacked the cabin." She stared at him, remembering the feel of the man's arm around her throat. Anyone could buy the same cologne as Pete's—anyone with money, she reminded herself again. And yet she'd never wondered until that moment where Pete got the money to buy expensive cologne or new pickups or live the way he did. He certainly didn't make a lot playing with the band. But his family had money, she reminded herself, sick at the doubts she was having. "One of the men tried to kill me," she said, needing to get it all out. "He wore the same cologne you wear."

Pete rocked back as if he'd been slapped. "What are you saying? That you believe I could do this to you?"

Tears rushed to her eyes. This was a man who'd professed his love for her, who'd asked her to marry him. "I think the person who hurt me wanted me to believe it was you."

"Why?" He looked pale under the hotel's lights. Pale and sick. "Why would someone do that?"

"I don't know." She felt as if she'd been punched. "I thought maybe you would know."

He looked away for a moment, and she had the strongest feeling he knew more than he was telling her. His gaze softened as he turned back to her. "Remember when we were kids on the lake?"

She nodded. It had always been the three of them and Max. "Do you remember the tree house we built?" She wanted those times back. They'd been so close. Like family.

"The tree house." Pete looked up at the ceiling. "I'd forgotten about the tree house."

"You and J.D. didn't always agree, but we pulled together and we got it built," she said, memories flooding her heart. "Remember how it was? We were all best friends."

"Times change," Pete said, jamming his hands into his jeans.

"You and I have always been friends."

"Yeah, friends." He grimaced; it had never been enough for him.

She bit her lip, knowing she shouldn't say any more, but needing to know, and more than anything, wanting to give him a chance. "The day Max was murdered, you were in Missoula with the band." She studied him, thinking of the years they'd shared. The words caught in her throat. "Were you, Pete?"

He closed his eyes for a moment, then looked toward the bar again. "You want me to write it in blood? Because I'm sure my word won't be enough."

"Tell me about the photograph," she whispered, her voice as lost as the look in his eyes. This was Pete. Pete Williams, a man she'd always trusted.

"The photograph?" Pete sighed as he pushed his hat back on his head. In the other room, the band started up again, only it was J.D. singing instead of Pete. And it was one of the songs that had made J.D. famous—"Good Morning, Heartache."

"Max called me and said he had to see me before I left for Missoula," Pete said slowly. "I knew something had been going on with him but he'd never wanted to talk about it before."

Denver held her breath, afraid of what Pete was going to say.

"But when I got to his office, he wasn't there." Pete looked her in the eye. "The photograph was on his desk."

"You took it and ripped J.D. out of the picture." It seemed like such a childish thing to do.

Pete shrugged. "He has it all, Denver. Everything. Including you. I'd let him have all his success and more if I could just have you."

Her heart ached at his words. In the next room, J.D. sang in that voice that had haunted her every dream for years.

"I'm sorry," she said quietly.

He nodded and touched a tear on her cheek with his fingertip. "Yeah, I know you are. But you're making a big mistake with him. He's back here, probably thinking you're what he needs." She could feel Pete's gaze on her face. "With J.D., nothing will ever be enough. Not even you."

Pete's words hit a chord in her. J.D. hadn't found happiness with his music. Did he see her as just another goal to be reached? The thought battered her heart.

"Haven't you ever asked yourself where J.D. got his start nine years ago?"

Denver caught her breath.

"Max." Pete spit out the word. "J.D. made a deal with Max. Money for the promise that he'd never come back for you. Max bought him off, and J.D. took the money and ran."

She let the air slip from her lungs, her wounded heart fighting to keep beating. "I don't believe you." Max wouldn't demand such a deal, and surely J.D. would never—

"You want to know what happened to that photo?" he asked as he started to walk away from her. "I ripped J.D. out just like I'd like to rip him from your heart."

As she watched Pete stalk away, she felt a fear, heart-deep, and an emptiness as cold and dark as a winter night. She staggered to the doorway of the lounge, stunned by Pete's jealousy of J.D. as much as by his claim that Max paid J.D. never to come back. Was J.D. that sure he would never want to come back, that he could never love her?

On stage, Pete announced that he and the famous J. D. Garrison were going to sing a song they had written together as teenagers. Anyone in the audience would have thought they were still the best of friends.

Their voices blended beautifully. Tears of sadness stung Denver's eyes. She'd known Pete harbored some envy when it came to J.D., but she had never realized how much. And it had nothing to do with music.

She stumbled down the hallway to the ladies' room and stared into the mirror. "Oh, Max." She washed her hands and splashed the achingly cold water on her face. She would get to the truth, she told herself as she left the room. Her resolve wavered, however, when she saw Deputy Cline in the shadows beside the stairway in the lobby. The music had stopped. And Cline was in deep conversation with J.D. They seemed to be arguing.

"What's wrong?" she asked, joining them.

Both men quit talking abruptly. Cline stepped back and pulled off his hat. There was a weariness about him as if he hadn't had much sleep lately.

"Denny," J.D. said, "it seems the deputy has frozen your uncle's assets until a deposit for $150,000 can be explained." His look warned her to be careful.

She frowned at Cline. "Why would you do that?"

The deputy attempted a sympathetic smile. "The money might have been acquired illegally."

"That's ridiculous," she snapped at him.

"Are you saying Max squirreled away that much?" Cline asked.

Money had never meant much to Max. "Obviously someone put it in his account to cast doubt on his character."

"One hundred and fifty thousand dollars?" Cline chuckled. "I wish someone would cast that much doubt on my character." He sobered. "Know anyone with that kind of money who hated your uncle enough to do that?"

Denver shook her head. Max didn't have any enemies that she knew of, let alone rich ones.

"It could be a smoke screen," J.D. interjected. "To lead you in the wrong direction."

Cline stood for a moment looking from one of them to the other. "Well, until we get to the bottom of it, that money stays right where it is. The Great Falls police have picked up a hitchhiker matching the description of the one seen with Max. They're holding him until I can drive up and talk to him."

Denver stared at Cline. "You can't still believe a hitchhiker killed my uncle. Not after this $150,000 has turned up. Unless you think the hitchhiker put it in Max's account."

Cline scratched his red neck. "I'm just covering all my bets. Maybe this hitchhiker didn't kill your uncle. But he might have seen who did."

"So you think that's a possibility?" Denver asked, amazed Cline had thought of it.

He grinned. "Anything's possible."

"When will you be talking to him?" she asked.

"First thing in the morning."

"I can't wait to hear what he has to say." Finally, maybe they'd have a lead. "Have you found Davey?" she asked, and realized belatedly that either way he would be a sore point with Cline.

"No, as a matter of fact, I have more important things to do than worry about a fifteen-year-old runaway," he snapped. "And one more thing, Ms. McCallahan. The next time you withhold information from my department, you're going to be the guest of the county. Got that?" He tipped his hat to J.D. and stomped off.

Denver turned her glare on J.D. "You told him about my ransacked cabin and the man who jumped us?"

"Someone had to. This is a homicide investigation, remember?"

"And a lot of good it did telling Cline," Denver said, daring him to argue with her. "Look what he came up with at Max's office. Nothing. He isn't going to solve this case and you know it."

"We can't be sure of that."

Tears rushed to her eyes. "I'm not sure of anything—or anyone. Not anymore." She turned to leave, but he grabbed her arm.

"You told Pete, didn't you?" he demanded.

She jerked away; her gaze snapped up to his. "I don't expect you to understand. I needed answers and I owed Pete that much."

J.D. slammed his fist against the wall. "Dammit, Denny, you may have just made the biggest mistake of your life."

"No, J.D., I did *that* the day I fell in love with you." She turned, tears blinding her, and ran.

Chapter Ten

J.D. caught her just outside the door and pulled her into his arms. He kissed her the way he'd wanted to from the moment he saw her with that lamp in her hand at Max's apartment. An electricity danced between them. Her body felt as wonderful as he'd expected it would. But nothing prepared him for the sweet taste of her or the desire that swept through him as they kissed. All the memories of the past melded with the present, shocking him with one simple earthshaking fact: he'd never felt this way about a woman before. They both stumbled back from the kiss. Denver looked as dazed as he felt.

"And what was that all about?" she demanded, her voice as shaky as his knees.

"I just wanted to kiss you," he answered truthfully.

She nodded as if she'd expected as much from him. "Answer one other question then. Where did you get the money to go to California nine years ago?"

He knew where this had come from. Pete.

"Did Max give you money?" she asked, her eyes begging him to say no.

J.D. looked her in the eye. "Yes."

"And you made a deal with him that you would never come back into my life, right?"

"Denny, you were just a kid when I left."

"I see." She started to turn away from him.

He grabbed her arm and pulled her to him again. "No, you don't see. But you're going to." He led her to his pickup. "Get in. And this time, Denny, don't argue."

With a regal air, she climbed into the cab, slamming the door behind her. He joined her from the driver's side. The neon of the Stage Coach Inn sign flickered across the windshield. He could hear her angry breathing and feel his own pulse accelerate out of fear. He'd found Denny again and he didn't want to lose her.

"I *did* take money from Max," he said. "He offered it to me to give me a start. I later paid it back with interest. But there was no deal." He touched her shoulder, her heat rushing through his fingers and into his blood. The effect this woman had on him!

"Max obviously wanted you out of town as badly as you wanted to go." He heard what could have been a laugh—or a sob—come from her. She turned her face toward the side window away from him.

"Denny, all I ever promised Max was that I'd never hurt you. He just wanted you to be happy," he said, his hand gently rubbing her shoulder. "And he knew that couldn't happen if you quit school and took off with me. I had nothing to offer you. I didn't even know where I'd be sleeping or eating or—" His laugh was low and self-deprecatory. "No, the big thing was, I didn't know if I had talent. I was betting everything on a talent I wasn't even sure existed. I couldn't have asked you to go with me even if we hadn't been kids, even if—"

She turned to look at him. "—you'd been in love with me?"

He felt her gaze warm his face and he smiled wryly. "I was too full of myself to know how I felt about anyone."

Denver's answering smile was as sad as the knowing look in her eyes.

"That day at the fire tower, I didn't realize what you were offering me," he said softly. "I do now."

They sat in silence for long minutes. "It's getting late," she said. "I'd better get to Maggie's."

"I'll drive you."

"No." She started to open the door, but he stopped her.

"Dammit, Denny, can't we stop fighting each other?" She met his gaze and held it, the hurt in her eyes softening.

"I need to be alone to think," she whispered.

He wanted to kiss her again right now. Her lips looked full and soft, her eyes shimmered, and it was all he could do not to take her in his arms. "You'd better get out of here before I kiss you," he said.

She opened the pickup door, then leaned back in to kiss him. He grabbed her and pulled her into his arms. The first kiss had been sweet and stunning; this one started a fire in him he knew could never be put out. He drew her closer, pressing his lips and body to hers, feeling a bond that filled the holes in his heart.

She pulled away first. "I have to think," she mumbled as she slipped out of the pickup.

He watched her go, surprised by what he found himself wishing for.

THE NIGHT AIR MINGLED with memories. J.D. grinning at her, holding her, threatening to kiss her. Denver forced herself to relive those first few months after his sudden departure. The hurt that had holed up inside her for so long finally moved on. Her heart soared, a kite in a strong wind, flying high into the night, free. She felt tears sting her eyes as the memories overwhelmed her. Memories of J.D. and Pete and Max. They'd always been connected, always been part of the happiest time of her life. Growing up on the lake with Max and the boys. Loving J.D. for as far back as she could remember.

Had Max really been trying to buy J.D. off, or had he just wanted J.D. to have a chance at reaching his dream? Max had always been proud of him. And Max had always known how Denver felt about J. D. Garrison.

She stopped on Maggie's steps recalling the kisses, the feel of his lips, the way her heart had pounded and her limbs had turned liquid. Just the touch of him made her insides ache.

The night caressed her, clear and cold, while the dark velvet sky, splattered with a shower of silver as silver as J.D.'s eyes, smiled down on her. She breathed in the night air, savoring it the way she savored J.D.'s kisses. A laugh escaped her lips; she hugged herself, smiling. The past suddenly gave her a sense of peace. And the future?

J.D. still had a hold on her as strong as ever. He'd warned her not to trust him with her heart. What did he know that she didn't? No, the future held no peace, only a restlessness that she knew wouldn't end with the capture of Max's killer. It wouldn't end as long as J. D. Garrison had her heart. And she realized now that that would be forever.

Denver opened the door to find Maggie standing in the middle of a ransacked living room.

"Look what they've done," Maggie cried. "What in God's name was Max involved in?"

J.D. SAT IN HIS RENTED pickup down the street from the Stage Coach Inn waiting for Pete. He fought to quell his anger at Pete for lying about the reason why Max had given him money and why he'd taken it. Was there nothing Pete Williams wouldn't do to keep Denny? What frightened J.D. was not knowing Pete's motives. Was it only out of love for Denny? Or was he trying to hide his role in Max's death? As much as J.D. had first fought the idea, he now considered Pete Williams a prime suspect.

The back door of the Stage Coach opened and Pete came out and climbed into his pickup. It was parked next to an old school bus. The entire bus had been painted black, including the side windows, and the name Montana Country Club had been slapped on the side in an array of colors. J.D. remembered a bus he'd driven during his early touring days that looked a lot like it. Instantly he felt guilty for his success.

J.D. waited, then fell in behind at a safe distance, following Pete north out of town. He wasn't even a little surprised when Pete turned onto the Rainbow Point road. He was headed for Denny's cabin. J.D. turned out his lights, letting the bright sky overhead keep him on the road between the tall lodgepole pines, probably much like Pete had done that night on his way to the shortcut road on Horse Butte.

J.D. parked at the edge of a snowbank, not far from where Pete had left his pickup, and followed, keeping the thin beam of Pete's flashlight flickering through the trees ahead of him in sight. It took J.D. a moment to realize where Pete was headed—to the large tree house the three of them had built one summer when they were kids.

J.D. moved closer. The flashlight beam bounced with each step as Pete climbed up the makeshift ladder. Then the light went out for a moment as Pete disappeared inside the tree house. Through the cracks in the walls, J.D. saw the light come on again and heard Pete rummaging around, apparently searching for something.

J.D. sneaked to the bottom of the tree and climbed up as quietly as he could. As he reached the trapdoor, he wished he had a gun. He didn't like guns. But right now, holding heavy, cold steel in his hand would have given him a real feeling of security. He slipped through the open trapdoor.

DENVER HELPED MAGGIE clean up the house. Like hers, it hadn't been ransacked as badly as Max's office and apartment. Just enough to make her and Maggie both feel violated.

"Are you sure you're okay?" Denver asked after they'd finished. Maggie had built a fire in the fireplace and collapsed in front of it.

"I'm just mad now," she said. "I want these people stopped."

"I was hoping you'd say that. There's someone I need to talk to—Lila Wade. She's the woman Max was working for right before his death."

"Yes, that's the one who suspected her husband of cheating on her," Maggie returned.

Denver explained what she and J.D. had discovered in the file, including the notation at the bottom. "I'm hoping Lila might be able to shed some light on it. Mind if I borrow your car? J.D. and I left my Jeep at the lake."

"Of course not." Maggie handed her the keys. "Are you sure you don't want me to come with you?"

Denver shook her head. "I don't want her to feel like we're ganging up on her."

PETE STOOD OVER an old box that had once doubled as a bench, leafing through a manila file folder by flashlight. The smell of the old wooden tree house flooded J.D. with memories of the three of them and the club they'd formed to protect their treetop fort. Just kids. Silly kids.

"Interesting reading?" J.D. asked.

Pete jumped, the file folder snapping shut in his hands. "I thought you'd be with Denver."

"Did you? Is that why you told her about Max giving me money?"

Anger showed in Pete's eyes and in the tight set of his jaw. "You forced me to do that because you wouldn't stay out of things. Your interference is causing me a lot of headaches."

J.D. sighed, suddenly tired. And afraid. "What's going on, Pete? I assume that's the case file everyone's been looking for. What's so important about it?"

Pete glanced at the folder in his hands. "You don't know how badly I need this. When I was talking to Denver tonight, she reminded me of the tree house."

Max had hidden it where he thought Denny would find it. Had he forgotten about Pete? Or had he trusted Pete so much it got him killed? "There was a time when we were best friends, when we trusted each other," J.D. said.

Pete gripped the file tighter. "That was before Denver fell in love with you and stayed in love with you."

"This doesn't have anything to do with Denny and me," J.D. said, realizing it probably had more than he knew to do with them. "Let me see the file."

Pete ran the back of his hand across his mouth. "I can't do that." His hand dropped to his jacket pocket.

J.D. swore as he stared at the pistol Pete pulled, then looked up at his friend's face. "Tell me you didn't kill Max."

"Would it do any good?"

"I don't believe you're a murderer."

"Why not? You already know I'm a liar."

"But not a killer," J.D. said with more confidence than he felt.

"Oh, I wouldn't bet your life on that, old buddy," Pete said, moving toward the trapdoor, the gun pointed at J.D.'s chest.

J.D. held his ground. "The name of Max's murderer is in that file, isn't it? Who are you protecting, Pete?"

"How do you know I'm not just protecting myself?" They stood only a few feet apart; J.D. could taste the tension between them. He estimated the distance and wondered whether he could reach Pete, take the gun away and not get either of them killed.

"Don't do it, J.D. There's been enough bloodshed."

"If you care about Denny, tell me what's in that file. She isn't going to give up looking for Max's killer and you know it."

Pete swore. "Can't you make her see how dangerous this is?"

"Just how dangerous is it, Pete?"

"It could get her killed."

J.D. shook his head. "Turn the file over to Cline."

Pete seemed amused by that idea. "Cline?" He glanced down at the folder. "This is about a lot more than just who killed Max, don't you realize that? Stay out of it, old buddy. And keep Denver out."

They stood staring at each other, across the years and the choices that separated them.

"Is that file worth dying over?"

Pete smiled. "Or killing over? Yes." He edged toward the door. "If this landed in the wrong hands . . ." He shook his head. "Take care of Denver. I can't protect her anymore. But don't break her heart again, old buddy. Not again." The

gun leveled at J.D.'s heart, Pete stepped to the trapdoor and
waited for J.D. to move so he could slip through it.

J.D. moved back, but at the last moment grabbed his
arm. "Dammit, Pete, I can't let you leave with the file."

Pete shook off J.D.'s hold. "But the only way you can
stop me is to take this gun away from me, and I can't let you
do that. Trust me on that, J.D."

J.D. looked from the pistol to Pete's face. Would Pete
really shoot him? "Tell me I'm not a fool to trust you."

Pete smiled, his eyes as blue as they'd been in his youth
and just as hard to read. "Oh, you're a fool, all right, J.D.,"
he said, and dropped through the hole into the night.

J.D. stood in the tree house, praying he hadn't made a
fatal mistake.

LILA WADE ANSWERED the door of her doublewide trailer
in a hot pink chenille robe and fuzzy bunny slippers. Most
of her short brown hair was still trapped in curlers; some
had escaped and stood on end, giving her a comical look.

"Yes?" she muttered, squinting as she held the door
open.

Denver introduced herself.

"I know who you are." Lila had partaken of at least a few
beers this night. "What can I do for you?"

"I'd like to talk to you about my uncle," Denver said,
hoping they wouldn't be forced to have this discussion on
the front steps. "It will just take a moment."

Lila made a face but opened the door wider for Denver to
enter. "Lester's going to be home soon, you know."

Denver didn't know. Lila motioned toward the couch,
and Denver sat down, dropping deeper than she expected
into the worn-out cushions. "I'm checking into some re-
cent cases my uncle was working on before his murder." She
tried to work her way to the edge of the couch but gave up.
"You hired him a few weeks ago to follow your husband."

Lila let out a snort as she picked up a bottle of bright red
fingernail polish and continued what Denver had obvi-

ously interrupted. "Don't ask me why I did it. I was telling Clara—Clara Dinsley, you know her—"

"She's the beautician at ClipTop."

Lila nodded, the polish brush dangling from her fingers. "I was telling her I thought that damned Lester was chipping around on me. And she suggested hiring Max. I guess she'd hired him once." She waved that away as another story. "So I did. It was just plain silly. Lester with another woman! He can't even handle the one he has." She let out a brittle laugh as she screwed the lid down tight on the polish.

"Where was Lester those nights you thought he was with another woman?" Denver asked.

Lila's face stiffened as if a mud mask she'd applied had suddenly dried. "Just foolin' around with the boys. Drinkin', stuff like that." She got to her feet, careful not to touch her nails. "Lester will be home soon. I don't want him finding you here."

Denver nodded as she pushed herself out of the couch. "Well, thank you."

"No problem. I hope I helped you some." Lila closed the door behind her. Denver walked to Maggie's car and, as she climbed in, turned to look back. She caught Lila peeking out the curtains. And she wondered just what Lester Wade had been doing those late nights. And why Lila had lied for him.

THE CALL FROM CALIFORNIA came just before J.D. showed up at Maggie's door. It was from a member of his band who'd tired of leaving messages at the Stage Coach and was trying to track J.D. down. Denver took the message. She handed it to J.D. when he came in. It read:

I hope things are going better, that you're writing some new songs, and that you've changed your mind. Hurry back.

J.D. read it, then crumpled the note and threw it into the fireplace. Denver saw the dark frustration in his eyes and doubted he'd written any new songs. He'd been too busy helping her. But what did "hope...you've changed your mind" mean?

"I understand if you have to go back—"

"You'd better get some sleep," he said, cutting her off. "We have to be at Grayling Pass before daybreak. I'm going to spend the night here with you and Maggie just in case—"

She nodded and went down the hall to the linen closet to pull out sheets and blankets for him. "Can't you tell me what it is, what's wrong?"

"Nothing's wrong." He turned his back to her and began making himself a bed on the couch with the bedding she handed him.

"Fine. Nothing's wrong. Everything's great." She spun on her heel and started down the hall.

"Denny."

She turned to find him silhouetted against the firelight.

"You don't understand." His voice, soft as a caress, tugged at her.

"No, I don't," she said, closing the distance between them. "Why don't you tell me? It's being here with me, isn't it? It's hurting your career."

He let out an oath and took her shoulders in his hands. "It's not you. It's the songs. They're gone." He dropped his hold on her and moved over to the fire.

She stared at his back. "What do you mean they're gone?"

"The music has been in my head ever since I can remember." He turned to look at her. "Then one day, I woke up and it wasn't there anymore. And I didn't care." His gaze met hers and held it. "Until I saw you again."

She stepped into his arms and he held her. The fire crackled behind them.

"Go to bed," he said softly, kissing the top of her head. "We need to get some rest."

She nodded and moved away, knowing nothing she could say would erase the pain in his eyes. Behind her, she heard J.D. collapse on the couch.

She stopped in Maggie's room to tell her good-night, then went into the guest room, stripped down and crawled into bed. For so long, her heart broken, she'd focused all her thoughts and energy on losing J.D. Now as she lay staring up at the ceiling, she felt only his hurt, his pain. If she followed her heart, she knew exactly where it would lead. To the man on the couch in the other room. She didn't care where J.D.'s heart was headed. He needed her. While she wasn't sure how to help him, as she drifted off to sleep, she promised herself when the time came, she'd be there for him.

Chapter Eleven

Long before sunrise, J.D. pulled off Highway 191 into a plowed area not far from Grayling Pass on the far side of Fir Ridge. "What's wrong?" he asked as the darkness settled around them.

Denver glanced back at the highway. "Nothing."

"I don't think we were followed, if that's what's worrying you."

She looked behind her again and he could tell she didn't believe that. "It's nothing," she said again. "Probably just the heebie-jeebies."

J.D. knew those well. He'd lain awake last night thinking about Denny. As he studied her face in the shadowy darkness, he wondered what the future held for them. That old spark of hope he'd thought dead stirred in his heart. For a while, he'd forgotten about liars and murderers; he'd even forgotten about Pete and the case file.

"Denny, last night, after you left the Stage Coach, I followed Pete out to your cabin. He went to that tree house we built."

"The tree house?"

"He found the case file Max had hidden there."

"So there *was* a case file." She grumbled softly under her breath. "Why didn't I think of the tree house? Only Max would hide it there. What was in the file?"

J.D. chewed at his cheek. "I don't know. Pete wasn't in the mood to show me."

"What?"

"He had a gun," J.D. explained. "But that was only one reason I didn't try to stop him."

He heard her chuckle. "So which one of us is the bigger fool?"

He grinned. "I'd say it's a toss-up." He rubbed his whiskered jaw and stared out into the dark. "What are the chances I can talk you into staying here and letting me get the information from Davey?"

Her laugh was low as she climbed out of his pickup. He concentrated on the dark for a moment, wondering if they were just as foolish to trust Davey, then followed her.

The faint starlight did little to illuminate the predawn sky. Denver fingered the tiny flashlight in her jacket pocket, but quickly rejected the idea. As J.D. handed down her cross-country skis and backpack from the pickup, she felt the blackness envelop her and the memory of Davey's wreck on Horse Butte came back in vivid detail like an omen. Her fingers shook as she snapped her boots into the bindings; she told herself it was just the cold.

She swung the backpack on, automatically pulling her long braid out from under the strap. Bending down to put on his rental skis, J.D. was an ebony-etched shadow in the night beside her. She was getting used to having him around.

It had snowed during the night. The earth lay cloaked in a soft white mantle. Away from the shadow of the trees, the snow glowed, clean and cold, a virgin tapestry. Denver skied to the top of the ridge and turned to watch J.D. glide toward her. Something in the way he crossed the snowfield tugged at her. His smooth, fluid grace. The power behind his gentle movements as he joined her on the ridge line.

"Where to, Sunshine?" he whispered, just inches from her. Blame it on the quiet seclusion of the hillside. Or the cold air that seemed to suspend them in time. Or the fact that J. D. Garrison hadn't called her Sunshine in years. Suddenly all she wanted was to be wrapped in his arms. To feel his warm breath on her neck. To have him kiss away the cold—and the fear.

Even in the dull light, she was afraid he had seen what she was thinking and quickly turned away. But too late. His gloved hand clasped her shoulder and turned her to him. In an instant, she was in his arms, her skis entwined with his. His lips grazed hers tentatively. His kiss last night had been urgent, then soft, sweet and loving. This was a combination of the two. His lips caressed hers, his tongue explored the warm wetness of her waiting mouth. She melted into him, surrounded by his strong arms and the warmth of his body, the wondrous feel of his mouth on hers. His tongue touched hers, teasing, tempting, then plunged into her again, seeking, savoring. Slowly he pulled back to look at her, his breath as ragged as her own.

"Oh, J.D."

He smiled ruefully and pointed to a large pine tree. "I think we'd better find a place to wait for Davey."

They crouched in the windblown hollow under the huge pine, hiding in the shadowy darkness beneath it. Denver focused her binoculars on the crest of the ridge. It was still too dark to make out anything but patterns of black. She rubbed her mittened hands together. Her breath came out in frosty white puffs.

"Cold?" J.D. whispered.

"A little." Just the closeness of him was enough to fog up her binoculars.

"Well, I'm freezing." He put his arm around her and gently pulled her to him. "You wouldn't let me freeze, would you?" She snuggled against him without protest and fought the sharp pang of desire that swept through her. His breath stirred the hair at her temple. She closed her eyes to the dark and listened to the rapid beat of his heart, her own answering with a thunder as she snuggled against him to wait for sunrise.

THE SOUND OF A SEMI coming up Grayling Hill woke her up. Denver sat up under the tree, banging her head on a limb and sending a shower of new snow cascading down on her. In the silence after the truck topped the hill, she heard another sound. The soft click of a car door closing. She glanced over to find the spot under the tree beside her empty. J.D. was gone.

Swearing, she raised her binoculars and scanned the wide stretches along the highway through the barren limbs of the aspens. The sky had lightened but not enough to distinguish much more than shapes. Then she saw them. Two figures, dressed in heavy coats and hats, unloading large packs from a light-colored van parked beside the highway. It was still too dark to recognize them, but one towered over the other. Could Davey be the smaller one? Denver scanned the hillside again. Where was J.D.?

After a moment, the van drove away, and she watched the two finish loading their equipment onto a sled. Something glinted in the waning darkness, then the skiers covered the sled with a tarp and started east along the ridge line toward Yellowstone National Park, the larger man pulling the sled behind him.

Denver watched with growing interest. These skiers were taking an awful lot of gear if they only planned to make the Fir Ridge Trail Loop through forest-service land and part of Yellowstone Park, ending on the outskirts of West Yellowstone. It was only a half-day loop, certainly not long enough for all the supplies and equipment they were carrying.

She lowered her binoculars. They could be planning to go into the back country of the park and camp for a few days. Except . . . She brought the binoculars up to her eyes again. Except that it was spring, a bad time for a long ski trip, what with the snow rotting in sunny places on the mountainsides and with the grizzly bears coming out of hibernation in hungry, ill-tempered moods.

Another semi downshifted for the long climb up the hill as the sky began to lighten over the dark purple of Mount Holmes peak. Denver cursed J.D. as she struggled to get out of her hiding place under the tree. How could he wander off now, of all times?

"You have such a way with words," said a voice above her. Strong arms pulled her easily from the shelter beneath the pine boughs, then dropped her unceremoniously in the snow. She stumbled and almost fell.

"Where have you been?" Denver demanded.

"Keep your voice down," J.D. whispered. "I just wanted to take a closer look."

"And?"

"And nothing. Just two men. Davey wasn't one of them. Let's go home."

Denver watched the silhouettes of the two figures move across the ridge line as she reached for her skis. "I'm going to follow them."

"I beg your pardon?"

"Shh. Something isn't right here and you know it."

"I know there's another storm coming in, Davey tricked us into getting up early, he's probably robbing your cabin right this moment, and at best, I know following these two men could be a waste of time. At worst—" His gaze locked with hers, warming her deep inside.

"Are you trying to tell me you don't think there's anything suspicious about those two?"

He glanced after the skiers. "Too much equipment, too early in the morning and too late in the season?"

She nodded. "Want to try to convince me it's a coincidence that Davey told me to be here at the same time those two showed up?"

"No."

She slipped on her pole straps, grinning at him. "Then I'm going after them."

"I never doubted it for a moment."

"Then why did you argue with me?" she demanded in a hoarse whisper.

"Habit?" He gave her a shrug and a grin. The grin made her want him to hold her again more than ever. "Maybe you ought to go back and let someone know what's going on."

"Nice try," she said.

As they skied after the pair, Denver wondered what would happen when they all arrived at their destination. She thought of Max's pistol in her backpack. It seemed little consolation as she skated her skis to gain speed, trying to catch sight of the men. She skied parallel to the trail and the men, keeping a good fifty yards to the south. Ahead of her, she watched J.D.'s back, his skis making a steady swish across the snow. She just hoped they weren't being drawn into a trap.

Not far up the trail, Denver realized they'd lost the skiers. The ridge line glistened in the silvery light of daybreak as she traced the horizon through her binoculars from Highway 191 across the gossamer-smooth snowfields to a thick stand of aspen several hundred yards ahead. Beyond the aspen grove, mountains cloaked in dense pines climbed toward the heavens. The nearest road to the east was thirty miles away. Someone could get lost in this remote part of the country forever, she thought as she turned to search again among the bare aspen limbs etched against the skyline. She'd just lost two of them.

"See 'em?" J.D. whispered beside her.

"No." She handed J.D. the binoculars and surveyed the countryside with her naked eye. "They couldn't just disappear," she whispered back. "They should be on the ski trail. Unless..." She glanced over at J.D.

He lowered the binoculars. "Unless they knew we were following them. Or they have some reason not to take the trail."

Denver scoured the ridge line again. "They couldn't have seen us. And this isn't the Bermuda Triangle. They didn't have that much lead time. They couldn't have just vanished." She reached for her poles to ski farther up the trail. Then she saw it.

A movement. In the aspens. She motioned to J.D. Suddenly a figure glided from the trees, a sleek silhouette of arms and legs in stride as he skimmed across the snowy opening. In an instant, another skier burst from the trees.

Denver gave J.D. a thumbs-up sign. "We have them now," she said softly, watching the men head east toward Yellowstone Park and directly into the pines and the approaching storm. They were making their own trail as they went.

J.D. grunted. "Or they have us."

"Don't try to change my mind," she advised.

"I'm smarter than that."

Denver gave him a look that said she doubted it, as she tucked her binoculars into the backpack next to her camera, survival gear, including her hairbrush, and Max's loaded pistol. As she zipped the top of the pack closed again, she eyed the approaching storm.

"It's pretty dangerous to ski into a storm, especially a spring storm," he said quietly.

A spring storm could drop several feet of snow in a matter of hours. People got lost every year; they went to sleep after wandering in circles and died of hypothermia. She and J.D. were breaking not one but two cardinal rules—they were skiing into a storm and they were alone. No one knew they were there. Except Davey. Wherever he might be.

Denver swung the pack onto her back and smiled at J.D. "Why worry about a little old spring storm? I'll bet those men are more dangerous than any storm you've ever run across."

He laughed. "Got your logic from Max, didn't you?"

Just the mention of Max made them look solemnly at one another for a moment, then up the trail after the skiers.

"Okay, Denny," J.D. acceded. He touched her cheek, his gaze assuring her that he was willing to take the risk with her, because of her. "Let's go get 'em."

Winter had wrapped the earth in a cold and silent package of white, and spring had done little to release its hold here in the high mountains. Picking up the ski tracks left by the men, she and J.D. followed at a safe distance, gliding their skis across the silken snow in a rhythmic swish. The air tasted cold and wet; the breeze played at the loose strands of hair that had escaped from her braid and her hat. She didn't look back as they skied away from the highway and deeper and deeper into the mountains. Instead, she concentrated on the skiers ahead. And J.D. directly in front of her.

Whatever trouble might lie up the trail, she was taking J.D. into it with her. That, she realized, worried her more than her own safety.

Daylight came slowly. First, flickers of gray rimmed the mountains, then filtered up into the atmosphere. The snow absorbed the light, then radiated it. But the new day brought problems; they could no longer follow as closely and had to drop back. The men were moving fast, probably rushed by the storm that now inched across the peaks toward them.

"You know something, Denny?" J.D. remarked at her side. They'd stopped for a moment along a hillside; their quarry had also stopped. The day had broken and was spilling around them, gray as the coming storm. "You've turned into quite the woman. I'm proud of you." He looked away. "They're moving again," he said, skiing off.

She smiled, then followed him.

A half mile up the trail, J.D. came to a sudden stop. "Get down!" He pushed Denver behind a snow-covered pine, but not before she'd seen the skier below them. He stood at the bottom of a ravine, his rifle raised, looking through the scope. In her direction.

"Tell me that wasn't a rifle," Denver whispered.

"It was a rifle."

She glared at him.

He shrugged in reply. "Something tells me we're not dealing with your average armed cross-country skiers here."

"Firearms are prohibited in Yellowstone Park," she said. "And they're headed for the park."

He glanced over at her and smiled. "Well, Denny, when we catch up to those two, I think you'd better tell them that."

She mugged a face at him. "Do you think he saw us?"

J.D. pulled her deeper into the shelter of the pine tree. "I don't know." She could see the worry on his face. "You have to admit that the chances are good these guys could be dangerous."

She cupped his bearded jaw in her gloved hand. "Convince me it's a coincidence that Davey told me to be here at sunrise."

He smiled at her. "I've never had any luck convincing you of anything." His gaze caressed her face. "You realize, of course, if that skier saw us, he's probably working his way back up the hill toward us."

"Or rounding up his friend to come get us," she whispered back.

"You always know just what to say to make me feel better." His look turned grim. "Seriously, Denny, this is a risky business. I think we're out of our league here."

"But we're on to something. You feel it, too. If we turn back now, we may never find out what's going on." He held her gaze. My God, did J.D. really believe Max was involved in something illegal? She looked at the mountains ahead, suddenly afraid of what they might discover there.

"If that skier didn't see us, he's going to be moving again," J.D. warned. Denver shifted and peered around the trunk of the tree.

"Damn. He's gone." Denver scanned the trees and the white snowy expanse ahead. "You all right?" she asked, adjusting her backpack. J.D. hadn't moved.

He looked at her with a straight face. "We're miles from the highway, heading into a snowstorm, following two men with guns. Of course I'm all right."

She tugged his ski hat down over his face, then poled after the skiers, following the tracks in the snow.

They'd lost valuable time and the thought of losing the skiers now was unbearable. Ahead she saw the clear-cutting that marked the Yellowstone Park boundary. At first she didn't see the man. Then she caught a glimpse of movement as white as the snow. He crossed the clearing, his dark-colored coat hidden under what looked like a white bed sheet, and was quickly sucked up in the pines on the other side. Yellowstone Park.

"Did you see that?" Denver pulled her camera from her pack. Her fingers trembled as she snapped on the telephoto lens. She had a feeling she was about to take some of the best photographs she'd ever taken in her life. The second skier crossed the clearing—also covered with a white sheet. Denver focused, then hit the motor drive, capturing the second skier's movements on film like an evasive ghost.

"Kinda makes you think they don't want anyone to see them enter the park," J.D. muttered. He stood watching her, a frown creasing his forehead. There was no turning back now, and Denver could see that in J.D.'s expression.

Denny slipped the camera back into her coat.

"You realize if there was some way I could protect you—"

"I've been protected too much in my life, as it is." She squared her shoulders and brushed a gloved finger along his bearded jawline. "From now on, I'm going to make my own mistakes. And by the way, I have Max's pistol. We're just as illegal as those two."

"Thanks for warning me."

The storm dropped over the tops of the pines like a thick drape, snuffing out the light, making the new day appear to dissolve into twilight. The air settled around them, heavy with moisture. Denver threw her pack over her shoulders again and adjusted it, then she and J.D. headed after the men. Time was running out.

She could feel the men's driving need to get somewhere. Her arms and legs ached to the point of numbness as the hours passed and she wondered how much farther she could go.

Not far into the park, the skier in front of them dropped down a hillside and stopped. Denver and J.D. skied into a stand of small pines. Denver slipped her camera from its shelter in her coat and handed J.D. her binoculars. As she focused on the skier they'd been trailing, Denver saw the larger skier join him and push back his ski mask, giving her a clear view of his face. She swore as she recognized him.

"It's Cal Dalton!" She snapped his photo, then focused on the other man. He still wore his ski mask, but he looked vaguely familiar. "Can you tell what they're doing?" she asked J.D.

Cal tugged at something and a camouflaged tarp fell away from a huge pile of what looked like limbs, tree limbs.

She focused the telephoto lens on the pile. They weren't limbs. They were antlers. Elk antlers. Denver moaned.

"Horn hunters," J.D. said, peering through the binoculars. "Looks like they've come for their cache."

The other skier stepped into view, his ski mask now pushed back as he started to load the horn onto the sled.

Denver's heart lurched. "It's Lester Wade."

Chapter Twelve

Pete had never liked Earthquake Lake, didn't like meeting here and wasn't thrilled about the feeling he'd had all day that something was wrong, terribly wrong. As he stood at the empty visitors center, he tried to focus his thoughts on Midnight. The boss had finally agreed to meet him face-to-face. No more having to deal with that crazy Cal.

But not even finally meeting Midnight could keep him from feeling uncomfortable here. He stared at the lake, trying to decide what it was about it that bothered him. A feeling of death hung suspended over the long narrow lake. Maybe it was all the dead trees, still standing like aging sentinels chest-deep in the icy water. Or maybe it was the ghosts of the people who'd died here that night in 1959 when the earth shook down a mountain on top of them, while behind the fallen mountain, the Madison River pooled like blood to form the lake.

The phone rang, making him jump. He stared at it, realizing that Midnight had tricked him again.

"You're late," the synthesized voice said on the other end of the line.

"I thought you said you'd meet me here," Pete complained.

Midnight let out that synthesized laugh Pete had come to hate. "You sound tense. Has something happened?"

"No." Pete tried to relax. "Everything's fine."

"You have Denver under control?" he asked.

"Sure." He only wished. He'd been trying to reach her all morning and there'd been no answer. Where in the hell was she? And more importantly, what kind of trouble were she and J.D. cooking up? At least he had the file now.

"What about the kid?" Midnight asked. "We find him yet?"

"Davey won't be doing any talking."

"Then everything is just as we planned?"

"Yeah." Pete was relieved when Midnight didn't ask him any more about Denver, but got straight to business. He'd stashed Davey at a friend's—not quite as permanent as Midnight would have liked, but Pete didn't have the stomach for more bloodshed.

"I have a buyer," Midnight said. "Wants a trophy elk and a deer. The guy's willing to pay $16,000 a piece. And we need more bear. Our Oriental entrepreneurs are paying $4,000 a pound for bear gallbladders. The little suckers are so damned easy to transport inside film canisters—let's hit them hard."

"Bear bladders," Pete muttered, mentally adding them to the list. He wondered where Midnight was calling from. Someplace safe, no doubt, the way he was running off at the mouth.

"Can you imagine wolfing down dried bear bladders?" Midnight pretended to gag. "Some aphrodisiac, if you ask me. Kind of like that stuff they make out of the horns— wapiti love potion, my behind. Supposed to have a rejuvenating property like ginseng, keeps you from aging or something. All I know is sliced-up elk horns and all those strange grasses they throw in and boil up make for some pretty vile brew. It sure didn't do anything for me as far as the ladies are concerned, but then I never needed it to start with." Midnight chuckled. "*You* might want to try it, though, Pete." He tried to contain his laugh and failed. "Or maybe give a little to Denver."

At times like this, Pete wished he'd never gotten involved with this operation. Or this man. But he had to admit Midnight was damned good at this business; that's why no one had ever caught him.

"And my buyer will take all the bear-paw pads you can get," Midnight continued. "They eat 'em, you know. Bear-paw pads." He groaned. "Can you believe that?"

The shadows running ahead of the storm collected in the dead pines. Pete wished they could hurry. He felt nervous and tired; all he wanted was for this to be over so he could go find Denver.

"Anyone seen any griz yet?" Midnight asked.

"Yeah, Cal got treed the other day."

Midnight swore. "Tell him to shoot the damned things instead of letting them run him up a tree. Jeez. We need more griz and bear claws for our jewelry customers, too." He chuckled. "That damned Cal. He's crazy, you know that?"

Unfortunately, Pete did. And he wondered if Midnight had ordered the hit on Denver the other night or if Cal had just improvised on his own. Another scare tactic.

Pete could hear Midnight's admiration for crazy Cal resonating in his counterfeit voice. "How is the shed-horn shipment coming? We can't miss the deadline or the price will fall."

"There won't be any delays." At least Pete hoped there wouldn't be. He could feel Midnight listening closely to him and tried to sound enthusiastic. "Cal says it's like the ultimate Easter-egg hunt out there this year. They're picking up a thousand dollars' worth of horn in about thirty minutes."

"My kind of sport!" Midnight declared. "You don't seem all that excited about business, though. I mean, we're making more money than the president of the United States and it's as easy as robbing an unguarded bank." Midnight laughed.

"I'm not sure Max would have agreed with that."

The laugh died. "Just get me the merchandise. And don't sound so damned unhappy about raking in money. It makes me nervous."

"When am I going to meet you?" Pete asked before Midnight could hang up. "Don't you think it's time we quit playing this little electronic phone game?"

Silence. "We will meet soon enough. In the meantime, make sure Denver doesn't become any more of a problem. And you know that case file you found of Max's?"

Pete held his breath. "Yes?"

"It felt like some of the information was missing."

Pete's heartbeat echoed, ricocheting against his chest so loudly he almost couldn't hear Midnight when he spoke.

"You wouldn't hold out on me, would you, Pete?"

"If you'd tell me exactly what it is you're looking for—"

But Midnight had already hung up. Pete swore. He didn't like working for a synthesized voice at the end of a phone line; it was time Midnight showed himself.

As Pete walked back to his pickup, snow began to drift down from the grayness overhead. He thought about the case file and the information he'd taken out. A little insurance. Then he thought about Max hiding the file, probably thinking it was his insurance. Max's death still bothered him, gave him nightmares even in the daylight. Maybe there was no insurance against a man like Midnight.

He returned to his more immediate problem. Denver. Where was she and what was she doing? He didn't even want to consider the possibilities.

POACHERS. CAL DALTON and Lester Wade. Denver groaned as she watched Cal raise binoculars and point them toward a wind-scoured slope across the ravine. At the edge of the storm clouds on the opposite mountainside, she could see a bull elk feeding on the snow-bare slope. The area was a winter elk range. And it didn't take an Einstein to figure the two below her had been collecting the antlers shed by the elk in hopes of smuggling them out of the park—a highly profitable but equally illegal enterprise.

"It all makes sense now," Denver said as she remembered Max's scribbles at the bottom of Lester Wade's file. "Pearl. Oh, J.D., don't you see? That's what Max meant.

The Oriental Pearl, the brow of the elk, the elixir of the Orient. The elk horn.'' She stared at him, her eyes widening. "Max was referring to the poaching operation.''

"That would explain a lot,'' J.D. agreed. "Like why he was spending time with Cal Dalton. And what Lester Wade was doing late at night when his wife thought he was chasing other women.''

"And why Lila lied,'' Denver added. "I'm sure she and Lester could use any extra money he made. She was probably just relieved Lester wasn't running around on her.''

"Most people don't consider picking up shed horns— even in a national park—much of a crime,'' J.D. remarked.

Denver focused the camera on Cal near another cache of horns and snapped his photo; the motor drive hummed as she captured the two on film as they loaded the sled.

"Davey must have reason to suspect Max's death is connected to the poachers,'' she said, lowering the camera. "Why else would he tell me to be here this morning?''

"He could have known Max was investigating Lester Wade and found out about the poaching.''

She looked over at J.D. as she dropped the exposed film into her backpack. Maybe it was just the way he said it or the way he wouldn't meet her gaze. "That explains everything except the $150,000 in Max's account.''

"Yeah.''

She began reloading the camera. Her fingers trembled with anger. And fear. "Poaching has become very profitable. Newly shed horns can go for more than ten dollars a pound. But not *that* profitable.'' She bit her lip, and shifted her gaze at him. "Max wasn't involved in poaching horn.''

J.D. put his arm around her. "You won't get an argument from me. Poaching wasn't Max's style.''

She leaned into him and gave him a quick kiss. "Thank you.''

His eyes sparkled as if he liked the idea of her kissing him for whatever reason. "Still, ten dollars a pound doesn't seem like much money for the risk involved.''

"That's the problem. There isn't much risk. Right now, the number of rangers in the park is at an all-time low. It's estimated thirty tons of elk antlers are being shipped to the Orient every year from the twenty thousand head of elk in this great Northern Yellowstone herd. The park's too large and there aren't enough rangers to stop the poaching."

"Well, it looks like Max tried," J.D. said.

She took more shots, getting Mount Holmes in the background so there was no mistaking where the horns—and the horn hunters—were. "With poaching laws so lenient, I just find it hard to believe that anyone would kill Max over a few shed horns. Even if they're caught, these guys would probably never see jail time. Just a fine."

Cal and Lester had taken off their skis and now wandered through the pines on the southern-exposed bare areas of the mountain. Both had their rifles slung over their shoulders. Denver kept photographing as they collected more shed horn.

J.D. scanned the hillside with the binoculars. "Denny, doesn't this look like an awfully large horn-hunting operation?"

She nodded. "Most are just a couple of guys carrying out a few days' horn on their backs after dark." She snapped more photos of the poachers and close-ups of the antlers, chocolate brown with ivory tips.

"If Max was investigating this poaching ring—"

"Then the case file is probably the one Pete found in the tree house." She turned to face him. "Pete could be covering for Lester, one of his band members, instead of himself."

"That's a possibility, I suppose. It doesn't explain Pete's pickup at Horse Butte, though."

"No, it doesn't." She wished he hadn't reminded her of that. He must have seen the disappointment on her face because he pulled her into his arms. She leaned into him, feeling his strength and warmth.

"Denny, I think we'd better get that film to the authorities."

She didn't want to move out of his embrace. But she knew she should get more photographs, enough to nail Cal and Lester but good.

The report of a rifle made her jump. She and J.D. scrambled to look around the tree. Cal was standing still, holding his rifle. Not ten yards away, a small black bear lay dead.

"Why the hell did you do that?" Lester demanded, his voice coming up the hillside.

"It's a bear. We're supposed to kill bears, remember?" Cal snapped.

"Not in the park in broad daylight! You're going to get us in trouble." Lester stomped back to the cache of antlers and worked to remove it by himself.

Denver lifted her camera, taking a couple of shots of Lester and the horn, then turning it on Cal. He stood over the dead bear, a knife in his hand. . . .

Then the storm came, in a rush. The sky blurred chalky white in front of her camera lens and snowflakes cascaded down from the heavens, obliterating everything in front her.

In the shelter of her coat, she reloaded the camera, stuffing the exposed roll into her pocket for safekeeping, then put her camera back in the pack.

"Ready?" J.D. whispered. Denver started to move from the shelter of the pines. She saw Lester glance up in their direction.

"Up there!" he yelled. "I just saw something."

J.D. pulled Denver down behind the bushy pine but through the branches she could see Lester pointing to the pines where they crouched. "There's never a dull moment being with you," J.D. whispered. "You ready to leave *now?*"

She nodded and grabbed her ski poles. The snow-laden pines would provide only minimal protection. In a moment, Lester would be making his way up the hill and he'd see their tracks. Even if they found a better hiding place, their ski tracks would lead the two men directly to them.

"Head down the mountain keeping to the south," Denver whispered. "When you hit Duck Creek follow it west to the summer cabins, then head to the highway for help."

J.D. grinned at her. "And where are you going to be?"

"I'm going to stay here and—"

He shook his head. "No way. You're going first." She started to argue. "I'll be right behind you, Sunshine. Covering your backside. Now git."

She swung the pack over her shoulder.

"Go on," J.D. urged. "And Denny—"

She looked into his eyes and for an instant had the feeling that this might be the last time. The thought tore at her heart.

"If we get separated, don't double back. Keep going. You hear me. You have to get that film to the rangers. And…be careful." He grabbed her and kissed her hard. Then gave her a shove.

Denver dived from the pines, skiing across the opening to where the mountainside dropped down toward the valley below. It wasn't the fastest way back to the highway and safety, and it definitely wasn't the safest escape route, but right now it was the only way out. Straight down.

She could hear voices behind her, and the sound of her skis on the snow. Neither Lester nor Cal could have reached the top of the hill yet, she told herself. Slightly off to her left, she saw J.D. skiing through the trees. A few more minutes and the horn hunters wouldn't be able to see them because of the storm. She heard the sharp crack of a rifle shot. Terror filled her.

She raced down the mountainside at the edge of her control, turning only to miss a stump, a fallen tree or a standing one. Out of the corner of her eye, she caught glimpses of J.D.'s dark ski jacket. Then nothing. Worry stole through her. She wished she had never gotten J.D. involved in this mess, wished he were still safe in California. "Stay with me, J.D.," she pleaded. "Stay with me."

Her vision blurred as the snow beat against her face and often blinded her completely. At best, she could make out the shapes of trees; at worst, she saw nothing but white.

She dipped down into a small gully and poled frantically up the other side, her heart pounding loudly in her ears. Off to her right, she heard the sound of a tree limb breaking and a grunt. Without taking time to think, she skied toward the sound. She tasted the metallic sourness of fear. What if J.D. had fallen? What if— Her skin went clammy and cold. What if they'd shot him? The thought ricocheted inside her head, out of control.

Denver stopped and pulled Max's pistol from her pack, listening. Silence. Large white flakes fell all around her, insulating the land in a cold, protective shell. She tucked the pistol into her coat and traversed the hillside, heading once more in the direction of the sound.

The wind whirled snow around her like a plastic-bubble winter scene from a five-and-dime store. She wondered how she'd ever find J.D. in this swirling white curtain of cold. Then Denver heard it. The faint swish of fabric against pine needles. "J.D.?" she called fearfully. "J.D.?"

Cal came out of the trees from her left. She went for the pistol in her coat. He lunged for her, ripping the gun from her fingers as his other gloved hand came around from behind to cover her mouth before she could scream.

"Well, well, well, if it isn't Denver McCallahan," he sneered. "We finally meet again. And on my turf."

Chapter Thirteen

Pete Williams pulled the pickup over to the side of the road and adjusted the tracking equipment on the seat next to him. He didn't want to believe it. He stared at the faint green beep, then out his window. Damn. How could this have happened? He slammed his fist against the steering wheel. He should have known. Stopping Denver McCallahan was like trying to lasso a runaway train. Especially now that she had J.D. as a running mate. But how had she found out? A leak somewhere. He remembered Davey and moaned. The little snot-nosed kid *had* talked before Pete got to him. Damn.

For a few moments, Pete sat staring at the falling snow, wondering what he'd be doing right now if Max McCallahan were still alive. He drove down the road to the phone booth at the old Narrows resort and dug out a quarter. Midnight was right about one thing. Denver was a problem.

He dialed the number he'd been given for emergencies. "It looks like I'm going to need some help."

"Where?"

"Grayling Pass at Fir Ridge."

WHITEOUT. J.D. STOPPED for a moment, hearing nothing. Snowflakes fell around him, cold and lacy white. The poachers had turned back, he told himself as he tried to see ahead. Nothing. Nothing but a solid white wall of snow. He'd lost sight of Denny. By now she could already have reached Duck Creek and the summer cabins. *Denny is a good skier. She can take care of herself.*

The words sounded hollow even to him. Fear filled his chest to overflowing. He couldn't lose Denny. Not now. He pushed off again, skiing down the hill, knowing sooner or later he'd hit Duck Creek. Then he'd find her. He refused to believe anything else as he skied forward.

The snow obliterated everything in his path. He couldn't see more than a few feet in front of him. Trees would appear suddenly and without warning. Rocks and stumps came at him out of the snow, large white mounds he had to dodge at the last moment. Just a little farther and he'd be off the mountain. "Denny." He whispered her name like a prayer.

The land before him seemed to flatten out and he thought the worst part was over. Then the earth dropped out from under him.

"DON'T SCREAM OR I'LL hurt you," Cal muttered harshly against her temple. Slowly he pulled his gloved hand away from her mouth.

Denver's first instinct was to scream bloody murder. She squelched it, though, fighting for a calm she didn't feel, because she knew now that Cal Dalton was capable of anything. If she screamed, it could bring Lester. Or worse yet, J.D. She didn't doubt Cal would shoot him.

"You're a pretty clever broad," Cal said. "What did you do, follow us from town?" A strange kind of admiration glowed in his blue eyes. "Take off your pack, sweetheart. I think I'd like to see what you've got in there."

Denver slipped the pack strap from her shoulders as slowly as possible, her mind racing. He had his rifle slung over his back with a leather strap and Max's pistol stuck in the waist of his pants. She knew he could get to either before she had a chance to escape. "Why don't you tell me what horn hunting had to do with my uncle's murder?"

Cal shook his head as he planted his ski poles in the snow and reached for the pack. "Horn hunting? I don't know what you're talking about." He opened the backpack. She knew in a moment he'd see the camera, and even as dense as Cal was, he'd figure out she'd taken photos of the poaching operation.

"You know, what you really want isn't in there."

He looked up, a smile slowly lighting his eyes as he let the pack slip from his fingers. "No?"

"No," she said softly.

He moved closer. "It's about time you came around."

She swung one of her poles, hoping to knock him off balance and into the snow. It might give her enough time—

Cal grabbed her wrist and twisted. The pole dropped into the snow at their feet. "You think I'm a fool?" he demanded hoarsely. One hand captured her face; the other dragged her to him. "I'm tired of playing games with you." He shoved her down into the snow and fell on her, his fingers tearing at the zipper on her coat. "You're about to find out what a real man is like." He laughed as he jerked her coat open. She didn't put up a fight as his hands slipped beneath her sweater. "And you're in for a treat, sweetheart."

She knew he planned to rape her. And then what? Kill her? With shaking fingers, she began to unzip his coat.

J.D. FELL OVER THE EDGE of the cornice, dropping through snowflakes and cold air, then hitting the snowfield and somersaulting. A branch slapped him; a rock dug into his ribs. He lost all perception as he tumbled downward. There was no sense of distance, or depth, only that endless falling sensation and a brilliant suffocating whiteness.

And just when he thought it would never end, he slammed into a snowbank and stopped. For a few moments, he lay still, crumpled and cold, his breath ragged. He brushed at the snow on his face and beard, simply breathing and trying to get his bearings. Then he felt the unmistakable pain in his left ankle.

First he'd escaped two rifle-toting horn hunters. Then he'd survived a fall off a cliff. And now his ankle was broken. He groaned. And where was Denny? Right now, all he wanted was to see her smiling face. To hear her laugh or speak his name. He closed his eyes. But that old sharp stab of fear that Denny was in trouble hit him hard between the eyes and he opened them again.

The snow fell around him. Quiet. Like death. He leaned over to survey the damage the fall had done to his ankle. He didn't even bother to worry about the scratches, scrapes and gouges. It was the ankle that would mean the difference between getting out of here and finding Denny or dying in a snowdrift.

It didn't hurt as badly as it had at first. But he wasn't sure if that was a sign he was about to freeze to death. Hypothermia. Good night, Irene. He untied his boot and felt along the ankle. He felt again, unable to believe his good luck. At least it wasn't a compound fracture. Maybe it was just a bad sprain, not even broken. It didn't hurt enough to be broken, he assured himself. He tied his boot up again and tried getting to his feet.

Bad idea. Pain raced up his leg. He fell back into the snow. Damn. If he couldn't even get to his feet to try to ski for help . . . No, he didn't want to think about that. Instead, he thought of Denver. That did the trick. He took his ski poles and determinedly worked his way up onto the one good leg. Carefully he put a little weight on his bad ankle and knew two things: his ankle wasn't broken, but he wasn't going far.

DENVER SLID HER HAND under Cal's shirt. She sank her other hand deep into the snow.

Cal leered at her. "Finally see the light, huh?" He laughed as he leaned down to kiss her.

Denver wrapped her fingers around a cold hard chunk of granite she'd dislodged under the snow. She brought the rock up with one swift movement and slammed it into the side of Cal's head. He looked confused for an instant. Then she gave him a shove and he fell over into the snow. His eyes slowly closed as if he needed a little nap.

"Finally see the light, huh?" Denver said, getting to her feet and zipping up her coat again. She snapped on her ski bindings Cal had so helpfully released, anxious to find J.D. as quickly as possible. She pulled the rifle from the snow where it had fallen next to Cal and slung it over her shoulder, but didn't take the time to look for Max's pistol somewhere in the snow. She heard Cal moan and was relieved she hadn't killed him. Then she picked up her ski poles and skied down the mountain through the falling snow.

J.D. POINTED HIMSELF what he guessed to be south. The land dropped away at a gentle slope. He hoped there were no more cliffs. The next thing he wanted to stumble into was Denny. And Duck Creek. Together they could find a cabin and take shelter from the storm.

Using the poles as crutches, he slid one ski forward, then the other. Pain. It beaded up perspiration on his forehead even in the cold. More than ever he wanted to lie down and sleep. His brain tempted him to do so. The thought of Denny kept him moving. He had to tell her something. And when he saw her it was the first thing he was going to do, tell her. *If* he ever saw her again.

"Denny." He realized he'd said her name out loud. And worse yet, he thought he heard her voice on the wind. He told himself he had to be delirious.

As he stumbled clumsily along in the storm, the wind whirled around him, giving him only teasing seconds of sight. Then he saw it.

He blinked with disbelief. A mirage rising from the desert! But instead of tall, cool shade palms and a pool of clear water, he thought he'd seen the side of a cabin in the woods. His eyes were playing dirty tricks on him, tormenting him. Could he really have reached the first of the cabins along Duck Creek?

The storm was a living force he had to battle to reach the mirage. He concentrated on Denny, her smile, her laugh, the defiance and determination that so often burned in her eyes, instead of the pain, fatigue and icy-cold wetness that enveloped him as he lumbered forward. It took all his powers of concentration to keep his legs moving.

He was so preoccupied that he almost collided with the corner logs of the building. A cabin. It had to be one of the summer homes along the creek. That would mean shelter and probably a fireplace. Surely he could find something to burn to make a fire. The thought of a warm, dry place—and Denny—pushed him on. Just a few more feet.

Hope soared, but quickly fell as he rounded the corner and saw that the structure was nothing more than part of an old cabin wall. He held on to the corner of the rotting logs. There would be little shelter in the crumbling edifice, little chance of keeping a fire going in the wind.

As if the wind were aware of his dilemma, it swirled snow around him in a low growl. He tucked his head down against its freezing sharpness. For a moment, he thought he heard Denny's voice on the wind again. Calling to him. The wind continued to whip the snow in tiny eddies. He raised his head to see the outlines of two other buildings looking like a ghost town in a desert sandstorm. The cabins disappeared again in the storm—or in his mind. He feared they had only been in his mind. Just like the sound of Denny's voice.

WHEN DENVER REACHED Duck Creek and the first boarded-up summer cabins, she stopped. Snow circled around her. Cold and tired, she urged herself to go on to the highway for help. But her heart wouldn't let her. J.D. If he'd made it to the highway, he'd already be getting help. And if he hadn't . . .

She peered into the storm, then, making up her mind, she skied to the larger of two cabins. The door was locked. But with a piece of firewood from the stack beside the cabin, she pried open a shutter, broke the window and let herself in. She thought about J.D. out in the cold and debated building a fire. The smoke could lead Cal and Lester right to her door. But she knew that if the two men made it as far as the cabins, they'd find her anyway. And she wanted the place to be warm if she found J.D. *When* she found him. She refused to consider any other possibility.

Hurriedly she got a fire going in the old stone fireplace, warmed her hands, then went back out in the storm to look for J.D.

SMOKE. J.D. THOUGHT for a moment he could smell smoke coming from one of the cabins that had appeared miraculously from out of the storm. He'd gone a few feet when he saw what had to be another mirage. A figure was coming out of the storm toward him. At first he thought it might be one of the horn hunters. He stopped, the cold and the pain freezing all thought. The sweet scent of smoke tantalized him; the wind whistled across the cabin's roof, dying in a low howl off the eaves. Then he heard her voice calling his name.

"Denny?" Snow whirled around him. The cabin was gone. So was Denny. A mirage. Only a mirage. He stumbled and fell into the snow. Too tired to move, he closed his eyes, remembering the feel of her in his arms. "Denny," he whispered and smiled. "I love you."

Chapter Fourteen

"Denny," J.D. whispered, snuggling deeper into the couch. She wrapped her arms around him, giving him her warmth. He still shivered from the cold. She tried not to think about what could have happened if she hadn't found him when she did. "I love you, Denny."

"Sure you do," she said, her voice breaking. She held him, wondering if it was the pain or the cold that was making him delirious. "I love you, too, J.D.," she whispered, knowing he couldn't hear her. A lock of his hair curled down over his forehead. She pushed it back and touched his forehead. Hot. The fire beside them murmured in hushed tones; outside, the storm canceled out any thought of escape.

Denver studied J.D.'s face in the firelight and felt a sudden chill of worry. What if the horn hunters found them here now, with J.D. so sick? She'd considered going for help, but couldn't leave him alone. They were safe from the poachers as long as the storm continued, she assured herself. But once it let up, Cal would be looking for them again. Looking for her especially.

She pressed her lips to J.D.'s forehead; his heat seared them. If only his fever would pass. Then, if he could ski on his hurt ankle. If... There were too many ifs.

He sighed in his sleep. "...love you."

Tears came to her eyes. "Oh, J.D."

She slipped from his arms and knelt to tuck more blankets around him. In the cabin's tiny kitchen, she rummaged through the cabinets and came up with an old can of coffee and some powdered milk. Not much, but better than nothing. Outside, she scooped up a pan full of snow, then set it on the wood stove to heat. She felt so tired. From fueling the fires all afternoon. From skiing for miles. From running. Running scared. She still felt scared. For J.D. For them both.

Denver leaned over the counter and watched the storm through a crack in the boarded-up window. Snow stacked silently higher; by morning everything would be obliterated. Through the chink she spotted an old shed. Hope fought back her exhaustion. She gulped down a cup of the horrible coffee, then pulled the pot to the edge of the stove. Quickly she threw on her coat and boots, picked up Cal's rifle, took one last look at J.D. to be sure he was still covered, and left.

The snow was now knee-deep. Denver stumbled through it to the weathered shed only to find the door locked. With the butt of the rifle, she broke the padlock, promising herself she would find the owner of the cabin and pay him for all the damage she'd done. Then she pushed open the door of the shed and peered into the shadowy, frigid darkness. As her eyes adjusted to the dim light, she smiled.

The one thing that might save them hunkered in the back of the shed, big, old and ugly—an ancient Ski-Doo snowmobile, much like one Max used to have. But what made it such a welcome sight was that it didn't require a key, only mixed fuel. She found a gas can, half-full, and several quarts of oil.

Denver wanted to start the snowmobile to make sure it ran, but knew that wouldn't be smart. If Cal and his friends were anywhere near, they'd hear it. No, she'd have to wait until the storm broke and just hope it would get her and J.D. to the highway. She mixed some fuel in one of the gas cans and filled the vehicle's tank, then left, closing the door firmly behind her. She and J.D. stood a chance. If the snowmobile still worked.

Trudging through the snow to the cabin, Denver held the rifle, ready for the slightest movement from out of the storm. All the way back, she expected Cal or Lester to appear. Smoke curled up from the chimney to blend with the grayness of the storm. On the porch, she took one last look out into the falling snow, then slipped inside.

J.D. had drifted off to sleep, no longer shivering. After checking the door to make sure it was bolted and the shutter was firmly nailed back over the broken window, Denver curled up on the couch beside J.D., Cal's rifle on the floor next to her, and waited for sleep to take her. She didn't have to wait long.

J.D. WOKE TO FIND A FIRE blazing in the fireplace and Denny asleep beside him on the couch. The heat made his eyelids heavy and he started to drift back into the fairyland of sleep. A flash of memory—skiing, the whiteout, Denny—forced his eyes open again. He pushed himself up on one arm and looked down at her. Strands of hair had come loose from her braid. They curled around her face, fiery red in the firelight. He brushed one back with his finger and glanced down to see that she'd found them both dry clothes. His fit better than the large old T-shirt and baggy jeans she'd scavenged up for herself. He thought about her undressing him and felt a heat that had nothing to do with the fire. Through a crack in the boarded-up windows, he could see the snow that still fell into the night.

He glanced around the sparsely furnished room, trying to put the scattered pieces of memory together. The hand-crafted log furniture gave him the eerie impression that he'd been dropped into another time. The old couch frame was built of slim lodgepole pines, stripped of bark and coated with varnish to a yellowed sheen. Even the rocking chair by the fireplace was handmade. An old guitar leaned against the wall by the fireplace. Behind him, a wall divided the cabin, but he could smell coffee and knew the kitchen was on the other side.

He slipped from the couch, careful not to wake Denny. The moment he put his left foot to the floor, he remembered his ankle. Swollen and bruised, it balked at holding his weight. Denver had wrapped it. He glanced down at her again, touched by her strength and courage. And her tenderness toward him. A man who had done nothing but hurt her. He took one of the fire tools and limped his way into the kitchen.

He poured himself a cup of coffee and looked at his watch, wondering if he'd lost hours or days. It wasn't even nine at night. But what night? Then he remembered what had woken him. A song. It played on the edge of his memory. He dug through the kitchen drawers until he found a pencil and some scratch paper. Taking his coffee with him, he went back into the living room and sat down on the hearth in front of the fire.

It took only a moment to tune the old guitar. He ran his fingers across the worn wood, wondering who owned it. Then he softly strummed a few chords, the song he'd heard in his dream coming back. He strummed some more, then scribbled notes hurriedly, afraid the music would escape.

DENVER WOKE TO MUSIC, soft and sweet as the warm flicker of the fire. She remained perfectly still, watching J.D. Completely lost in the music, he didn't notice. As he began to sing softly, Denver let the sound lull her. The words, as gentle as a caress, brought tears to her eyes. Did he really mean the lyrics he sang? Would he truly give up everything just to be with her? She pushed herself up on one elbow to watch him play.

He stopped abruptly, killing the sound with his hand across the strings, when he realized she was awake.

"You wrote a new song," she whispered into the quiet that followed.

He nodded, his gaze polished silver as he put down the guitar and came to kneel beside her. "It's about you. It's called 'On My Way Back to Denver.'"

Her heart jitterbugged. "You're feeling better?"

"Yes." His look heated her face hotter than the fire.

"You were delirious earlier." From the way he was staring at her, she wondered if he still wasn't. "Talking crazy."

He grinned. "Was I? What did I say?"

She looked away. "Not much."

His hand cupped her chin and turned her face to his. "Did I say I loved you?" The firelight caught in his eyes. "When I was in the middle of that storm, I realized—"

She touched a finger to his lips. "Don't say anything you'll regret later."

He smiled sadly. "Oh, Denny, I already have so many regrets. I can't stand to add another one. I love you." He cradled her face in his hands. "I love you, Denver McCallahan. I've always loved you in some way. But now..."

Tears filled her eyes to overflowing. She pulled away, getting up to go stand in front of the fireplace. Behind her, she heard J.D. sigh. She picked up her hairbrush from the hearth where she'd left it earlier and stared down at it. "We've been through a lot the past few days. This kind of danger sometimes makes people—"

He laughed softly. "Face how they really feel about each other?"

"'Confused,' is the word I would have chosen." She turned. Just the sight of him made her weak.

"Come here, Denny."

The fire burned hot, radiating heat across the room. She stood before the flames, her braid partially undone, her hair curled around her face. Firelight shone through the thin, worn T-shirt. She breathed raggedly, her eyes dark, her face in shadow.

J.D. caught a glimpse of the expression on her face and fought for breath. "Come here, Denny," he said again, sliding up to sit on the couch.

She took an unsteady step toward him, his name on her lips, and dropped to the floor to kneel at his feet. He touched her hair, soft and warm. Slowly he began to unbraid it. The strands parted beneath his fingers, silken and smooth. He freed them and took the hairbrush from her hand. She turned her back to him and he began to brush the shimmering auburn waves in long, slow strokes. Again and again he ran the bristles from her scalp through the dark crimson tapestry to where her back curved to jeaned bottom. He heard her moan or maybe it was the sound of his own desire.

She leaned back into him with each stroke. Her hair fanned across his thighs; his fingers ran through the strands of liquid fire. "Denny," he whispered. She arched back to look at him; her breasts stretched against the thin cotton T-shirt. Nipples hardened into dark points beneath the cloth. He buried his hand in her hair and pulled her head back. His mouth dropped to hers, first tentatively tasting the wetness between her lips, then plunging into the warm, moist darkness. He felt heat where the back of her head rested and told himself he should stop. As much as he loved her, he didn't know what would happen to them tomorrow. He wanted to promise her happiness with him, but he couldn't. He didn't know what his own future held.

He lifted his lips from hers. Her eyes closed; she moaned softly and reached for him. Reason evaded him. He bent to take one nipple in his mouth. His tongue moistened the thin cloth. He captured the nipple gently between his teeth.

Her body jerked, making his heart pound like beats on a drum. He pulled away to look into her eyes. The fire that had been simmering in his groin burst into flame. If he was going to stop, he'd better stop now. If he slid the T-shirt up over her breasts, if his mouth touched her bare skin, he would never be able to.

"Damn, you're so beautiful, so desirable," he murmured. The wanting in her eyes mirrored his own and they begged him not to stop. Slowly he inched the T-shirt up over her firm, flat stomach, then over the smooth, rounded breasts, nipples silhouetted rosy pink in the firelight. He tossed the T-shirt aside and pulled her into his arms. Her hair spilled out like a dark red river across the icy whiteness of her shoulder to her breasts. He buried his hands in it and tilted her head as he pulled her down into a kiss.

Denver opened her mouth for J.D.'s demanding kiss and moaned as his lips devoured hers. She reached for the buttons on his shirt, wanting desperately to feel his chest against her naked breasts. He groaned as she began unbuttoning his shirt.

She freed the last button and slid the shirt off his shoulders. He pulled her to him. Her breasts pressed against his warm chest, setting her skin on fire as his mouth savored hers again. He dropped a kiss at a time to her neck, then her breast. She shuddered as his mouth closed over her nipple.

His eyes flamed in the firelight; her body glistened from his kisses. "Please, J.D.," she cried, needing him inside her, needing to feel his body on hers.

"Oh, Denny, you're so beautiful," he whispered as he covered her mouth with his, her body with his.

With a cry, she felt him fill her. He came to her like the storm, slowly at first, like tentative snowflakes drifting earthward from the swollen clouds above. Kisses fevered and wet-slick. Bodies burning, slithering touches, cries and caresses. Then stronger, a pulsating need, a pressing and probing like the wind at the windows. The clouds opened. She rose with him, again and again, a gale of sensations wracking her body.

"J.D., oh, J.D.," she moaned. The storm swept her along in a blinding whiteout until she cried out beneath him, felt his body pulse and tremble with the first shock of their combined passion and thought she would burst from the joy of loving him.

Bodies gleaming in the firelight, the snowstorm raging outside the cabin, she reached the zenith of another storm, heard the thunder within her. She wrapped her arms around him and held her to him as the storm subsided. He smiled down at her; her heart filled like a helium balloon.

"Never in my life have I felt anything like this," he whispered at her temple. He raised his head to press a kiss to her swollen lips. "Never," he said, locking onto her gaze. "I love you, Denny."

She pulled him down to her again, smiling as she kissed him, leisurely exploring his mouth.

"You knew that day at the fire tower, didn't you?" he asked, trailing his fingers across her skin.

"That I loved you and would never love another man the way I did you?" She smiled. "Yes."

He shook his head, his eyes dark with his need for her. "I thought for so many years that all I needed was my music. But something was missing. I just didn't know what it was until I saw you again."

She lay in his arms, more contented than she'd ever thought possible. His skin felt warm and smooth against hers. She glanced toward the window, wishing they never had to leave this cabin. The snow still fell thick and white against the darkness.

"We're safe here," he said, caressing the silken skin at the base of her throat.

"Until the snow stops."

The fire popped softly. Shadows danced across the ceiling to a music Denver had never heard before, but had unknowingly longed for. She looked up at him, her eyes soft and dark. He smiled as he bent to kiss her. This time the music started slowly, then caught time with the beat of her heart as she came to him again.

Later, they lay wrapped in each other's arms as the fire died down. J.D. stared up at the shadowy darkness, listening to Denny breathing gently beside him, trying not to think about poachers or murderers. Instead, he closed his eyes and concentrated on the soft, warm feel of her skin against his, rather than on what they would have to do once the sun rose over the mountains and the storm ended.

Chapter Fifteen

April 19

At first she thought it was the steady beat of her heart. Or a flushed grouse coming out of the brush in a flutter of frantic wings. She thought she was dreaming again.

Denver sat up and looked around, forgetting for a moment where she was, but not who she was with. She smiled down at J.D. asleep beside her on the couch. The firelight played on his peaceful face, across the expanse of his chest, his skin golden in the glow. He stirred, eyes opening, his gaze as loving as his body had been as it drifted over her. Then he, too, heard the sound and sat up abruptly.

Through the crack in the shutter, Denver could see it was still dark out. But the storm had stopped and the fallen snow shone like freshly minted silver. The sound grew stronger, a steady throbbing now.

J.D. swore as he jumped up and hopped to the window to peer through the broken shutter. "A helicopter."

"Maybe it's someone looking for us?" she asked as she joined him, clutching a blanket around her.

"Who knows we're here, Denny?" He pulled her into his arms and stroked her hair, his hold fierce and protective. Tears sprang to her eyes as he wrapped the blanket around them both. Yes, who did know they were here? Davey? Cal. Lester.

"If the horn hunters have a helicopter..." she began.

"Then this is quite a sophisticated poaching operation."

Denver looked up into his face, thinking about other horn hunters she'd read about. Greedy poachers, who shot down the elk to cut off the newly grown more potent and prized antlers still in velvet, leaving the elk to bleed to death. Dangerous men. Like Cal.

"That means they have unlimited resources, Denny."

The sound of the helicopter grew louder. "Think there's a chance they won't find us?" she asked hopefully.

J.D. raised an eyebrow.

"That's what I thought."

She hurried back to the couch and began to dress in her ski clothes. When she looked up, J.D. was still standing by the window.

"You go," he said, limping over to her. "I'll just slow you down."

"I'm not going anywhere without you," she said, stopping to meet his gaze. They stared at each other, the fire crackling softly, the steady *whoop whoop* of the chopper moving nearer.

He smiled, shaking his head at her. "Why do I keep forgetting just how determined you are?"

"I don't know." She returned his smile. "I found a snowmobile in the shed. I'm not sure if it runs, but either way, we're leaving here together."

He closed the distance between them. Eyes wistful, he wrapped his arms around her and kissed her hard, taking her breath away. As he pulled away to dress, Denver assured herself it wouldn't be their last kiss.

J.D. HELPED DENNY OUT the back of the cabin through a window, then leaned against the building in the deep snow. His ankle ached with each step; he balanced on his good foot, knowing he wouldn't be going far if the snowmobile didn't run. He'd have to force Denny to go on without him because there was little doubt in his mind what the occupants of the chopper had in mind. Darkness still hung over the treetops but the new snow shone bright as moonlight on water.

"Why haven't they landed?" Denver whispered.

The chopper made another pass over the cabin, back-tracking west. Through the trees, J.D. could see other cabins along the creek. "I think they can't figure out which one we're in." He pointed up. The smoke from their fire formed a gray haze that stretched all along the creek. And the storm had obliterated all their tracks in the snow. The pilot of the chopper didn't know where to land. Yet. "You ready?"

Denver nodded. He could see the fear in her eyes and knew it had nothing to do with her own safety.

"Let's go," he whispered.

They broke through the drifts to the shed. In the distance, they could hear the helicopter heading back. J.D. pulled the shed door open just enough for them to squeeze through, then slipped into the darkness after Denver, and pulled the door shut behind him.

It took a moment before he spotted the large old Ski-Doo at the back of the shed. He handed Denver his pack and the rifle. "It's now or never," he said, feeling something in his heart pull like fingers on a guitar string.

The sound of the chopper grew louder. A beam of bright light cut through a break in the haze like a laser, skittering across the outside of the shed. "They've got a spotlight," she said. "If the smoke clears—"

J.D. grabbed the handle on the rope starter and pulled. The Ski-Doo engine coughed once. The helicopter hovered overhead. He pulled again. The engine coughed a couple more times. He choked it. The steady beat of the chopper grew louder and closer.

"They're putting down," Denver cried.

He gave the starter another yank, putting all his weight into it. The engine sputtered, rumbled to life, coughed a few times, but kept rumbling. He released a breath. The Ski-Doo's headlight flickered on, illuminating the tiny shed.

"Ready?" he asked.

Denver nodded and smiled. It sent his heart soaring, and he promised himself that if they ever got out of this, he'd make her smile like that the rest of her life.

Denver pushed open the shed door. Through the trees, he could make out the silhouette of the chopper touching down in a clearing not far away and knew they had seen the snowmobile light. He gave the throttle a twist, and Denver jumped on behind him, wrapping her arms around him as they roared out of the shed. The chilling spray of new snow showered them as the snowmobile broke through the first deep drifts and headed west.

J.D. spotted Pete running from the chopper, a rifle in his hands, saw Pete's mouth open but didn't hear the words over the high-pitched whine of the snowmobile's engine. But he knew Pete was yelling for them to stop. J.D. knew Denny saw Pete, too. He felt her tighten her hold on him. J.D. gave the Ski-Doo all the throttle there was to give and they burst through the snow and into the pines, the single light on the vehicle cutting a swath through the darkness and the trees.

J.D. glanced back, afraid of what he'd find. But Pete was pushing through the deep snow headed back to the chopper. "I'm sorry, Denny," J.D. yelled over the roar of the snowmobile. She hugged him tighter, burying her face against his back.

Damn Pete. Damn him for hurting Denny. J.D. could only hope that Pete wasn't the one who killed Max. He feared that would destroy her.

Denver fought the anger and disappointment that pulled at her mind and body. Pete. Pete with a rifle trying to stop them. For an instant back there, she thought maybe he'd come to rescue her. But how could he have known they might be in one of the cabins along Duck Creek? Only if Cal had told him.

She tried not to think how it all fit together as she and J.D. sped west toward the highway. The snowmobile broke through the deep new drifts, sending snow flying. Its headlight punched a bobbing hole in the darkness, while behind them she knew the chopper would be coming. She huddled against J.D.'s back, feeling his warmth and his love. It gave her strength. She tried to imagine living without him again. And couldn't.

She felt J.D. turn around and knew the helicopter must be tracking them.

"We have to kill that headlight," he yelled. She nodded against his back as he brought the snowmobile to an abrupt stop, the engine putt-putting, and climbed off. They'd have to break it; the light wouldn't shut off except when the engine did. She handed J.D. the rifle. He limped around to the front. In one swift movement he brought the rifle butt down into the headlight. The darkness settled around them. They both turned at the sound of the chopper coming up quickly behind them.

Hurriedly, J.D. jumped back on and hit the throttle. They shot into the darkness of the pines. The spotlight from the chopper flickered across the treetops, then flashed off. The steady *whoop whoop* of the blades disappeared in the roar of the Ski-Doo's engine as they raced through the snow, zigzagging in the night shadows, trying to lose the helicopter. Denver tried not to think about what had happened to the idyllic Montana life Max McCallahan had given her. Instead, she held tight to J.D. and the love they'd shared.

"DAMMIT." PETE LEANED back against the chopper seat as he surveyed his latest disaster. "What's that over there?" He pointed off to his right.

"Looks like another snowmobile light," the pilot said.

Pete swore again. They'd lost Denver in the trees and the dark. And now someone else had joined in the hunt. "It's got to be Cal. I should have known he wouldn't stay out of this." Cal had skied out for a snowmobile, convinced he could find Denver before Pete did. Now he was backtracking, trying to pick up Denver's trail, and it looked like he had.

"I better radio the boss." The pilot reached for the radio, but Pete stopped him.

"No. I'll handle this." The pilot looked skeptical. "Just follow Cal. He's going to lead us straight to Denver. And then I'll take care of her."

"I really think—"

Pete shifted the rifle in his lap. "Don't think. Just do what I tell you." The pilot hesitated. "Denver should have been stopped a long time ago. I'm going to do it now before she and that damn J. D. Garrison blow everything. Trust me. You'll probably get a bonus."

The pilot laughed at that, but banked the chopper back over the lone snowmobile headlight. Pete watched it bob through the trees; Cal was following Denver's snowmobile tracks, hunting her like a rabid dog. The vast snowfield glowed virgin white in the darkness. Only the pines provided shaded sanctuary. Denver was out there somewhere. Denver and J.D. Pete gripped his rifle and waited for Cal to track them down.

DENVER SAW THE LIGHT fluttering high in the trees ahead of her. It took her a moment to realize what it was. Another snowmobile. She tightened her hold on J.D. as he set about outracing it. She estimated they were no more than five miles from the highway; all they needed was a fighting chance. But with a helicopter overhead and a snowmobile following in their tracks, she entertained little hope of that. The vehicle behind them was also gaining quickly. Newer and faster, it probably carried one rider; she could guess who it was.

The light flickered over them as the other snowmobile drew closer. J.D. turned, his lips brushing her ear. "I'm going to jump off. You keep going. Will you do that for me, Denny?"

She heard the pleading in his voice. This was no time to argue. They couldn't outrun the other machine. She nodded.

The light grew brighter as it neared. The poachers had no intention of letting them reach the authorities. Denver felt

J.D. shift his weight; then he was gone. She held the throttle down and kept going.

J.D. TUMBLED OFF, ROLLED a few times in the snow, but came up with the rifle strap still snug across his chest. He eased it off, then crouched low behind a small pine adjacent to Denny's snowmobile tracks. The approaching light bobbed across the white expanse from a pocket of darkness along the edge of the pines; its engine screamed. J.D. stayed down, the rifle ready. In those few seconds before the snowmobile came alongside him, his brain tried to convince him that the driver was someone Davey had sent for them. Maybe Maggie or Taylor. Even Deputy Cline. He couldn't shoot before he was sure. But as the rider roared up, there was no mistaking him. J.D. raised the rifle to fire, but there wasn't enough time. Swearing, he grabbed the barrel end and swung as Cal Dalton roared past.

The rifle hit Cal in the chest with a blow that sent him flying backward from the snowmobile and shattered the rifle stock. The machine sputtered a few feet without its rider holding down the throttle, then stopped. J.D. limped over to Cal and picked him up by the front of his coat.

"All right, you bastard," he said as Cal's eyes flickered open. "Denny told me what you tried to do to her. You have one chance to tell me who's behind this."

A sneer curled Cal's lips as the sound of the helicopter drew closer. "I'll have Denver yet."

J.D. glanced at the snowmobile idling a few feet away, its light shining like a beacon. He slammed Cal down into the snow, making the man grimace with pain and his breathing come out in a wheeze. He pushed his boot into Cal's chest. "Who killed Max?"

The wheezing grew louder. Cal tried to push off the boot but finally gave up. "Pete." He closed his eyes; his arms dropped to his sides. "Pete Williams." J.D. gave him a shove with the boot and limped over to the snowmobile. He could hear the helicopter, see the spotlight slicing through the darkness ahead as it searched for Denny. He wished he hadn't sent Denny on ahead, worried he might have sent her into worse danger. As he started to gun the engine and catch up with her, he heard the unmistakable sound in the pines close by.

The old snowmobile came out of nowhere, bursting through the snow-filled branches of the pines, airborne. Denny landed the Ski-Doo just inches from Cal's inert body. For the first time, J.D. was glad she hadn't listened to him. He stumbled through the snow, his ankle be damned, to pull her off the machine and into his arms. He kissed her, crushing her lips as well as her body against his.

"Boy, am I glad to see you," he murmured in her ear.

She clung to him for a moment, her only answer, and he saw her looking at Cal, lying passed out cold in the snow. "Did he say anything—"

"No," he lied. Not now. He'd tell her later, after they'd gotten away.

He listened for the helicopter, surprised he couldn't hear it. Hurriedly he picked up the broken rifle from the snow and Denny followed him to the newer snowmobile. He smashed the light and climbed on in front of her.

They had sped through the snow for a few hundred yards when J.D. brought the vehicle to a stop. He pointed ahead to a spot where the terrain narrowed down to only a trail between Duck Creek and a granite bluff. Beyond it he could see a set of headlights flash along Highway 191. "Is there another way out of here?"

Denver shook her head. He could feel her trembling and knew it wasn't from the cold. "Not without crossing the creek. Why, what's wrong?"

He couldn't put his finger on it. The heebie-jeebies. "Nothing." He gave the snowmobile gas and raced toward the bluff.

They'd almost reached the narrow trail wedged between water and rock when Pete stepped out, blocking the road and their escape. He held a pistol in his hand. The barrel pointed at J.D.'s heart. And ultimately Denver's.

Denver let out a cry as Pete stepped in front of the snow-mobile. She saw the pistol and the expression on Pete's face. She thought for a fleeting moment that J.D. wouldn't stop. That he'd run into Pete and plunge him into the creek or into the wall of granite. But not before Pete had gotten off at least one shot.

J.D. brought the snowmobile to a skidding halt. And Pete reached over the windshield to turn off the engine, the gun still trained on them.

"I knew you couldn't run me down," Pete said to J.D. He sounded tired and he looked worse than he sounded. "At least I hoped you couldn't." Pete shifted his gaze to Denver.

"Let us go, Pete," J.D. said, his voice as cold as the morning. "It's all over. We know about the poaching. We know who killed Max."

Denver wondered for an instant if J.D. was bluffing. Then she realized what Cal had told him back there in the snow. That Pete had killed Max. "Pete, no."

Pete looked her in the eye. "Don't believe it, Denver." He sighed and rubbed his face with his hand, fatigue showing in every line of his body. "We don't have much time, so please listen. I wish I could tell you everything but I can't. You have to trust me." His gaze settled on Denver again. "You have to give me a few days."

"You can't possibly expect us to trust you," Denver cut in. "Not after everything that's happened."

Pete glanced behind him where the chopper was probably waiting for him, then back at her. "Isn't saving your lives enough reason to give me a couple of days?"

"What difference could a few days make except to give you time to get your damned horn shipment out?" Denver demanded. "J.D.'s right, Pete. It's over. Turn yourself in. Don't make me—"

Pete shook his head. "I wish it was that simple. Give me the film, Denver."

She swallowed the lump in her throat. "What film?"

"You'd never go anywhere without your camera—especially not after what Davey must have told you about the operation. Just give me the film, okay?"

When she didn't move, he jerked the pack from her back and, still holding the pistol on her, opened it. He dug around, slipping a completed roll of film into his coat pocket, then cracked open the camera and ripped out the partially exposed film. He studied Denver while he felt around in the bottom of the pack for more.

"J.D. told me about Max's case file you found in the tree house," she said. "It was the horn-hunting case, wasn't it? But why kill Max?"

"Give me a few days and I'll tell you everything. Right now, I don't have any more answers than you do."

"I want to believe you, Pete." She felt tears rush to her eyes. "But I can't. Not anymore. You've lied to me too many times."

He stared at her for a moment, then handed back the pack. "I told you not to look for Max's murderer. You should have listened to me, Denver. Now you leave me no choice." He pulled a two-way radio from his coat pocket. Static filled the air. "Come on in. Let's get this over with."

With a slow *whoop whoop*, the chopper's blades whirled to life on the other side of the bluff. In seconds, the helicopter rose over the treetops, then moved toward them. Snow whipped at them as sharp and cold as ice shards. *It's now or never*, J.D. thought, and instantly felt Denny's fingers on his waist, warning him to be careful. Under different circumstances, it would have been funny, *her* warning him.

He looked into Pete's face, searching for some hope, finding none. What he found there was more frightening than the pistol Pete had trained on them. Defeat. A dangerous combination when mixed with the gun in Pete's hand.

Shooting for speed, J.D. pulled the starter on the snow-mobile and the throttle. Unlike the antiquated machine, this one started in a heartbeat, the roar of its engine drowned out

by the deafening whir of the chopper. The snowmobile
leaped forward.

Pete had only an instant to make up his mind. J.D. saw his
decision in those speeding seconds. He pulled the trigger,
but the shot went wild, ricocheting off the rocky bluff.
He dived into the icy creek as the snowmobile just missed
barreling over him. J.D. didn't look back; he pointed
the snowmobile northwest, toward Grayling Pass and his
pickup. The helicopter thrummed behind them. Over the
tops of the trees, daybreak pried at the darkness.

Chapter Sixteen

Denver didn't expect the pickup to run. She sat shivering as J.D. hurriedly cleaned the snow from the windshield and slid in behind the wheel.

"Cross your fingers," he said, pulling her to him before he reached for the key.

"They had to have tampered with the engine." She watched the shadows pooling beneath the pines in the first light of day and wondered where the helicopter was.

"If it doesn't run, we take the snowmobile and go on into town."

She nodded, doubtful how far they'd get. Pete was out there somewhere. And Cal. Even a fool like Cal would know they'd head for town if the pickup didn't run. And not even the pickup was a match for a helicopter.

The engine made a slow, sluggish attempt to turn over. J.D. tried it again. He grinned at her as it started, but neither the grin nor the running engine reassured her. Why hadn't Pete disabled the pickup? Because he hadn't expected them to escape?

She watched J.D. test the brakes, knowing he, too, was questioning their luck. If the pickup was going to blow up, wouldn't that have happened right away? He backed the truck up to the highway. She stared out the window, expecting to see Cal's face—or Pete's—appear without warning.

The promise of dawn danced across the mountainside, playing hide-and-seek among the shadowed pines. No helicopter spotlight poured from the gray sky overhead. No snowmobile came flying out of the trees.

"Where are they?" Denver wondered aloud.

J.D. pulled her closer. "We have two choices. We can run or we can go to the Feds. It's up to you, Denny."

She nodded, feeling time slip like sand through her fingers. Emotions stirred within her. Anger pushed at the cold and exhaustion, at the disappointment and disillusionment. Not Pete, her brain kept arguing. No, not Pete. "I want to stop them." She glanced up at J.D. "We can't chance going into West Yellowstone, but there's a district ranger who has a weekend place down by Hebgen Dam." Tears blurred her eyes; she fought them back as he pulled her to him.

He kissed her, a warm, soft, reassuring kiss, then he hugged her closer. "I just want you to be safe, that's all, Denny." He pulled onto the highway and headed south. "Who is this ranger?"

"Roland Marsh."

"Roland Marsh?" J.D. asked with a frown. "Denny, I've heard that name before. It's unusual enough—" He hit the steering wheel with the palm of his hand. "That's it. I saw that name and a telephone number written on a piece of paper in Max's wallet."

Denver looked out into the waning darkness. "Maybe Marsh was his government contact person." But if that was the case, Max hadn't been very careful, carrying that note around in his wallet. But Max had been terrible at remembering phone numbers.

"Let's see if Marsh is at his cabin, and then we'll go to Ennis on the Quake Lake road," J.D. said. "I don't think they'll expect that, do you?"

She shook her head, more interested at that moment in the road ahead. She could tell J.D. didn't want to pass Fir Ridge any more than she did. As the pickup climbed the far side of the hill, Denver held her breath. She imagined the helicopter sitting in the middle of the road.

But when they topped the crest, there was nothing there. Their headlights caught the leafless quaking aspens and the gravestones as the cemetery slipped by in a flash of headlights. Then they were past, the pickup rolling toward the Duck Creek Y. No snowmobiles chased after them. No helicopter was waiting.

"They must have given up," J.D. said. "Pete has the photographs—he probably feels safe now."

Denver closed her eyes, not believing that any more than she knew J.D. did. Whatever was going on wasn't over.

J.D. took her hand in his, squeezing it as if he thought he could squeeze the warmth back into her, could squeeze out the pain. "I'm sorry about Pete, Denny."

Tears stung her eyes. "How could he get mixed up in poaching, especially with someone like Cal?"

J.D. sighed. "I've asked myself that same question."

She squeezed his hand back. He brought her hand to his lips and kissed her palm. "Thank you," she said, letting her gaze settle on his handsome face. "For being here."

He grinned. "My pleasure."

The white world outside glistened as the new day continued to break around them. She leaned against J.D.'s strong shoulder and closed her eyes. Pete. His face came to her, so clearly she almost reached out to him. But it wasn't the face she'd seen in the middle of the trail in front of the snowmobile. It was the face of her friend—Pete Williams. Smiling at her. Promising to help her forget about J.D. Telling her to trust him. How could she have been so wrong about him? She opened her eyes. If they gave the death sentence for deception, Pete Williams would get the chair.

The highway remained empty, just a stretch of snow-packed pavement splashed in daylight. J.D. drove up the mountainside to Roland Marsh's cabin. It sat pushed back into the mountain, the front windows looking out over the still-frozen dam arm of Hebgen Lake. The drapes were closed, everything quiet, but smoke was curling out of the chimney. Denver felt a chill she couldn't explain. Why hadn't Pete or Cal tried to stop them? Because without the photographs, they had no proof. She was certain that Pete and Cal would move the caches of antlers as quickly as possible. It would be her word and J.D.'s against theirs.

As they walked up to the house, Denver could tell that J.D.'s ankle hurt him. Her heart wrenched watching him. This had to end. She pulled his arm over her shoulders and tried to take some of his weight.

As they stumbled up the not-yet-shoveled steps to the front door, Denver had the feeling that they were being watched again. Was she losing her mind or had they been followed? J.D. tapped at the door. If Pete had somehow followed them here, why didn't he make his move now? What was he waiting for? She pushed her hands deeper in her coat pocket; her fingers touched something slick and cold. A roll of exposed film. Then she remembered. She'd put a completed roll of film she'd taken of the poachers in her pocket. Pete hadn't stolen all the film after all.

"J.D., I forgot this last roll—"

Just then the porch light flashed on and the door opened.

Ranger Roland Marsh tugged at his faded blue bathrobe and squinted at the bright light. Slim, with graying short hair and a cropped silvery mustache, Marsh looked to be in his late fifties. Sleepy blue eyes blinked from behind angular wire-rimmed glasses. "Yes?"

"We're sorry to bother you this early," J.D. said, glancing over his shoulder at the highway below.

Marsh blinked again, the last of the slumber leaving his eyes. "Please, come in," he said, stepping aside. He smiled as he motioned for them to sit down. "J. D. Garrison. My wife's not going to believe this. She's quite a fan of yours. She'll never forgive herself for not being here."

J.D. sat down on the edge of the couch. Denver joined him.

"And Denver McCallahan." Marsh beamed at her. "This is an unexpected surprise."

"I didn't think you'd remember me," Denver said. A year ago, she'd done some photography for a park-service brochure.

He took a chair across from them. "I was so sorry to hear about your uncle. A terrible loss."

Denver clung to the couch with a feeling of relief soaking in. He knew Max. That could explain his name being in Max's wallet. Solid ground. Finally they had someone who would help them.

"Now, what can I do for the two of you?" Marsh asked, still smiling as if he expected their visit to be a social one.

"We've stumbled across a poaching ring," J.D. said.

Marsh frowned.

"We followed two horn hunters into Yellowstone Park at Fir Ridge," Denver added.

"Horn hunters?"

"They're part of what we suspect is a very large poaching ring," J.D. said.

Marsh shook his head. "I've never heard of a horn operation on this side of the park. Gardiner, yes, with all the elk that winter-range in that area, but not West Yellowstone. You're sure about this?"

"I was hoping you knew about this poaching ring," Denver said, near tears. "I was hoping Max—"

"We think Max found out about the poachers," J.D. finished for her. "We thought he might be working with you because your name and number were in his wallet."

Marsh shook his gray head, his brows furrowed. "This is the first I've ever heard of such a thing. I've seen residents this time of year picking up horn along the park boundary, but—"

"These are huge caches of antlers *in* the park," Denver explained, giving him the location. "We saw one of the poachers shoot a bear. Unfortunately, the poachers saw us, too."

"They tried to kill us," J.D. added.

Marsh stared at him. "You can't be serious."

"They tried to keep us from getting out of the mountains with the information," Denver assured him.

"I'm sorry if I sound skeptical," Marsh said quickly, "but with the low fines poachers get if they're caught...I mean, why would they try to...kill you?" He looked shocked. "I can't believe this."

J.D. took Denver's hand. His fingers moved slowly, reassuringly over her palm. She concentrated on his touch.

"We have proof," Denver said, reaching into her pocket with her free hand.

"Proof?" Marsh asked.

"Photos of the antler caches, the horn hunters and one of them standing over the bear he shot," she said, and handed him the roll of film.

He stared down at it for a moment, then pushed himself up from his chair and started for the kitchen. On his way he dropped the film into his robe pocket. "Let me get us some hot coffee or tea."

Denver pulled her hand free of J.D.'s and followed the ranger. "I'm sure they'll try to move the antlers as quickly as possible."

Marsh stopped in the kitchen doorway so abruptly she almost collided with him. "As you have the men on film, does that mean you also recognized them?"

Denver swallowed. She didn't want to tell him about Pete but she knew she had to. "As you'll see in the photographs—" Through the kitchen door, she spotted something that stopped her heart in midbeat and silenced her tongue. Then she found her voice again. "The storm blew in and the visibility wasn't great. Then they saw us."

Denver turned to find J.D. staring at her in puzzlement. She fought the tears that burned her eyes, feeling more weak and tired than she'd ever been in her life.

"Of course, the storm," Marsh said. "So we might not have a positive ID of the men on this film?" He studied her with an intensity that made her heart pound with fear; he had to know she was lying. Would he try to keep them from leaving? "You must be exhausted," he said as he shifted in the doorway. "You could stay here if you like."

"No, thank you. I want to go back to my place at the lake and wait there," she said, feeling like a mechanical doll as she moved toward J.D. He got up and limped to her side, his arms encircling her with what should have given her a feeling of safety. Her eyes felt full of sand; her muscles ached. She wondered if she'd ever feel safe again. "You'll call when you've found the antlers?" she asked.

Marsh nodded, looking relieved. "I'll be in touch with you by this afternoon."

"Thank you so much for your help, Mr. Marsh," J.D. said as they made their way to the door. Denver reached for the doorknob.

"Just a moment," Marsh said behind them. Denver stopped, her heart pounding. She turned, afraid of what she'd find. Marsh was holding out a scratch pad and a pen. "Would you mind giving me your autograph for my wife?"

J.D. took the pad and pen. "What's your wife's name?"

"Annabelle." Denver watched J.D. scribble on the pad. He handed it to Marsh, who read it and smiled. "You two be careful," he said as they left. "And don't worry. I'll take care of everything."

"I'm sure you will," Denver said as J.D. took her arm. They walked quickly toward the pickup, J.D. limping at her side.

"What in the world was that all about?" he demanded the moment they were out of earshot.

"Just keep walking. The sooner we get out of here, the better. *If* we get out of here."

J.D. shot her a look of surprise. "Were we followed?"

"No." They reached the pickup and climbed in. "That's just it. We weren't followed." She tried to laugh but it came out a sob.

J.D. looked at her as if she'd gone mad as he started the pickup and headed down the mountain.

"We walked right into a trap." She leaned back against the seat and closed her eyes, fighting fresh tears of pain and frustration. "Pete's hat. I saw it on the counter in Marsh's kitchen." She opened her eyes. "Pete was there."

J.D. stared at her. "How could he have known where we were going? How could Pete have beaten us there?"

"Marsh's lake place was the closest, and he *is* the district ranger."

J.D. glanced in the rearview mirror, then at the highway ahead. "They'll be watching us. If we turn toward Ennis, they'll know we're double-crossing them. We have to head back toward town to make it look as if we're going to the lake cabin."

"But at the Duck Creek Y, we'll go north to Bozeman," Denver said, sitting up straighter. "We'll go to Bozeman and then . . ." She looked over at J.D. "Then what?"

He put his arm around her and pulled her closer. "It looks like we're on our own, Sunshine."

"J.D.," Denver said thoughtfully, "How *did* Pete find us at the cabin on Duck Creek? And beat us to Marsh's? Are you thinking what I'm thinking?"

He swore. "A tracking device. They've got us wired."

"Not *us*," Denver said, looking down at her wrist and the watch Pete had given her the day after Max's death.

Chapter Seventeen

The moment Pete left Marsh's, he turned on the tracking unit. He held his breath as he watched the monitor. The last thing he'd expected Denver to do was go to her cabin and stay out of trouble. But the steady beep verified that J.D. and Denver were on their way toward West Yellowstone and the Rainbow Point turnoff to the lake.

He smiled and relaxed a little. Maybe everything would work out after all. He doubted they'd cause any more trouble for a while. And right now, he had more urgent worries. Such as saving his own neck. Midnight hadn't told him where they'd be loading the last of the shed horn for the shipment. Pete hoped this oversight wasn't personal, that Midnight just mistrusted everyone. But it made him worry. He didn't like working for a man he'd never met; it would be too easy for Midnight to double-cross him.

DENNY WOKE CRYING.

"It was just a dream," J.D. said, pulling over to the side of the road and taking her in his arms. "Just a bad dream."

She snuggled against him. "It was so real."

"Dreams are like that sometimes." He thought of his own nightmares in strange motel rooms in the wee hours of the morning. They were more real than life. And because of that, much more frightening.

She sat up and looked around as if she didn't recognize the countryside. They were just coming out the Gallatin

Canyon. The early-morning sun hung over the Bridger Mountains, glazing the new snowfall in blinding brightness.

They'd flagged down a bread truck at Duck Creek Y on its way into West Yellowstone. Denver knew the driver and asked him to take the watch to the sheriff's office *after* he'd made his delivery rounds. If he thought the request strange, since he had to make a large loop through the lake area before going into town, he didn't say anything. J.D. had then headed the pickup for Bozeman, and Denver had fallen into an exhausted sleep.

"Was the dream about your father and mother again?" he asked.

She nodded. "But this time, the past and present were all mixed up. You were there, and Maggie." She shook her head. "And Cal Dalton. Like I said, it was all mixed up."

He reached over to push a wisp of hair back from her cheek and kissed the spot. She seemed to avoid his gaze.

"You said you were in this for the long haul."

"I am," he assured her, taking her hand.

"Then...I think it's time I find out about this dream." She searched his face. "I was thinking I might try hypnosis like you suggested. There is something in that dream that keeps bothering me and has ever since Max's murder. The bank robber was wearing a ski mask but there is something about him, something I just can't put my finger on. I keep thinking if I could just see it a little more clearly..." She glanced toward the foothills glowing in the sun. "I keep seeing something silver spinning in the man's hands." She shook her head and smiled at him. "I know it doesn't make any sense. I just feel the answers are in that dream. But I promised Max I'd leave it alone, that I'd never try to remember."

"Sometimes there are good reasons to break a promise," he said, hoping that was true as he turned his attention to the highway ahead. "What do you say to a hot bath, some new clothes. And breakfast first?"

She nodded. "I want to call Maggie, too. You don't think she went to Missoula after we warned her not to, do you?"

"Are you asking if she's as stubborn as you and Max?"

She elbowed him gently in the ribs.

"And don't forget Cline. He's probably gotten that hitchhiker to confess by now," J.D. said.

This time she elbowed him a little harder.

AFTER A LARGE BREAKFAST, Denver used the phone at a gas station on the east end of Bozeman. When Maggie didn't answer at the Missoula number or at her home in West, Denver called Taylor at the Three Bears.

"Maggie?" Taylor said, sounding a little surprised. "I guess she hasn't come back from Missoula."

Denver shot J.D. a look. So she'd gone to check out Pete's alibi on her own. Denver swore under her breath. Maggie had probably picked up that stubbornness from all those years around Max.

"I think she just needed to get away for a few days," Taylor said, confirming her suspicions that Maggie hadn't even told him what she was up to. "I'll tell her you called when I see her."

When he saw her. "So you're staying around for a while?" she asked.

He chuckled softly. "It looks like it. I was thinking I might buy a business here."

Denver couldn't help smiling. She'd resented his attentiveness to Maggie at first, but only because she felt as if he was cutting in on Max. But Max was gone. And Maggie was alone. She supposed if Taylor wanted to settle in West, it would be all right.

"I'm going to be out of town for a few days myself," she told him. "I'll catch Maggie when she gets back."

Then she dialed Cline's number. The dispatcher said he wouldn't be back until later in the day.

PETE STARED AT the tracking monitor for a few moments, then at the sheriff's office, and swore. Denver had done it.

Somehow she'd realized the tracking device was in the watch he'd given her. He swore again. She'd suspected him of being a liar and a murderer, and now she knew just how low he'd go.

The two-way radio squawked and Cal's voice filled the pickup's cab. "Come in, Cowboy."

Pete could tell by the tone of Cal's voice that he'd told Midnight about what had happened and Midnight wasn't pleased. He picked up the headset. "What do you want?"

Static. "Somebody wants to talk to you. Now."

Great, Pete thought. And what was he going to say when Midnight asked him, "Where is Denver McCallahan?"

Good question. He wished to hell he had the answer.

J.D. LEFT DENVER SLEEPING on the queen-size bed that took up most of the motel room. They'd both spied the bed the moment they walked into the room. He'd taken one look at her and knew she wanted him as badly as he did her. He'd waited until she fell asleep before he'd gotten up and gone into the bathroom to shave off his beard. For a long time, he stood in front of the mirror staring at himself, wondering how long he'd been hiding beneath the beard.

"Oh, J.D.," Denver cried when he came back into the bedroom. She jumped up to take his face in her hands. She studied him for a long moment, her eyes brimming with tears, and then she kissed him. "I'd forgotten what a wonderful face you have."

They made love again in the big, soft bed, then reluctantly got dressed in their new clothes for the appointment with the psychologist they'd found in the yellow pages. The doctor specialized in hypnotherapy.

Trembling, Denver leaned against the wall as they took the elevator up to his office on the third floor of the old Bozeman Hotel building. The other night when the man in her cabin had tried to choke her, she'd known fear, but she'd never experienced sheer terror. J.D. gave her hand a reassuring squeeze as they entered Dr. Richard Donnley's office. "I'm here for you," he said. She smiled in answer, hoping that would always be the case.

The doctor was a tall, thin man with kind eyes and a soft voice. His office was much like him, with a soft and peaceful feeling. Denver sank into a comfortable, overstuffed love seat. J.D. sat beside her, holding her hand.

"It's true that dreams can be a way for the subconscious to communicate with us," Dr. Donnley said carefully after Denver explained about the nightmares.

"Does that mean that under hypnosis I might be able to remember more?" she asked.

"Sometimes you can access a memory through hypnosis," he agreed. "But the whole area of memory retrieval is very controversial."

"Controversial?" J.D. asked.

"It's rare that you get a pure memory," the doctor explained, steepling his fingers against his chin. "It will only be *your* perception of what happened."

"Does that mean what I recall under hypnosis won't be real?" she asked in surprise.

"It will be the way you remember that day, which may not be exactly the way it was," he replied.

"I saw the robber's face when he turned. He wore a mask and he had something in his hand...."

"Even if you recognized him, it wouldn't be admissible in court," he said.

J.D. squeezed her hand. "Her memory isn't enough to have him arrested—let alone convicted, right?"

"Exactly." Dr. Donnley brushed a speck of lint from his pant leg. "There is another point to consider. You may not be able to see the man's face in your dream because you couldn't see it that day in the bank."

"But I feel so certain the dream is trying to tell me something," Denver cried. "It must be the identity of the murderer."

"Not necessarily so," the doctor said. "It's not unusual in a case like this for you to want so desperately to recognize him that you start believing you can. We won't know until we hypnotize you. And there is a good chance that if it's too painful, your subconscious might not *let* you remember."

"So what do you think, Sunshine?" J.D. asked. He smiled at her, a lock of his hair hanging down over his forehead. "You still want to do this?"

She nodded. "I have to. I have to know."

DENVER LEANED BACK in the chair, eyes closed, hands curled in her lap. She felt herself drifting in the darkness. The feeling was not unpleasant. It soothed, as did Dr. Donnley's softly spoken words. Deeper and deeper. Her body felt heavy; her breathing slowed until she feared she'd forget to take a breath. Then she forgot to worry about it as she floated in the peaceful darkness, content.

"Let's go back to that day when you were five," Dr. Donnley said. "You and your parents were going to the bank. Do you remember?"

Denver nodded, although she didn't feel her head move.

"What did you do before you went to the bank?"

"We picked up my father from work." Her voice sounded far away. "He's a policeman."

"So he's still in his uniform when you go into the bank. Tell me what you're doing as you go into the bank."

"Skipping. And singing." She sang softly, the words still there after all these years. "You are my sunshine, my only sunshine..."

"Where are your parents?"

"They're behind me. I stop skipping."

"Why?"

"There are people on the floor. Something is wrong. I turn around to tell my parents. But I can't."

"Why?"

"I see the other policeman."

"What other policeman?"

"The one on the floor. He's reaching for his gun. It's still in his holster. And I hear my father call my name. I run back to him. I'm afraid."

"What's happening now?" Dr. Donnley asked.

The words poured out as she watched it happening in her head. "My father pulls his gun. He grabs my shoulder with his other hand and pushes me hard. It hurts. He pushes me as he yells at my mother to get down. I hit the floor and slide. The floor is cold and hard. I hit my chest on the desk leg. It hurts so bad."

"You're all right, Denver," the doctor assured her.

"It hurts. I can't breathe." Denver felt tears rolling down her face, then the fear, the panic. "I can't breathe!"

"You're all right. You're not there. It's just a memory. Take a deep breath. There now. What do you see?"

"Nothing. I'm on the floor by the desk. I can't see anything." She sobbed quietly for a moment. "I hear my mother scream. I crawl under the desk. I can see the robber. He's standing by the counter. He turns. He has a shotgun in one hand and something in the other. It's shiny. I can't tell what it is. I look at my father. All I can see is his legs. But I can see the other policeman on the floor. He has a gun in his hand. He's pointing it at my father. I hear the gunshots."

Dr. Donnley kept talking, his voice soft and reassuring. "What is happening now?"

"I hear people screaming. Now I hear the shotgun go off. My father is on the floor beside me. His eyes are open. There is blood on the floor. Blood everywhere. People are crying. I'm crying. I slide farther under the desk and watch the robber leave. He stops for a moment beside the desk."

"Can he see you?"

"No."

"Can you see what he has in his hand?"

She shook her head. "He leaves. And I see my mother. She's on the floor, too." The sobs rose from deep inside her, a well of sorrow. "A lady helps me out from under the desk. She hugs me and tells me my parents are dead."

"It's all right to be sad. It's all right to cry."

Denver cried until there were no more tears, until she could hear the music and feel her mind drifting in the darkness again.

"Think back, Denver. Are you sure you don't know the man wearing the mask?"

She shook her head, remembering only the mask and the flash of silver she'd seen in his hand. But as she looked into the darkness, she saw another face. "I know the other one."

"What other one?"

Denver focused on the darkness. She stared into the man's face. Into those bottomless eyes. Her heart seemed to race out of her chest. She couldn't catch her breath. "Ooohh."

"You're all right, Denver."

Her eyes flew open. She jerked up, pushing herself back into the chair as her gaze darted around Dr. Donnley's office. "I saw him!" she cried. He'd been younger then, not much more than a teenager, and thinner. But there was no mistake about that hair, those eyes or that awful, cold look of his. "It was Cal. Cal Dalton. He was the cop on the floor. But he's dead."

J.D. HELD DENNY. The sun poured into the front seat of the pickup. She felt good against him, warm and safe in his arms. He stroked her back, his chin resting on the top of her head.

"It was Cal," she whispered. She'd been saying it over and over again. "But he was on the floor of the bank, surrounded by blood. He was dead. How could that be?"

J.D. hugged her to him. "I don't know."

Dr. Donnley had warned her again about the questionability of memory retrieval. The man she'd seen might have been someone she connected with evil, he'd explained. She'd said herself that this man had tried to rape her. It would be understandable that she'd put his face on a man who might have killed her parents.

But Denver had argued that she'd recognized him as he was more than twenty years ago. Was that possible? she'd asked him.

Dr. Donnley had smiled sympathetically and told her there was much they didn't know about the mind and warned her not to take much stock in the things she'd remembered. He'd suggested further hypnosis.

J.D. believed Denny had seen Cal's face, but like the doctor, he was skeptical as to what it meant. She'd been through so much lately. It didn't seem impossible she should put Cal's face on a dead man's.

"I can't explain it, but I know I saw Cal," Denver insisted now as she leaned back to look into J.D.'s eyes.

"Maybe it was someone who looked like him," J.D. said reasonably. "Maybe even a . . . relative."

"I never thought of that." She smiled.

He knew that smile. "Let me guess, we're going to Billings to investigate a robbery?"

THEY DROVE INTO THE Magic City, the sun high overhead, the city's famous rock rims drenched in warm sunlight against a clear blue Montana sky. The largest city in the state, Billings sprawled across the valley, jumping the Yellowstone River, then running south as far as the eye could see. Denver had been quiet all morning, and he knew she was anxious about what they'd find. She nestled against him, her face set in an iron-willed determination that constantly amazed him.

The library was a huge brick building just off a one-way street downtown. They waded through the 1969 city directory—the same year as the bank robbery—then the years before and after. Denver's disappointment showed in her eyes when they didn't turn up even one Dalton in the years before or after.

"We just keep hitting one dead end after another," she complained, slamming shut the 1971 directory. "So much for the relative theory."

On impulse, J.D. flipped through the 1969 directory again, only this time to the *C*'s. He ran his finger down a column.

"Take a look at this, Sunshine," he said, turning the directory so she could see. "William Collins."

She stared at him, then at the name. The one that matched the fingerprints Max had taken at his birthday party. "You don't think—"

"There's only one way to find out."

Denny slid into his arms, pressing her lips against his neck, before they walked to the pickup. She felt warm, her familiar scent making him want nothing more than to be alone with her.

The *Billings Register* was in a large old brick building on the south side of the city, which was part of a city renewal plan. As soon as they walked in, J.D. still limping, heads turned. Denver seemed confused at first as to why everyone was staring at them, and then realized they were staring at J. D. Garrison, country and western star.

"I keep forgetting just how well-known you are," she said.

At that moment, J.D. wished he wasn't. The woman at the front desk asked him for his autograph. Denver insisted he give it to her. "We need the morgue," J.D. said. The woman dragged her eyes away from J.D. to point down the hallway.

They pulled out the roll of microfilm from 1969 and sat down. J.D. held Denver's hand for just a minute. It was cool and he could feel it trembling.

"The summer of 1969?"

She nodded.

The pages blurred by. He wanted to hold her, to make this easier on her, but he doubted there was anything he could do to lessen her anxiety.

The first story about the robbery came up on the screen and Denver covered his hand on the knob to freeze it.

A masked bandit killed two people and wounded a third during a holdup that netted more than a million dollars at State Bank this morning.

Denver's grip on his hand tightened; she took a ragged breath. "Wounded a third?"

Chief of Police Bill Vernon said the male robber wearing a ski mask came into the bank shortly after it opened. At gunpoint, he forced bank personnel onto the floor while one teller sacked the money.

A spokesman for the bank said this branch doesn't normally have that much cash on hand but was transferring money from the oil fields.

The shootings occurred when an off-duty police officer, still in uniform, came into the bank with his family. The police officer was killed, along with his wife, and a security guard was wounded during the shoot-out that followed.

"Oh, J.D., the guard wasn't killed," Denver cried. "Does it give his name?"

J.D. shook his head as he scanned down the rest of the article.

The robber escaped with more than one million dollars. No arrests have been made. Chief Vernon said the investigation is continuing.

J.D. started to scroll to the next story when Denver stopped him. "Look," she said, pointing to the date of the first article.

He stared at the numbers and felt a sudden chill. "June 14, 1969. It's the number from Max's notation at the end of the Wade file."

"The date of the robbery article in the *Billings Register*," Denver said. "Bil 69614. He'd already connected the poaching and the robbery or at least suspected a connection. Better make a copy of the stories," Denver added.

J.D. nodded, dropped in a dime and hit the copy button. Then he turned to the next robbery story.

Police Chief Bill Vernon confirmed today that the victims of the State Bank holdup last week were Timothy McCallahan and his wife, Linda. Both were shot during the robbery, which netted more than one million dollars.

He felt her tremble and pulled her closer. "Are you sure you want to read this, Denny?"
She nodded.

Timothy McCallahan, a Billings police officer, was off duty at the time of the robbery, but still in uniform. Witnesses say he entered the bank and, realizing what was happening, went for his gun.
Also wounded during the shootout was bank guard William Collins. Collins is in satisfactory condition at Billings Deaconess Hospital.

Denver let out a cry. "William Collins?"
But J.D. had already scanned ahead to the next robbery story and the accompanying photograph. A young Cal Dalton smiled at the photographer from his hospital bed. "Just what we thought."
"William Collins is Cal Dalton!" Denver exclaimed. "We were right!"
J.D. pulled her into his arms and swung her around in a circle, hopping on his one good leg. She laughed, her head thrown back, her eyes bright, and he yearned to see that kind of happiness in her face always. Then he kissed her. At first lightly, then with a need that made him weak with wanting her. He released her when an older woman came into the morgue. They both sat back down at the microfilm

table and waited innocently for the woman to leave, then they looked at each other and burst out laughing.

After a moment, they turned their attention back to the photograph of William Collins a.k.a. Cal Dalton. Cal was much younger but there was no doubt that William Collins and Cal Dalton were one and the same. "Do you realize what this could mean? If you were right about Cal being the bank guard, then there's a good chance you were right about Cal shooting at your father, instead of the masked bank robber."

Denver moved in closer to read the story. "You're saying it was an inside job?"

"That would explain why Cal still had his gun."

"This could be what we've been looking for," she said. "It could explain why Max was hanging around Cal, why he'd run a fingerprint check on him."

"But Max never got the results," J.D. observed.

Denver tilted her head up in speculation. "I wonder if Max knew something or was just suspicious? I guess it doesn't matter. If Cal even *thought* Max was on to him..."

He nodded, thinking the same thing. "It could have been enough to get Max killed."

They quickly scanned later newspapers for news of the robbery. The articles became shorter and shorter as the weeks went by. Both the bandit and the money still had not been found. William Collins a.k.a. Cal Dalton recovered from his gunshot wound and was released from the hospital. Then the robbery just died away.

"I'd sure like to talk to this Chief Vernon," Denver said as they put the microfilm away.

He smiled as he took her hand. "Then I guess we'd better find him."

AT THE POLICE STATION, a young lieutenant told Denver that Chief Bill Vernon had retired. "But if it's an old case, he'll remember it." He wrote down an address on the west end of town.

Bill Vernon was a tall, silver-haired man with an arrow-straight back and keen gray eyes. "The State Bank robbery in '69." He nodded his head. "Remember it well." He offered them chairs and coffee. They turned down the coffee but sat down on the couch. "Want to tell me what makes you interested in such an old case?"

J.D. covered Denver's hand with his own. "Denver's father and mother were killed in the robbery."

Vernon's eyebrows shot up; his expression softened with sympathy. "You're the little girl?"

Denver nodded, feeling like that frightened little child again. Chief Vernon had the answer she needed. Who had killed her parents? She'd always believed it was a stranger. Now there was a possibility she knew the man.

"Timothy McCallahan was one fine policeman," Vernon said.

Tears welled in her eyes. "Thank you."

"A terrible tragedy." Vernon shook his head, his gaze distant. "That was one case I wanted to crack more than any other in my career. We knew there was someone on the inside but couldn't prove it."

Denver stole a look at J.D. "We think William Collins was the inside man."

Vernon nodded. "I still do, too. The gunshot wound should have proved it."

"The gunshot wound?" J.D. asked.

"Collins was shot with a standard-issue police revolver," Vernon said. "He said he was in your father's line of fire and was shot by accident."

"Then my father did shoot him?" Denver asked. "I remember the guard pulling his gun and pointing it at my father, and then I heard the shots."

Vernon rubbed the back of his neck, studying her. "So you do remember some of it?"

"Some. I'm just not sure how much of it is real," she said, thinking of the flashing silver.

"We knew the guard had to be in on it, but he wasn't the brains behind the holdup. He wasn't smart enough," Vernon said.

That certainly fit Cal Dalton a.k.a. William Collins, she thought.

"The case was never solved?" J.D. asked.

Vernon shook his head. "Got away free as a bird. Money and all."

Denver thought of the memories that had surfaced during her hypnosis session. "There's something I need to know. Did William Collins kill my parents?" she asked, bracing herself for the answer.

Vernon shook his head. "They were both killed by the bank robber. Witnesses said the man carried a sawed-off shotgun. That is consistent with the pathologist's findings."

Denver took a deep breath and let it out. In the park across the street, two young boys worked to get a Ninja Turtle kite airborne. "Is there any way to trace the money from the robbery?" she asked, thinking of the $150,000 in Max's account.

Vernon shook his head.

"And if you could prove William Collins was in on the robbery?" J.D. asked.

"Accessory to murder." The old police chief smiled. "Fortunately, there's no statute of limitations on murder, and there is nothing I'd like better than to nail Collins."

Denver thanked him. As she got up to leave, she noticed a photograph of several policemen on the wall. She moved closer, recognizing a younger version of Chief Vernon. Then her gaze took in a young policeman on his right. Her pulse thundered in her ears. "Who is that man?" she asked, her voice cracking.

Vernon stepped up behind her. "That's Bill Cline. He and I went to the academy together."

"He didn't happen to work for the Billings Police Department in 1969, did he?" Denver asked, holding her breath.

Vernon frowned. "Bill? No, he was never on the force here."

"Just a thought," Denver said, breathing again.

Vernon opened the door for them. "No, in 1969, Bill Cline was working in security."

"Here in Billings?" J.D. asked.

Vernon shook his head. "Up in the oil fields. He was an armored-car driver for Interstate West, a company that transferred oil money."

Chapter Eighteen

"I'm telling you he's our bank robber," Denver argued as they left Vernon's.

"Cline?" J.D. started the pickup and headed back into the city. "He's a lot of things—"

"He's an obnoxious redneck, male-chauvinist, know-it-all jerk," she said, daring him to disagree.

J.D. laughed. "Yes, he's all of that and probably a lot more you're just too polite to name."

She grinned at him.

"But a bank robber and murderer? Let alone the brains behind a million-dollar heist?"

That stopped her. She'd never thought of Cline as smart, but maybe she'd misjudged him. Maybe all that redneck bluster was an act. "Think about it, J.D. Cline called Pete the morning after Davey's accident on Horse Butte to warn him. And Cline would have known about a large oil-money transfer to the bank."

"So would a lot of other people," J.D. countered. "And Cline likes Pete and he isn't that wild about me."

"Are you going to tell me it isn't strange that Cline and Cal Dalton ended up in the same town?"

"Cline's been the deputy sheriff in West Yellowstone for years," J.D. said reasonably. "Dalton or Williams or whoever he is has only been in town how long?"

"A few months," Denver admitted. "But maybe he went there because of Cline."

J.D. pulled up to a light and looked over at her. "Isn't it more likely that he went there because of the horn?"

"He could have come for both," she muttered under her breath.

"The question now is, what are we going to do?" he asked.

"About Cal?"

"About food." He grinned at her. "I'm starved."

She laughed, snuggling against him. "You're always starved."

"Always starved for *you*," he said, planting a kiss on the top of her head. Her hair smelled clean and fresh and made him want her more than food.

He drove into an older neighborhood in the south end of town and found an authentic-looking Mexican café. They took a booth by the window and ordered two combination plates and two beers.

"Sheila Walker thinks she's traced the money trail to Max," Denver said after the waitress left. "If that money in his account is from the robbery, then the person who put it there has to be someone involved in the crime."

"Or someone who knew where the money was hidden."

Denver frowned. "I never thought of that."

"Or the money might be from horn hunting," J.D. said. "It might have been put in his account just to make Max look guilty."

The waitress put two frosty mugs of beer down in front of them. The place was empty at this time of day. J.D. felt safe for the first time in days and knew Denny did, too. He didn't want to talk about murder or robbery or horn poaching. He just wanted to look at Denny sitting across from him. He pressed his leg against hers under the table. She responded in kind with a smile, took a sip of beer and flipped through the robbery stories they'd photocopied.

J.D. reached across the table to take her hand. With his thumb he traced her life line. Then her love line.

"What do you see?" she asked, pushing the newspaper stories aside.

"I see a long, interesting life filled with adventure," he said, and she laughed. "And lots of children."

She raised one eyebrow and grinned at him. "Lots?"

"At least two."

"Two's a nice number. And is there a man in my life?"

"Of course." He frowned. "Well, I hope so."

"Is he tall, dark and handsome?" she asked, looking down at her palm.

"He'll pass."

Her eyes glinted with mischief. "Then maybe I already know him."

The waitress came back with a bowl of chips and salsa and J.D. reluctantly let go of Denver's hand.

She took another sip of her beer and licked the foam from her lips as she looked out the window. "You understand that I have to find Max's killer before I can—" She turned to him.

"Yes, but what if that person's never found, Denny? How long are you willing to put your life on hold?"

She picked up the newspaper accounts of the robbery again. "Don't ask me that, J.D. You know this is something I have to do. I owe Max." He watched her leaf through the newspaper articles. If she couldn't clear Max's name— Suddenly she stopped in midmotion, her fingers trembling as she clutched an article in her hand. "Look at this."

J.D. leaned over to see the page she was gripping.

"Sheila Walker," Denver whispered. "That reporter who keeps wanting to talk to me. She covered the robbery. No wonder she thinks she's found the money."

"I'M SCARED," Denver said to J.D. as she hung up the phone. He leaned against the doorway of the phone booth. Just the sight of him made her heart go pitter-patter. She ran her fingers through the curly hair at his nape and breathed in the heady scent of him.

"You didn't reach Maggie?" he asked.

She shook her head. "She should have been back from Missoula by now. As much as I don't want to do it, I have to call Cline and see if he's heard anything." She dialed, then spoke to the dispatcher, who put the deputy sheriff on immediately.

"Where the hell have you been?" he demanded. "I've been trying to get ahold of you for two days."

Her heart leaped up into her throat. It was Maggie, she thought. "Why? Has something happened?"

"We've caught your uncle's murderer."

Denver fought for breath. "What?" J.D. stared at her face, concern making his eyes the color of pewter.

"The hitchhiker," Cline said with obvious satisfaction.

"The hitchhiker?" she repeated, dumbstruck.

"He had the murder weapon on him and he confessed. Case closed." Cline let out a long I-told-you-so sigh. "And as far as that other little detective work you and Garrison did," Cline continued, "Roland Marsh and I went back in to the park, where you said you saw those elk-horn caches."

She gripped the phone. "You and Marsh?"

"No horn. No sign of any poaching. No dead bear. If I were you, I'd stick with that photography hobby of yours."

She started to hang up, but Cline's next words stopped her.

"And by the way, I'm not your damned secretary, missy. Everybody and their brother have been calling here."

"Who's everybody?" she asked, hoping there'd be a message from Maggie.

"Pete. I told him to wait until the dance tonight and if you didn't show up..."

She'd forgotten she'd promised to go with Pete. The Montana Country Club band was playing for the Spring Fling at the old railroad station. It seemed like a lifetime ago when she'd made the date.

"Pete said to call him. Something about Maggie."

"Maggie?"

"And that reporter woman," Cline said distastefully. "Sheila Walker. You're to call her at Max's office. Said it's a matter of life and death." He let out an irritated sigh. "Get an answering machine, will ya?" He hung up.

Denver stared at the phone, then quickly dialed Maggie's number. No answer. She rang Pete's. Still no answer. Finally she called Taylor. "I'm trying to find Maggie," she said carefully.

"Isn't everyone?" Taylor said, not sounding all that happy. "I've been looking for her myself. I thought she'd call me when she got back."

"Then she *is* back?"

"That's what Pete told me. But I have to tell you. I'm worried about her. Pete sounded like she might be in some sort of trouble."

"I'll keep trying Pete's number," she said, fighting panic. "If I hear anything, I'll get back to you."

"Wait a minute, where are you?" she heard him ask, but she broke the connection and dialed Max's office number. What if Sheila really had found out something? The phone rang and rang. No Sheila. Denver hung up and stepped from the booth into J.D.'s arms.

She fought her growing fears as she recounted first the conversation with Cline, then the one with Taylor. "Pete has Maggie. I'm sure of it. She must have found out Pete wasn't in Missoula the day Max was killed." She made a face. "Cline said he and Marsh went to look for the horn. Said they didn't find it or a trace of the dead bear. What does that tell you?"

He ran a hand through his hair and looked up at her. "That we're going back to West Yellowstone."

"If Pete has Maggie and we can't trust Cline—" J.D. swore and pulled Denver into his arms. "We have no choice but to go back," she agreed.

"I was hoping you'd say that."

Chapter Nineteen

Maggie sat in a chair by the fire pretending interest in the flames. She reviewed her options, wondering what Max would have done under the same circumstances, reminding herself that she'd never had Max's flare for the dramatic— or his total disregard for danger.

"How long do you plan to hold me here?" she asked the man beside her, trying to keep the fear from her voice.

Lester Wade smiled in answer. He was small, with soft brown eyes, but Maggie couldn't miss the hard edge to him. Or the pistol he cradled in his lap.

Maggie had gotten back from Missoula anxious to share her news with Denver. She'd verified at The Barn that Pete Williams hadn't been in Missoula the afternoon of the murder with the rest of the band. But when she'd rushed to Denver's cabin, she'd found the barrel of a gun—held by one of Pete's band members—waiting for her.

"Where's Denver?" Lester had demanded.

Maggie wished she only knew. Worrying about Denver made her feel braver.

Lester jumped when the phone rang. He picked it up. "Yeah?" He listened, frowning, then hung up. "Lucky for you, lady. They've found Denver. It sounds like she's headed back."

"Headed back here?" Maggie felt sick. Was she being used as a decoy to get Denver to the cabin?

"Don't worry about it," Lester said, sitting across from her. "Everything's going as planned now."

"What a relief," she said, but Lester didn't get the sarcasm. The plan seemed to be that Lester and some others would be skipping town tonight with enough money to retire someplace warm. She'd overheard that much when Lester was on the phone earlier. "Do you mind if I stretch my legs?"

Lester looked worried. "Stay in this room, don't touch anything and don't move too fast."

"I'm too old to move too fast."

The man had no sense of humor, Maggie thought as she got to her feet. She caught a movement outside the window in the growing darkness. A figure popped up for a moment and disappeared again. She moved to block Lester's view as best she could. A scraggly boy in his teens with large brown eyes peered into the window. He motioned for her to keep quiet and disappeared again. It wasn't exactly the cavalry but it was help. Possibly.

"Could I have a glass of water, please?" she asked.

Lester eyed her suspiciously.

"I promise not to try to drown myself in it."

He shot Maggie a humorless smile and moved cautiously into the kitchen. All the time he let the tap water run, he kept the pistol trained on her. She wandered away from the window, pretending to warm her hands in front of the fire. Lester filled a glass and brought it to her. He put it down on the hearth and stepped back as if he thought she'd try to jump him. He must think that kind of behavior ran in the family.

He headed back to his chair, but never reached it. His head jerked around at a sound in the hallway, the pistol raised ready to fire. Maggie caught a glimpse of the young man's head and knew Lester had, too. Quickly grabbing a log from the wood box, Maggie closed her eyes and swung. A gunshot whined through the cabin, echoing off the walls, and someone screamed.

FROM THE TOP OF Grayling Pass, J.D. could see the lights of West Yellowstone glowing in the distance like a small aurora borealis. He let up on the gas as they topped the hill in the van they'd rented in Bozeman and began the drop down into the wide valley.

"About this plan of yours…" he said, glancing over at Denver.

"The blueberry syrup plan?" She shrugged. "It's biodegradable and environmentally safe. That's about all I can say about it."

She'd had him stop in Bozeman, rent a van, and buy four gallons of blueberry syrup, a bottle opener and some wire.

J.D. looked over at her, his gaze softening at just the sight of her. "I hope this works."

"Have a little faith, Garrison," she said.

Out of the corner of his eye, he watched her chew at her lower lip and smiled at the familiarity of it. When he wasn't touching her, he loved looking at her. Her bravado right now made him love her all the more. But offered little reassurance. They were driving straight into a trap and she knew it.

J.D. honked as they crossed the Madison River bridge, making Denver smile. "I have to tell you these past few days with you have been—"

"Paradise?" she asked, laughing up at him.

He grinned. "Being chased by killers, hit on the head with hard objects, shot at with big-game rifles. Yes, Denny, it's been a little bit of heaven."

"Don't forget that fall into the bathtub."

"How could I?"

"If you're trying to say I'm not boring, I thank you," she teased, her gaze on the highway ahead.

"Boring?" He laughed. "Oh, Denny, you are anything but boring." His heart ached. "No matter what happens tonight—"

She touched her finger to his lips. "I know."

He pulled her hard against him. "This has to work."

They drove into West Yellowstone at one-thirty in the morning. Summer's Coming, read a sign at the Conoco station. If there were any signs of summer in this still-hibernating tourist town, J.D. couldn't see them.

He turned up Geyser Street. "J.D." Her hand squeezed his arm; he followed her gaze down the block to Max's office. "There's a light on. Sheila must be there."

"We don't have much time," he said as he parked the van. He felt a sense of urgency; they had to be at the dance before two. "Let's find out what she's got to say."

A chill crawled around his neck as they walked up the steps. J.D. took Denver's hand. The light was on only in the apartment above; it spilled down the stairs into the office, giving the room an eerie glow. No sounds came from inside. Nothing looked amiss. Except for the front door. It stood open, letting the night in.

"I don't like this," Denver whispered.

"No kidding."

IT TOOK MAGGIE A MOMENT to realize where the screaming was coming from.

"Hey, lady! Are you nuts?" the young man in front of her yelled. She closed her mouth, swallowing the last of the scream, and nodded. She'd never been more nuts in her life.

"Thanks," the kid said, uncovering his ears. "That's quite a set of lungs you've got."

"I used to scream professionally," Maggie told him.

He grinned at her. "You must have made a fortune."

Maggie smiled. "You have to be Davey."

"You've heard of me?" He sounded pleased.

Maggie noticed then that the front door stood open and Lester was gone. In the distance, she could hear the roar of an engine dying away down the road. Davey picked up the pistol from the floor.

"Max told me about you," she said, taking the gun from him as if it was a dirty diaper. He was the kind of kid Max had always loved to take under his wing; she suspected he was a lot like Max had been at that same age. "And of course your reputation for trouble precedes you."

"Oh, yeah?" He grinned, obviously pleased. "You want me to go after that guy?"

"No," Maggie assured him as she went to the phone. "I want you to stay here with me in case he comes back. And I want you to tell me who killed Max."

Davey shrugged. "Sure. A guy Cal calls Midnight."

"Midnight?"

He shrugged again. "Yeah, he offed Max to keep him from dropping a dime on him and Cal."

She remembered Max taking a stack of old detective-story paperbacks up to his office. "I've got this kid working for me. I'm just trying to help him with his reading," Max had said.

"Dropping a dime, huh?" she said to Davey.

"You know, dropping a dime—making a call to the cops," he replied.

"I know. And how did you find out all this about Midnight and Cal?"

He grinned. "I hang out. I listen. I do what Max did. I've been tailing Cal ever since Max bought it."

"You're lucky you didn't get yourself killed. And what else do you know about this Midnight person?" she asked.

"He's running a poaching ring here and sending illegal stuff all over the world. Lester and Cal have been stealing antlers and animal stuff out of Yellowstone Park for him. You wanna hear about the animal stuff? It's pretty gross."

She declined and picked up the phone to drop her own dime.

Davey looked uncomfortable. "You're not going to call the cops, are you?"

Maggie dialed the number. "I won't mention your name."

He nodded and headed for the fridge. "I hope you have better food than the place where they were keeping *me.*"

The moment Deputy Cline came on the line, Maggie poured out what little information she had based on what

Davey had told her, adding the part about her own kidnapping by Lester Wade. She didn't mention Davey. Cline listened without saying a word.

"Stay there," he said when she'd finished. "Lock the doors, don't let anyone in and don't answer the phone." He hung up. She stared at the phone, hoping she'd done the right thing by calling Cline. But she couldn't throw off the uneasy feeling Cline had given her. Why hadn't he seemed more surprised by the information?

She dialed Taylor's number. He answered on the first ring, and she quickly recounted what had happened.

"Are you sure you're all right?" he asked.

She assured him she was fine.

"Where is this Lester person now?"

"I don't know. Deputy Cline sounded like he might know, though."

"You called Cline?"

She couldn't miss the worry in his voice. "You don't think—"

"I'm sure you did the right thing." Taylor didn't sound sure at all. "I'll keep an eye on Cline. Just stay there."

She hung up, relieved she'd called Taylor. Max had once told her the reason he didn't get along with the deputy was because Cline bent the law when it suited him. But not even Cline would bend the law to protect a murderer, would he? Unless *he* was the murderer.

Just as she finished locking the doors, Davey came out of the kitchen with a large bag of chips, a jar of salsa, a couple of turkey and cheese sandwiches and two Cokes.

"Hungry?" he asked with a grin.

DENVER EXPECTED MAX'S files to be ransacked again. But as she stepped in, she realized it looked just as it had the last time she and J.D. had been here.

"Sheila?" Denver called out.

A sheet of silence as thick as ice lay over the house. Not even a breeze stirred the pines outside. Denver followed J.D.'s gaze to the stairs and felt him squeeze her hand. As she trailed after him, her pulse thundered in her ears. The stairs creaked under their weight as they climbed slowly into the light above.

On the landing at the top, Denver slipped and would have fallen if J.D. hadn't caught her. "What is it?" he whispered.

"Something's on the floor." She moved her foot to find a dark stain. She bent down to touch it gingerly with a finger, knowing what it was before she felt the sticky substance. "I think it's blood."

J.D. let out a groan; his hand tightened on hers. "Stay here."

She watched him cautiously push open the door to Max's apartment. He swore angrily.

"Tell me it's not Maggie!" she cried, hurrying up behind him.

"It's not Maggie," J.D. assured her, trying to hold her back. She pushed past him and stared down at the figure on the floor.

Sheila Walker lay on her side in a pool of blood. She was very dead.

J.D. DIALED THE SHERIFF'S office. Denver stood at Max's office window staring out into the night. When the dispatcher came on the line, she informed him that Deputy Cline wasn't in and couldn't be reached by radio right now. Was there a message?

"Tell him there's been a murder at Max McCallahan's. Upstairs. Her name's Sheila Walker."

Denver headed for the front door as J.D. hung up. "Where are you going?" he demanded, following her out to the porch.

"I don't want to be here when Cline gets here. He'll try to stop us. We have to fix the band's rigs and find Maggie."

J.D. checked his watch. He couldn't believe he was going along with her blueberry-syrup plan. "We still have time." He pulled her into his arms, cradling the back of her head in his hand. Just the touch of her hair brought back the memory of them together. His heart ached with worry that he might lose her.

"I can't quit now," she whispered against his shirt. In the distance, J.D. could hear the wail of a siren.

"I know." He released her; she stepped back and looked up at him. Her expression tore at his heart. They would never find happiness until Max's killer was caught.

J.D. took her hand and they ran across the street to the van. His ankle still hurt but felt stronger, he realized. With the headlights off, he quickly turned down the alley into the dark pines. Moments later, a patrol car came to a screeching halt in front of Max's office. The blue light on top spun, flickering against the night sky. J.D. pulled the van to the end of the alley and, heading toward the old depot, turned on the headlights.

DENVER COULD HEAR the music from the dance as J.D. pulled the van under a large pine on a logging road behind the depot and killed the engine. The festive sounds of the party drifted on the cool night air, belying the danger.

Denver glanced at the dashboard clock. It was 1:48 a.m. "Wanna flip for the bus or the pickup?"

J.D. shook his head. "You can have the bus. You'd probably cheat on the coin toss anyway."

She started to open her door, but he pulled her into his arms. His kiss promised her things she could not bear to think about. The feel of his lips, the taste of him, made her crave more. When he released her, she looked into his eyes, seeing the love she'd always dreamed of. How badly she wanted to forget this mess and just take off with him. But she knew Max's murder would always haunt her. And she had to find Maggie.

"I'll see you in a few minutes," she whispered and kissed him quickly. "For luck."

Then, pulling two gallons of the blueberry syrup, wire and a pair of pliers from the back, she headed for the band's old school bus before she could talk herself out of it.

It felt like a lark, something she and Pete and J.D. would have done when they were kids. But she neared the bus cautiously, only too well aware of what was at stake. The bus was parked behind the depot-turned-community center, secluded by virtue of the darkness and the large pines that loomed over it. Denver stopped for a moment to look back at J.D. He carried the same equipment she did, only he was working his way toward Pete's pickup parked around front, and she realized why he'd given her the bus. It was safer.

Laughter rippled on the breeze, mixing with voices. But no music. The band must be on a break. A few partygoers stood on the back steps of the old railroad depot, smoking and talking. It was too dark to see their faces—only the glow of their cigarettes was visible. She hung back in the shadows until they returned inside when the music started up again. Taking one last look around, she climbed under the bus.

J.D. CRAWLED BENEATH Pete's pickup, pulling the supplies with him. The sounds of the dance drifted around him. He listened for closer sounds as he checked his watch. Almost 2:00 a.m. The dance would be over soon. He reached for the first plastic gallon of blueberry syrup and the wire. Cutting a piece of wire, he tied the container to the undercarriage of the pickup, then carefully made a small hole in the plastic. The syrup began to drip. He reached for another gallon and attached it with more wire to the first in piggyback fashion, making a hole between the two gallon jugs. He watched the slow, steady drip of syrup for a moment, and smiled. He'd laughed at Denny's idea in the beginning.

"Well, it might not be as good as Hansel and Gretel leaving bread crumbs," Denny had said. "But at least the syrup should leave a trail we can follow on a snow-packed highway in the dark."

J.D. listened to the night sounds for a few seconds, thinking he'd heard a noise nearby. Nothing. He slipped out, brushed snow from his jeans and turned to find himself staring down the barrel of a shotgun.

DENVER FINISHED "syruping" the bus and looked around for J.D. Not seeing him, she headed back to the van according to plan. Her heart jackhammered at the thought that their plan might actually work. Now it was up to the FBI to stop the poachers; she'd called them from Billings and told them about the blueberry-syrup trail she planned to leave for them. But she couldn't be sure they'd taken her seriously. She'd warned them not to contact Marsh or Cline, and that could have been a mistake.

Now she couldn't wait to get back to the van—and J.D. More than ever, she wanted this whole thing to be over so they could be together. Once Maggie was safe—

Something moved ahead of her. Denver slowed, searching the pools of blackness beneath the pines and the shadows that sprawled across the aging snowbanks.

"J.D.?" she whispered.

A large dark shadow stepped from the trees. Just in time she caught the scream that rose in her throat. "Deputy Cline!" Her heart thundered against her ribs. "What are you doing here?"

"I believe that's my line. You're the one sneaking around in the dark." He nodded to the wire and pliers. "Like to tell me exactly what you've been up to?"

She took a step back in the snow, but he restrained her with a hand on her arm. "A hitchhiker didn't kill my uncle."

"Don't you think I know that?" he demanded. He motioned toward his patrol car parked in the pines down the road behind the depot. "You're coming with me." His fingers bit into her flesh.

"You're behind all of it?" Denver burst out, jerking her arm free of Cline's grasp as she tried to get her wobbly legs to move.

"You fool woman!" he snarled, reaching for her again.

She stumbled back. He grabbed her shoulder and spun her into him. She heard the metal clink of handcuffs and his mumbled curses as she fought to escape, but she didn't stand a chance against his strength.

Denver didn't hear the other person approach. It wasn't until Cline's grip loosened and he crumpled to the ground, that she realized she'd been saved. Again. She looked up to see Taylor looming over her. She fell into his arms, tears overflowing at the mere sight of him. "We have to quit meeting like this," she said on a sob.

He laughed softly. "I guess you're all right if you see any humor in this," he said, holding her at arm's length.

"This is twice that you've come to my rescue." Then she heard it. The rumble of the bus engine. Through the pines, she could make out two distinct figures. Cal was forcing someone into the back of the bus. "Oh, my God, they've got J.D."

Chapter Twenty

"I have to help J.D.," Denver cried, turning back toward the depot as the bus started to pull away.

Taylor caught her arm. "That won't help him, Denver. That could get him killed."

She spun around to face him. "You don't understand."

"Yes, I do. I talked to Maggie and she told me all about the poaching ring."

Relief rushed through her. "Maggie's all right?"

"Davey Matthews is with her at your cabin."

"Davey?" She felt like she'd fallen down a well.

Taylor looked at the unconscious Cline. "Davey told her about the poaching ring and some guy called Midnight, who he thinks killed your Uncle Max."

"Midnight?"

"Unfortunately, Maggie also called Deputy Cline and gave him the same information. That's why I've been following him. I've never trusted him."

She nodded, feeling a weight come off her shoulders. Taylor hadn't believed Cline's killer hitchhiker theories, either. No wonder he'd been hanging around Maggie's. She stared at the deputy, trying to imagine his face covered with a ski mask. It would explain a lot of things. Max would have trusted Cline. And the deputy had done everything to make it look like a hitchhiker was the murderer in order to keep her from looking for the real culprit.

"What can we do?" she pleaded as the band's bus pulled away from the old stone depot.

"One thing we can't do is let the deputy tip off the poachers. Help me move him."

They dragged Cline over to a tree, where Taylor gagged and handcuffed him.

"Come on." Putting his arm around her shoulders, Taylor led her to his Suburban. "We've got to call someone for help. How about the district ranger?"

"Roland Marsh?"

J.D. SAT HELPLESS in the back of the bus while Lester taped his wrists and ankles. Cal leaned against the opposite wall, holding a shotgun on him.

"Is that necessary?" Pete yelled back.

Cal swore. "Just drive."

J.D. tried to talk through the tape already covering his mouth.

"Worried about Denver?" Cal asked, guessing his concern. "We're taking good care of her." He laughed, then leaned over to check the job Lester was doing on J.D.'s ankles. "Use more tape. We don't want any trouble out of him."

J.D. noticed Pete looking at the road behind them in the rearview mirror as if he expected company. Cal must have noticed it, too.

"You got a problem, Williams?"

"I just want this night to be over."

Cal glanced back down the main drag. "Don't we all."

Just before they'd left the parking lot, Cal had checked the bus with an electronic device for detecting bugs. All the time he was doing it, he was watching Pete as if he thought Pete might have bugged the bus. J.D. could feel the tension between the two of them. Nothing like a falling-out among thieves, he thought. And here he was right in the middle of it. But where was Denver?

He caught a glimpse of the community church off to his left and realized they were headed north out of town. He prayed that Cal was wrong, that Denny was all right and that she'd gotten away.

"You're sure the boss is going to show?" Pete hollered as he got the old bus rattling down the highway.

"You worry too much," Cal yelled back. "By now, Midnight's got Denver and he's taking her to the semi." He smiled at J.D.'s reaction. "You don't like the idea of him having your girlfriend?"

J.D. felt his heart collapse from the sudden weight of worry on his chest. Denny with a man called Midnight. The leader of a poaching ring at best. At worst, a murderer.

"Stop that or I'll stop you," Cal said when he caught J.D. fighting the tape on his wrists.

Lester finished taping J.D.'s ankles. Cal inspected the job, then the two of them moved up to the front of the bus.

J.D. strained to hear their conversation. They seemed to be arguing but he couldn't be sure about what. He looked around for something to use to cut the tape.

"WE CAN'T GO TO MARSH," Denver said, climbing into the passenger side of the Suburban. The band's bus turned at the corner and headed north. "He's working with the poachers."

Taylor swung around to face her. "Are you sure?" She nodded and he swore, then apologized for it. "This whole thing is totally out of control."

"We have to follow the bus," Denver said. "I'm sure they plan to move the horn tonight. There's a tracking device on the bus. It's not as high-tech as the one Pete used on me, but hopefully it will work."

Taylor looked puzzled.

"I'll tell you all about it on the way," Denver assured him.

"Are you sure you want to do this?" he asked, checking the two rifles on the rack behind their heads.

"Yes, they have J.D. And who is there we can trust?"

"No one, I guess." He reached under the seat and pulled out a .38. He laid it on the console between them without a word, then turned onto the street, heading in the same direction as they'd last seen the bus going. "I think you'd better start at the beginning," Taylor said.

She filled him in. Starting with Lila Wade hiring Max to see if Lester Wade was cheating to the cryptic words at the bottom of Lester's case file, and all the way to the *Billings Register*'s morgue and Sheila Walker's murder. "Anyone who's gotten too close is dead," she finished.

Taylor didn't say anything. Instead, he studied her face, a frown creasing his brow. "It's all so hard to believe. You say Pete and this district ranger are in on it?"

She stared at the empty highway ahead, trying to pick up the blueberry-syrup trail, trying desperately not to think about her disappointment in Pete. "Pete used some sort of tracking device to follow me to Marsh's."

Taylor looked at her and swore, this time not apologizing for it. "Does J.D. know all this?" She nodded. "Then his life is in as much danger as yours is."

She thought of J.D. in the hands of murderers, and dread made her heart pound so that each breath was a labor. She picked up the syrup trail in the Suburban's headlights on the outskirts of town. A thin, dark blue line of drops along the snowpack shone in the lights; somewhere ahead, the band's bus lumbered down Highway 191 headed north.

"No wonder Pete and Cline tried so hard to dissuade me from looking for Max's killer," Denver said, seeing everything more clearly.

"So Davey's the one who tipped you off about the poaching ring," Taylor said, shaking his head. "Awfully brave kid, huh, especially after he was almost killed on Horse Butte that night. Then tonight he rescued Maggie from this Lester Wade character."

"I don't know what we would have done without him. I wouldn't have found out about the poaching and Cal and put it all together." They dropped over the hill past Baker's Hole Campground. There was no sign of the bus's taillights, just the steady line of blueberry syrup down the center of the lane.

"And you think it's all tied in with a 1969 bank robbery?" Taylor asked, sounding incredulous.

"Cal's the connection, although his real name is William Collins." She explained what she'd seen under hypnosis and what she later learned from Chief Vernon. "I think Sheila Walker figured it out and that's what got her killed."

He shook his head. "It's hard to believe Deputy Cline is this Midnight person."

"I know," Denver agreed, thinking about the small cabin he lived in at the edge of town. "I wonder what he did with the money from the robbery."

"Maybe he has it hidden somewhere for the time when he retires," Taylor suggested. They crossed Grayling Pass and dropped down the other side, the syrup drops growing smaller and farther apart. "Your blueberry-syrup trail just ended, kid."

Denver stared at the road for a moment, then behind her. "Didn't we pass a side road back there?" she asked, looking into the darkness. "They must have turned off."

"Or your syrup ran out."

She didn't even want to consider that possibility.

Taylor turned the Suburban around and pulled off on what looked like an old fishing-access road, nothing more than a snowy, narrow dirt road leading into the trees. But more than one set of dual tire tracks had already broken through the snowdrifts.

Taylor turned off his headlights and followed the tracks in the snow along the river. On a rise above a wide clearing, he stopped and killed the engine. Denver stared at the snowy meadow in front of them and the semitrailer sitting in the middle of it. The rear doors of the trailer were open, and in the faint glow of a lantern's light, she could see that the refrigerated trailer was only half-full. Huge piles of antlers waited to be loaded.

Parked in the pines off to the right was the band's bus. Where was J.D.?

A sudden chill stole up her spine as she looked over at Taylor.

He'd picked up a quarter from the tray on the dash and was spinning it between two fingers. It shone silver, flickering in a blur of light.

IN THE BACK OF THE BUS, J.D. strained to hear. Pete had brought the bus to a rattling halt, and the three of them had climbed out, slamming the doors behind them, still arguing about, of all things, grizzly bears. Cal opened the back door of the bus, checked the tape on J.D.'s ankles, then slammed the door again. A few moments later, J.D. heard the thump of something hard on metal not far from the bus. He pulled himself up. In the golden glow of lantern light, J.D. watched the three men load elk antlers into the back of an open semitrailer.

He eased himself down to work on the tape wrapped around his wrists, only to stop a few minutes later to listen again. He could have sworn he heard another vehicle coming up the road. The boss and Denver? He thought of the blueberry syrup; he only hoped it had worked and the FBI would be able to find them. He fell to work on the tape again, running it back and forth against the dull ridges in the metal floor—the sharpest things he'd found in the rear of the bus.

SHE STARED, SPELLBOUND by the spinning silver, stunned by its significance.

"Max would have been proud of you, Denver," Taylor said as he looked at the scene in the clearing. She noticed he touched the brake pedal with his foot twice. The coin spun around and around his fingers, a shiny blur. "You're a damned good investigator."

In the clearing below, three men came out of the trailer for more antlers. Denver recognized Pete, Cal and Lester. She stared at them, her heart racing, then looked over at Taylor.

"I never would have thought your blueberry-syrup trail would work," he said, shaking his head.

Denver went for the pistol between them and quickly turned it on Taylor, her hand shaking. "I remember," she whispered as the earth seemed to cave in beneath her. He caught the coin in his fist and looked surprised she had the pistol on him. She stared at him, two nightmares playing in her mind. In each she saw the strange light, the spinning silver. "It was you," she said. Just the other day at Maggie's, she'd watched him spin a toothpick and thought it a nervous habit. Why hadn't she realized then what it meant? "You were the masked robber. You were the one who killed my parents."

Taylor feigned shock. "Whatever would make you say such a thing?"

"The coin."

He looked at the quarter in his hand. "The coin? It's just a silly habit."

Denver nodded, the pistol wavering but still aimed in the general direction of his heart. "You picked up a coin from the counter that day at the bank and stood spinning it while you were waiting for the teller to bag the money. I saw you do it the other day at Maggie's with a toothpick."

He gave her a slight bow. "Very astute."

She watched him glance in the rearview mirror at the road they'd just come down. Was he expecting someone? Denver darted a glance at the trio loading antlers, then at the bus. "Where's J.D.?"

"He's not in the bus, if that's what you're thinking. I instructed Cal to tie him up and leave him in the woods. Only when the horns are safely on their way to the coast will I let the authorities know where to find you both."

"You've thought of everything," she said softly, not sure she believed him. He'd killed everyone who'd tried to stop him; he wouldn't let her and J.D. live. Not now.

She considered getting out to search the bus herself, but knew the pistol in her hand or even the rifles behind her wouldn't be enough to hold off four men. She just had to believe that wherever J.D. was, he was safe. And wait for the FBI to follow the same syrup trail she had.

"You were never in the army with Max, were you?"

He shook his head. "Everyone in town has heard Max's army stories. It was easy enough to find out what I needed to know and bluff my way into your confidence."

"And the robbery? What did you do with the money?"

A smile twisted his lips as he began to spin the coin again. "I spent it, of course."

Tears filled her eyes. "You killed my parents because of money." She felt her finger tighten on the trigger; Taylor's eyes narrowed for a moment.

"No one would have been hurt if your father hadn't come in when he did." He actually sounded as if he believed that.

"And Max? Was he to blame for his own death, also?" she demanded, fighting tears of pain and anger.

"Max found out about the poaching. Cal realized it was just a matter of time before Max put it all together and realized that he was really William Collins, the former bank guard. Cal got panicky, and rather than have him turn state's evidence against me, I took care of Max. I needed Cal to finish my work here in West Yellowstone."

Her heart ached as she stared at him. "Max must have trusted you to let you get so close that day at the dump."

He smiled. "For a few moments there, even Max believed we'd been in the army together."

"You tricked him into meeting you at the dump and then you killed him. After you'd put the money in his account."

He shrugged. "I thought with a few rumors and some money, Deputy Cline would think Max was the leader of the poaching ring." The coin spun in a silver blur. "I fed Sheila Walker enough information to make her think maybe Max pulled off the bank job or at least was in on it."

Denver tried to steady the heavy pistol. "Anyone who knew Max knew he was too honest for that."

"Not all plans turn out the way you hope they will."

Denver caught him looking in the rearview mirror again. The pile of antlers was shrinking. Was he expecting someone? Roland Marsh? Or Deputy Cline? "Suggesting going to Marsh was just a test, huh? And Deputy Cline is—"

Taylor grinned. "A chauvinist and a fool, but certainly not a man smart enough to operate a poaching ring the size of mine." He watched as Cal picked up a large rack and added it to the pile in the truck. "This is only part of a huge smuggling network. I set Cal up here just to keep an eye on him. And it has its moments. Did you know a bear is worth more dead than alive? It's like selling the parts from an expensive car."

With horrifying clarity, Denver realized Taylor was only telling her this because he planned to kill her, as well. She glanced down at the pistol in her hand.

"Right again," he said, smiling at her. "It isn't loaded. You are very good at this."

She let him take the pistol from her trembling fingers. Taylor reached into his pocket and brought out six shells and began to insert them into the empty chambers, watching her closely. Slowly she dropped her hands to her sides in defeat. He relaxed a little and she saw her chance. She grabbed the door handle and pushed, throwing herself from the Suburban. The momentum sent her sprawling into the wet snow. She kicked the door shut and scrambled to her feet. On the other side, she heard Taylor yell at Pete and Cal as he climbed hastily out of the driver's side of the Suburban. Denver ran toward the bus hoping to reach it before Taylor could fire at her.

She was almost past the semi when someone tackled her from the darkness. She screamed as she fell with a force that knocked the air from her lungs.

"I got her," Cal Dalton called as he held her down. "I got her."

Denver looked over her shoulder to see Pete standing above her, a rifle in his hands. The expression on his face was one of total fury.

Chapter Twenty-One

J.D. pushed himself up the back of the bus seat. He swore in frustration as he saw what was happening. He dropped back down, working harder at the thick tape around his ankles. Just a little— The fibers in the thick, sticky tape finally gave way...

Just as a shot exploded in the spring night.

IT HAPPENED SO FAST, Denver wasn't sure at first that she'd seen it.

Pete pointed the rifle at Cal. "Get away from her." His voice sounded far away. Cal looked up at him, no doubt expecting the rifle barrel to be aimed at her instead of his back.

Taylor came into view behind Pete; in those split seconds, Denver saw him raise the pistol. She screamed a warning but the explosion drowned it out.

Pete flew forward, hitting the ground hard. He rolled onto his side. Cal kicked the rifle away from him and Denver saw the bright red stain spreading across Pete's right shoulder.

He looked up at Taylor, resignation in his expression. "It's all over, Midnight," he said, his voice filled with pain. "The Feds will be here any minute. Do you think I trusted you enough to believe the location you gave me? I put a tracking device on the semi."

Taylor smiled. "Cal swept the bus and the semi. Forget about the Feds." He glanced toward the bus. "Where's Garrison?"

"Tied up in the back," Cal said. "Pete wouldn't let me dump—"

"You stupid—" Taylor swung the pistol on Cal, then seemed to change his mind. "Go get him. Lester, you keep loading horn." Denver started to get up but Taylor waved her back down with the pistol. "That would be very foolish, my dear. I realize now that it would have been a lot easier if I'd killed you at the bank years ago."

Denver leaned over Pete. His shoulder glowed bright red, a flower bursting into bloom from between his fingers as he gripped it. Pain deformed his handsome face. She pulled off her gloves and placed them on the wound beneath his hand. He smiled faintly, tears in his blue eyes.

"Move out of the way, Denver," Taylor ordered.

She glanced over her shoulder at him. "You aren't going to kill him."

Taylor looked pained to say he was. "He's working with the government, my dear. Obviously part of a sting operation if Roland Marsh is involved."

"Oh, Pete, I'm sorry," she said, realizing she had helped give him away by telling Taylor about Marsh.

Pete smiled ruefully. "He planned to murder us all in the end anyway. Once those antlers were loaded he was going to kill us. He's too greedy to share any of the wealth, especially now that things have gone badly."

"How true." Taylor raised the pistol, and shoved Denver aside. "Any dying request?"

At that moment, Cal came from out of the darkness, running hard, breathing heavily as if he were being chased.

"What the hell is it?" Taylor demanded.

"J.D.'s gone."

"What?" Taylor glanced frantically around the clearing. "He can't have gone far. Find him."

Cal didn't move. Instead, he stared at the night, a look of fear coating his face as thick as any mask.

"What's wrong with you?" Taylor demanded. "I said go find him."

Cal licked his lips, his eyes darting into the darkness of the pines. "She's out there. I heard her."

Taylor followed Cal's gaze to the shadows beyond the semitrailer. "What the hell are you talking about?"

Pete's laugh was low.

Taylor swung around to face him. "What's going on?"

"The mama grizzly," Pete grunted, grimacing from the pain. "Cal killed a cub this morning on the other side of that stand of trees and wounded the sow. When he found out this was the shipment location..." Pete coughed, closing his eyes for a moment. "He's convinced she's coming back to get him."

Taylor picked up Pete's rifle from the snow and tossed it to Cal. Then he grabbed the man's coat collar and shoved him hard. Cal fell to one knee, then awkwardly got to his feet again. "Find J. D. Garrison or *I'll* kill you." Cal looked from the pistol in Taylor's hand to the dark woods, and then back.

"Bears aren't like people," Taylor said, his voice almost compassionate. "They don't hold grudges, Cal. There's only one danger out there in those woods and that's J. D. Garrison."

Cal swallowed hard, glancing furtively into the trees. "That sow was the biggest I've ever seen, and wounded like that—"

"She crawled off somewhere and died," Taylor persisted, looking at his watch. "Just find me Garrison, then I'll give you..." He looked around. "...Denver. She's yours." Cal's eyes widened and he grinned, then he crept off into the darkness.

Denver moved closer to Pete, hoping to shield him from Taylor. "Run, J.D., run," she whispered. Beside her, Pete took her hand, motioning for her to be careful. She stared at him, startled when he led her fingers to the hunting knife in the top of his boot. He looked almost apologetic for suggesting it. She nodded and slipped the knife into the top of her own boot before Taylor turned around. "You can't possibly believe you can get away with this," Denver said to him, trying to block a straight shot at Pete.

Taylor looked almost sad, and for a moment she thought he might regret what he'd done. "I'll get away just like I did last time." He settled his gaze on her. "Except this time I won't leave any loose ends."

A scream tore open the night. Cal screamed again from the darkness beyond the semi. It was a terrified howl that made Taylor jerk Denver to her feet and hold her like a shield in front of him. He pointed the pistol in the direction the sound had come from, his hand shaking. "Cal? Cal!" Taylor swore as he dragged her around the back of the semitrailer. Lester wasn't in sight. Taylor released her just long enough to extinguish the lantern.

After a moment or two, Denver could make out shapes. One was too black, too big and moving too fast to be human. "The mama grizzly," she whispered in horror as she realized the bear had Cal down in the snow. With horrifying clarity, she could hear the low growls between Cal's screams. Taylor tightened his hold on her as he yelled for Lester to close the doors on the trailer. "You have to help Cal," she pleaded.

"I have to get this shipment to the coast."

Another figure moved among the pines. Denver saw J.D. lift a rifle to his shoulder and fire three quick shots in succession at the huge grizzly. Silence followed.

"J.D.?" Taylor called, pressing the barrel of the pistol against Denver's temple. "Come out where I can see you or I'll have to kill your girlfriend." Denver held her breath as J.D. stepped from the trees, Taylor's rifle from the Suburban in his hands. She felt Taylor's arm tense as he recognized the weapon. "Fool, there were only three bullets in that rifle and you wasted them on Cal!" He swung the pistol to fire at J.D.

"No!" Denver screamed and lifted her boot for the knife. She grabbed it and drove the blade into Taylor's thigh. The pistol exploded in her ears, the shot going wild. Taylor shoved her away as he grabbed for the knife stuck in his leg. Denver fell, hit the snowy ground and rolled away from him.

After that, everything happened so fast, and yet she would always remember it in slow motion, a flashing sequence of motor-drive shots, each in focus, each as permanent as a photograph. Taylor pulling the knife from his thigh and cursing, throwing the knife into the darkness and turning the pistol on her again. A shotgun report roaring in her ears. Taylor spinning around in surprise to find J.D. holding a sawed-off shotgun in his hands. Then Taylor staring down at his trouser legs and the bright red flow of blood, his words a cry in the night—"You should have made it count, Garrison." Taylor smiled as he brought the pistol up again, trying to steady it as he staggered on his wounded legs. First pointing it at J.D. and then swinging it on Denver again. Next, stumbling back, his legs refusing to hold him. His eyes widening as he saw the cache of antlers still beside the semitrailer. Swearing, then laughing as he must have realized what was going to happen. J.D. running for him. Taylor squeezing the trigger as he fell. The shot hitting somewhere in the trees overhead. J.D. reaching for Taylor but not being able to keep him from falling. And Taylor impaling himself on one large sharp tine in the pile of illegal antlers.

Denver watched it all in horror. Right to the end when Taylor looked over at her, the pistol slipping from his fingers, and smiled at the irony.

J.D. SWEPT DENVER UP from the snow and carried her to the Suburban. Her hands were ice-cold, but she didn't seem to notice. And he realized she'd been running on pure adrenaline. He could only guess what Taylor had told her, but whatever it was had her wired long before the terror of the night had even begun. "Are you all right?" he asked, knowing better.

She nodded. "Pete—"

"He's going to make it."

Denver looked around her as if blinded by the night. In the distance, he could hear the whine of a siren headed their way. He took off his coat and wrapped it around her.

"It's over, Denny," he murmured. The sirens grew closer and lights flickered in the trees as the first of the park-service four-wheel-drive vehicles pulled into the clearing.

Marsh jumped out, picked up Pete's white hat from the trampled snow. Behind him, Cline swore. Denver began to cry. J.D. pulled her into the protective circle of his arms. "It's going to be all right now," he whispered. "It's finally going to be all right."

Epilogue

When J.D. and Denver entered Pete's hospital room they found District Ranger Roland Marsh and Deputy Bill Cline beside his bed.

"We were just talking about you, Miss McCallahan," Marsh said, and smiled. "You're quite the heroine this morning." He paused. "Pete says you saved his life last night."

She met Pete's blue-eyed gaze. "I think it was the other way around." He looked pale and older, as if his boyish good looks had taken on a sudden maturity.

"Thank you," Pete said, his voice weak. His gaze moved to J.D. standing behind her. "You, too, J.D. I owe you my life."

Cline grumbled under his breath. "They both almost got *me* killed."

Marsh laughed. "You're lucky all you got was a bump on your head, Bill. If Taylor hadn't been afraid of blowing his cover in front of Denver, you'd have been dead right now," he reminded the cop.

"How's Cal?" Denver asked.

"He'll live to stand trial," Cline said. "In the meantime, he's been very talkative. So was Lester after we found him."

"And Taylor?" she asked.

Marsh shook his head. "He was dead when we got there."

Denver stepped to the side of Pete's bed. Marsh and Cline moved down to the end. "How are you?" she asked Pete.

"I'll live. Roland was just telling me about the blueberry-syrup trail they followed to find us last night."

"We thought it was oil at first," Marsh said.

"Not biodegradable," J.D. answered. "Denny's idea."

Marsh smiled over at her. "That was smart, calling the FBI. We'd have been there sooner but we got a false lead from Taylor. I'm sorry we couldn't have confided in you, but we didn't know who was behind the operation and we couldn't take any chances."

"So you were in on it from the beginning?" J.D. asked.

Marsh nodded. "When Max found out about the poaching ring, he turned it over to us. With Pete on the inside, we went after the leader. We knew it wasn't Cal Dalton."

"And I suppose it was Max's idea for Pete to go under cover?" Cline asked.

"No, Pete volunteered for the job," Marsh said. "It was fairly easy for him to get in once Pete knew Lester was involved. Max was dead set against it. He tried to stop Pete that morning—"

"Well, that explains why Max was so upset," J.D. said.

"Why *did* you take that chance?" Denver demanded of Pete.

"I overhead Max on the phone with Marsh one afternoon at Maggie's." Pete avoided her gaze. "I thought I could make some brownie points with you—as well as with Max." He coughed, grimacing with pain. "But my infiltrating the ring didn't help Max."

"Meanwhile, Max continued to investigate Cal," Marsh said. "I didn't know he'd run a fingerprint check on him. Unfortunately, Max made Cal nervous, and when Cal got nervous, Taylor got *real* nervous."

"Taylor was worried that if Max found out about the 1969 robbery, he might get Cal to turn state's evidence," Denver confirmed. "So he came here pretending to be an old friend and killed Max."

"I imagine we were easily deceived because there were dozens of Max's old friends turning up for his funeral," Pete said.

"And Pete had just gotten into the poaching ring. He hadn't met Midnight yet," Marsh continued. "So we had no idea it was Taylor. But Max must have been pretty nervous himself about Cal, because he hid the case file."

"Then why didn't he take his gun that day?" Denver demanded.

"From what we can gather, Max thought he was meeting Pete at the dump that day," Marsh said. "Or at least Pete and some old friend."

"I just don't understand how Taylor hoped to get away with killing Max?" J.D. asked.

Marsh chuckled. "Well, for starters, he didn't realize what a tenacious young woman Denver is. And secondly, he'd already gotten away with robbery and murder in Billings. He probably didn't think anyone could stop him, especially a small-town deputy like Cline here."

"I beg your pardon?" Cline objected.

They all laughed. "You know what I mean," Marsh amended. Cline didn't look as if he did. "When Cline started looking for the hitchhiker, Taylor thought he was home free. Then, Denver, you started investigating Max's death."

"Any one of you could have stopped me," she cried. "Why didn't you tell me the truth?"

"Believe me, I wanted to," Pete said. "But we knew whoever this Midnight person was, he'd be suspicious if you *didn't* try to find Max's killer."

"So Cline was in on it the whole time?" J.D. asked.

The deputy nodded, beaming as if he'd just won an Oscar.

J.D. frowned. "If Pete wasn't at Horse Butte—"

"It was Cal," Cline said. "Taylor sent him out to Denver's to help Pete look for the file. Cal found Pete passed out on the couch, saw Denver's note and called Taylor. Taylor told him to use Pete's pickup to get Pete in so deep they wouldn't have to worry about his loyalties.''

"And I didn't realize what had happened until the next morning when I got a call from Midnight," Pete said. "I'm sorry about trying to drug you, Denver. By then, I *was* in deep."

"And the hitchhiker?" Denver asked.

"He existed," Cline said. "We just invented the one who confessed. And we were looking for him in case he witnessed anything. He didn't."

"I assume Cal tore up Max's office, my cabin and Maggie's," Denver said.

"He and Lester," Cline added.

"But I smelled your cologne that night at my cabin," Denver said to Pete.

He nodded. "It seems Lester and Cal also searched my apartment. Cal helped himself to some of my cologne." He took her hand. "No wonder you were so afraid of me."

"So it was probably Cal who hit me on the head that first night at Max's," J.D. said.

"It's a good thing you have such a hard head, Garrison," Cline commented, but Denver detected an almost grudging compliment in the remark.

She closed her eyes for a moment. Her head swam. "That sawed-off shotgun J.D. found under Taylor's rear seat—"

"It's the same one that killed your parents," Marsh confirmed.

J.D. turned from the window. "What kind of fool would keep a murder weapon?"

"A lot of criminals like to keep a souvenir," Marsh said. "And I'm sure he saw some poetic justice in killing the daughter with the same gun more than twenty years later."

Silence filled the room to overflowing. Marsh took the hint and excused himself to make a phone call. Unfortunately, Cline didn't; the ranger almost had to drag him out of the room.

"I still think women should stay in the kitchen," Denver heard Cline say as he left. She smiled to herself. Right now, staying in J.D.'s kitchen, raising his children, baking cookies and doing the wash sounded wonderful, not that her camera bag would ever be far away.

"I owe the two of you an apology," Pete said, motioning for J.D. to come closer. "I did everything I could to keep you apart. You were right. I never called J.D. about the funeral."

Denver took his hand. "Pete—"

"Let me finish. I thought that you'd eventually get over J.D." He glanced at J.D., who had come to stand beside his bed. "I realize now that is never going to happen." Pete offered his uninjured left hand. "Friends?"

J.D. took his hand. "Friends." He turned to Denver. "I'll be outside."

She stood for a moment listening to the sound of birds singing beyond the open hospital window. "Thank you for trying to help Max."

Pete waved her thanks away. "I did it for all the wrong reasons." He took a breath and let it out slowly. "J.D.'s the right man for you, you know."

She smiled as she leaned over to plant a kiss on Pete's cheek. "Some day you're going to meet a woman who'll knock you off your feet and you'll wonder what you ever saw in me."

He laughed softly. "That's going to have to be *some* woman."

"She will be."

"Denver..." Pete pulled some folded papers from the table beside his bed. "I found this in Max's Oldsmobile. It's his will." She stared at the papers. "He wrote you a letter, too." Pete grinned. "Wishing you and J.D. happiness. Max knew you'd end up together, I guess." He met her gaze. "Be happy."

She smiled, tears in her eyes. "I'm going to try, Pete."

J.D. FOUND HER SITTING on a bench in a courtyard at the north end of the hospital. He stood for a minute just looking at her, marveling at everything they'd been through.

Quietly he sat down on the bench beside her and looked out at the Bridgers. The sun brightened the pines still laden with snow and brushed the rocky cliffs to gold. The air smelled of spring, and he realized, like the day, he held new hope for the future.

"I can't believe it's finally really over," Denver said, glancing at him.

"Are you all right?"

She nodded as she looked at the city of Bozeman sprawled below them. "Pete gave me Max's will." She handed him the letter. It was short and to the point. "He hopes the two of us will be happy. And he wants us to name one of our kids after him."

J.D. laughed as he handed back the letter. "We do make quite the team, don't we?"

She nodded. "Max would have been impressed, wouldn't he?" Tears welled in her eyes. "I miss him so much."

"I know." He took her hand; his thumb gently caressed the tender skin of her palm. "But I have a feeling he's still watching over you."

She brushed at her tears with her free hand and smiled. "I swear sometimes I can almost smell those awful cigars he smoked when he was working on a case."

The breeze stirred her hair; her lower lip trembled with emotion. J.D. touched her lip with his fingertips, wanting to make the same journey with a kiss. He pulled his hand back. "Denny." It came out a tortured groan. "How can I ask you to give up your life here, knowing how much you love it?"

"Because a long time ago you promised Max you'd do what was best for me," she whispered.

He said nothing; he didn't even dare breathe.

She cupped his jaw with her hand. "I think you know what's best for me."

He brushed her hair back from her temple. "You realize that means being on the road for months at a time and—"

She stopped him with a kiss. "Do you really think it matters where we are, as long as we're together?"

He took her face in his hands and kissed her eyelids, her cheeks, her lips. "I want you so much, Denny. I've never wanted, needed anything so badly." She raised an eyebrow; he grinned. "No, sweetheart, not even the music."

She laughed. "That's good, J.D., because I hate playing second fiddle to a guitar."

He held her for a moment, just breathing in the familiar scent of her. Was it possible? Was it really possible? "What about your camera shop and the cabin?" he asked with apprehension.

He watched Denny look toward Gallatin Canyon, the way home to West Yellowstone and the place she loved. "Maggie's taking Davey on to finish raising. The two of them have offered to run the shop for me. And the cabin will always be there for us." When she turned to him again, she smiled. "As for Max . . . well, he'll always be with me, too, J.D., no matter where I am." She leaned up to kiss him gently, her lips warm and inviting. "And it's not like I'm going to put my cameras away. I'm going to start a photo book."

"A photo book?" he asked, seeing that old adventurous glint in her eye.

"For our children. It's going to be photographs taken of their father's tours in the years before they were born. I want them to know right from the very beginning that their father is a musician."

He swallowed hard. "Our children." How he loved the sound of that. "They're going to love the lake." As much as we did, he thought. And he could see them, tanned by the sun, standing in front of the cabin Max had built for Denny, smiling into the camera. "We'll be back."

She smiled. "I know."

He kissed her then, putting as much of his love as he could into only a kiss. The sun warmed his back and caught in her eyes, making them sparkle. "Marry me, Denny," he whispered. "Say you'll marry me before you come to your senses."

Her laugh filled the spring air, the most beautiful music he'd ever heard, strong as their love and just as lasting. She looked to the heavens as if listening for a voice to guide her. Then she smiled and nodded.

It was the first time he'd ever seen her at a loss for words, and he knew it wouldn't last. He swept her into his arms and kissed her. The future waited on the horizon, beckoning them with promises like none he'd ever dreamed. His heart filled with songs yet to be written as he took her hand in his, and together they walked into the new day.

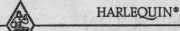

Deceit, betrayal, murder

Join Harlequin's intrepid heroines, India Leigh
and Mary Hadfield, as they ferret out the truth
behind the mysterious goings-on in their
neighborhood. These two women are no milk-
and-water misses. In fact, they thrive on

Watch for their incredible adventures in this
special two-book collection. Available in March,
wherever Harlequin books are sold.

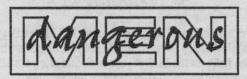

HARLEQUIN®

INTRIGUE®

Brush up on your bedside manner with...

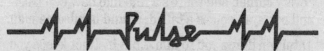

Three heart-racing romantic-suspense novels that are just
what the doctor ordered!

This spring, Harlequin Intrigue presents PULSE, a trilogy of
medical thrillers by Carly Bishop to get your blood flowing,
raise the hairs on the back of your neck and bring out all the
telltale of reading the best in romance and mystery.

Don't miss your appointments with:

#314 HOT BLOODED
March 1995

#319 BREATHLESS
April 1995

#323 HEART THROB
May 1995

On the most romantic day of the year, capture the
thrill of falling in love all over again—with

Harlequin's

Bachelors

They're three sexy and *very single* men who run
very special personal ads to find the women of
their fantasies by Valentine's Day. These exciting,
passion-filled stories are written by bestselling
Harlequin authors.

Your Heart's Desire by Elise Title
Mr. Romance by Pamela Bauer
Sleepless in St. Louis by Tiffany White

Be sure not to miss Harlequin's Valentine Bachelors,
available in February wherever
Harlequin books are sold.

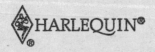

Harlequin invites you to the most
romantic wedding of the season.

Rope the cowboy of your dreams in
Marry Me, Cowboy!

A collection of 4 brand-new stories,
celebrating weddings, written by:

New York Times bestselling author

JANET DAILEY

and favorite authors

Margaret Way
Anne McAllister
Susan Fox

Be sure not to miss Marry Me, Cowboy!
coming this April

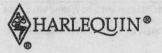 HARLEQUIN®

MMC

HARLEQUIN®

Don't miss these Harlequin favorites by some of our most
distinguished authors!
And now, you can receive a discount by ordering two or more titles!

HT#25577	WILD LIKE THE WIND by Janice Kaiser	$2.99	☐
HT#25589	THE RETURN OF CAINE O'HALLORAN by JoAnn Ross	$2.99	☐
HP#11626	THE SEDUCTION STAKES by Lindsay Armstrong	$2.99	☐
HP#11647	GIVE A MAN A BAD NAME by Roberta Leigh	$2.99	☐
HR#03293	THE MAN WHO CAME FOR CHRISTMAS by Bethany Campbell	$2.89	☐
HR#03308	RELATIVE VALUES by Jessica Steele	$2.89	☐
SR#70589	CANDY KISSES by Muriel Jensen	$3.50	☐
SR#70598	WEDDING INVITATION by Marisa Carroll	$3.50 U.S. $3.99 CAN.	☐
HI#22230	CACHE POOR by Margaret St. George	$2.99	☐
HAR#16515	NO ROOM AT THE INN by Linda Randall Wisdom	$3.50	☐
HAR#16520	THE ADVENTURESS by M.J. Rodgers	$3.50	☐
HS#28795	PIECES OF SKY by Marianne Willman	$3.99	☐
HS#28824	A WARRIOR'S WAY by Margaret Moore	$3.99 U.S. $4.50 CAN.	☐

(limited quantities available on certain titles)

	AMOUNT	$
DEDUCT:	**10% DISCOUNT FOR 2+ BOOKS**	$
ADD:	**POSTAGE & HANDLING**	$
	($1.00 for one book, 50¢ for each additional)	
	APPLICABLE TAXES*	$_____
	TOTAL PAYABLE	$_____
	(check or money order—please do not send cash)	

To order, complete this form and send it, along with a check or money order for the
total above, payable to Harlequin Books, to: **In the U.S.:** 3010 Walden Avenue,
P.O. Box 9047, Buffalo, NY 14269-9047; **In Canada:** P.O. Box 613, Fort Erie, Ontario,
L2A 5X3.

Name:_____

Address: _____ City: _____

State/Prov.: _____ Zip/Postal Code: _____

*New York residents remit applicable sales taxes.
 Canadian residents remit applicable GST and provincial taxes.

HBACK-JM2